Table for Five

ALSO BY IZZY BROMLEY

The Coach Trip

ALSO BY IMOGEN CLARK

Postcards From a Stranger

The Thing About Clare

Where the Story Starts

Postcards at Christmas (a novella)

The Last Piece

Reluctantly Home

Impossible to Forget

An Unwanted Inheritance

In a Single Moment

Table for Five

IZZY BROMLEY

LAKE UNION
PUBLISHING

Text copyright © 2024 by Blue Lizard Books
All rights reserved.

No part of this book may be reproduced, or stored in a retrieval system, or transmitted in any form or by any means, electronic, mechanical, photocopying, recording, or otherwise, without express written permission of the publisher.

Published by Lake Union Publishing, Seattle

www.apub.com

Amazon, the Amazon logo, and Lake Union Publishing are trademarks of Amazon.com, Inc., or its affiliates.

ISBN-13: 9781662511455
eISBN: 9781662511448

Cover design by Emma Rogers
Cover image: © Greens87 © Watermelon Sugar / Getty Images

Printed in the United States of America

Table for Five

1

'I'm afraid we're letting you go, Abigail.'

Cheryl, head of HR at McDougal & Wright, tips her head to one side and gives me her best sympathetic look, complete with full eyebrow raise.

It takes a moment for her words to sink in. When she says 'letting go' the first thing I think of is that Banksy picture, the one with the little girl and the red balloon. I see myself floating just out of reach and wonder how high I will get before my string snags on a tree.

Then I realise Cheryl is still talking to me.

'We will pay you three months' pay in lieu of notice and your accrued holiday pay in accordance with your contract.'

She pushes a piece of paper across the table towards me and taps the number at the bottom with the end of her pen, but I'm still two sentences behind her and struggling to catch up.

Losing my job?

Me?

This makes no sense. I love my job. I'm great at my job! I'm the backbone of the team, the one who can be relied upon to have thought of the thing that everyone else has forgotten. When I go on holiday, they count the days down until I get back, or so I'm told. 'Nothing ever runs quite as smoothly when you're not here, Abbie.'

These are actual words spoken by my old boss. Indispensable is the descriptor that is used of me more than any other.

They can't just sack me. I'm a vital cog.

I try to focus on the numbers but they bounce across the page like little Mexican jumping beans and I can't get them to stay still long enough to read them. I pick the paper up and focus hard on the total until it settles. It's a scarily small number.

With a gargantuan effort, I try to swing my mind back on to what is going on here.

'But you can't get rid of me for no reason,' I say.

I don't know much about employment law but I'm sure that's right.

Cheryl pulls a different face, not so sympathetic now.

'As you have less than two years' service then I'm afraid we can,' she says. 'What I can say is that Mr Frobisher is keen to build his own team rather than move forward with the one he inherited.'

She holds my gaze for a split second longer than she needs to and at once I get the subtext here. I haven't done anything wrong and she knows it. Frobisher just wants yes-men at his beck and call and I definitely don't fit the bill.

Then it all starts to make sense. If I think about it, he's been gunning for me ever since he arrived as director of marketing in a blaze of testosterone and unnecessarily strong aftershave. And suddenly I can see the direction of travel here. The clients I work with will be sidelined. There'll be no more high-end cosmetics or luxury treats as he moves the needle towards the technology products that he's more interested in.

Obviously, I'm not what he wants for his number two, which I imagine would be a carbon copy of himself. At my quarterly review he muttered something about looking the part, being taken seriously in a corporate environment. I hadn't taken much notice. I've always dressed like this and it's never been an issue. Well, maybe at school, but I'm thirty-one now, quite old enough to decide what I wear.

However, apparently, that's not the case at McDougal & Wright.

'But I love my job,' I say, as if that's going to make one iota of difference. 'And there've never been any complaints about my work.'

Cheryl's professional mask slips and something a little more compassionate crosses her face. Her voice becomes gentler.

'I'm afraid the decision has been made, Abbie.' She swallows and looks down at her notes as if she's re-finding her place on her 'How to sack someone' checklist. 'Termination of your employment will be with immediate effect.'

'Immediate effect,' I repeat, more to process what she's just said than anything else. Sacked right now. Just like that. 'Can't I go back to my desk and collect my things, say goodbye?'

Cheryl shakes her head. 'That won't be possible. We'll have your personal possessions sent on. Here is your copy of the paperwork, Abigail.'

She stands and hands me a manila folder. Our meeting is apparently at an end.

My head is spinning. I came to work as normal this morning, expecting to be confirming the make-up artist and caterer for next week's ad shoot, and now it's twenty past nine and I no longer have a job.

I stand too, suddenly filled with an urge to run.

'Thank you,' I say.

Thank you!! The woman just sacked me. But it's an automatic response. What can I say? My mum and dad did a good job of bringing me up.

And then I leave McDougal & Wright for what I assume will be the very last time. Cheryl actually escorts me off the premises so there's no danger of me sneaking back in. We stand at the front desk and she relieves me of my door pass like I'm a criminal. I sense the girls on reception watching us, eager for the gossip, but I don't make eye contact. I just want this humiliation to be over. Cheryl, pre-warned and efficient, has already collected my bag and coat from my desk and she hands them to me. At least she has the good grace to look sheepish.

'Good luck, Abbie,' she says in hushed tones, and finally I see in her face that this has been almost as difficult for her as it has for me, but I'm too shocked to care. I don't reply and push out into the street.

The dank drizzle that was in the air when I arrived at work half an hour ago has turned into a proper downpour. Rain is bouncing from the pavements and splashing up around my ankles. I reach in my bag for my umbrella and then realise that it's hanging on the back of the door near my desk.

With a fleeting thought for my hair, today a tall quiff and full victory roll combo, I step out into the torrent, but then I'm not sure what to do next. I should be at my desk, working on the new campaign for the most delicious chocolate truffles you'll ever eat, but instead I'm standing in the chilly rain without my beautiful polka-dot umbrella. Where should I go? The flat? Mum and Dad's? The pub? I have no clue what to do.

As I dither, the rain bucketing down on me, I see a white van heading my way. The driver looks barely old enough to have a licence. He steers his van towards the kerb and I think for one mad moment that he's going to offer me a lift to get me out of the rain. As he approaches he locks eyes with me and I see him grin. Then he accelerates and powers straight through an enormous puddle of cold, dirty water that has settled in the gutter at my feet.

I can't get out of the way fast enough. My suede shoes and camel swing coat with fur collar, and quite possibly my life, are ruined.

2

I look down at my coat, speckled with brown spots of muddy rainwater and a large patch the shape of Africa down one side. If I'm going to rescue it, I need to get handy with a damp sponge pretty quickly. This makes my decision for me. I shall head home.

The bus stop isn't far. Obviously, it isn't one with a shelter – the gods are not on my side today – so I position myself as far from the kerb as I can and wait. The hairspray that I used to create today's style is giving way, unable to withstand the quantity of water that is landing on it. My carefully curled quiff flops down over my face. Usually this would be a disaster but right now I have bigger things to worry about.

I sit on the bus in a daze. What am I going to do without a job? What will I tell people when they ask what I do? 'Hi. My name is Abigail Finch and I'm a marketing account executive, a job that I worked really hard to get and which I love. Except I don't actually have a job at the moment, but it wasn't my fault that I lost it.'

I can see the expressions on the faces of my friends and family, read what will be written there. 'You've always gone on about your marvellous bloody job, all those ad shoots in cool places, all those parties with clients, all that glamour. And you never stop going on about how fantastic you are at it, but you couldn't have been that great because they've just sacked you without so much as a by-your-leave.'

I reach for my phone to post a quick story about the outrage of it all and am already scripting a caption in my head and thinking about the best camera angle for not showing the mess on my coat. This is what I do, after all. Record my super-shiny life online for all my friends to coo over. I'm not bragging, not really. It's just that extremely cool things happen near me a lot. It goes with the territory.

But then I think it through. If I announce my misfortune to the world, where will that leave me? Who's going to take me seriously when I'm no longer the person with the job that's just that bit cooler than yours? I'll be no one. A nonentity. The loser who was sacked because her face didn't fit.

My cheeks start to flare and I feel the heat travelling all the way down my throat to my chest. What will everyone say when they find out? My mortification will be absolute, especially as I might have made just the tiniest fuss about how amazing my job/life is. And I'll have to confess that all the freebies will have dried up too. They're not going to like that.

I think of a conversation I had last time I was out with my girlfriends, how I hinted that I was up for promotion, which, to be fair, I genuinely thought was true, and my stomach clenches. How stupid am I going to look now? Actually, if being swallowed by the earth was a genuine option, I'd be signing up right this minute.

No. That seals it. I can't make an announcement. Not yet. The rumour mill will go wild and I don't want everyone talking about me – not when I can't control the narrative. I leave my phone where it is.

Then the feelings of humiliation give way to anger again and I feel my whole face tighten, my lips pinching into a tight little knot. I must look like a woman possessed, but, honestly, how dare he? How can he think he'll just sack me simply because I was already at the company when he arrived and I didn't fit his cookie-cutter mould of an account exec? That's not how it's supposed to work and it's no way to run a business. I'm great at what I do, some might even say brilliant, but he's made me look like a fraud, like I've been lying all this time, and that's simply not true and definitely not fair.

Well, he'll be sorry. Just wait until I've been gone a few days, a week at most. Then he'll see exactly what he's lost. No one can organise a campaign like me. I'm the one who makes things run like clockwork. If I'm not there it will all fall apart. Plus, the clients think I'm great. I'm their go-to person. And Frobisher might object to the way I dress, but my clients love it. What is 'inappropriate' and 'non-corporate' to him is quirky and fun to the people who actually pay the bills. I bet he doesn't realise that you don't just build those kinds of relationships overnight. He'll never find someone to replace me. Hell, he'll need two people to do what I did. He'll see.

But of course whether this is true or not is immaterial. I'm still sacked.

By the time I get off the bus and head for home, the anger has blown through and I'm see-sawing between fear over what I will do next and yet more humiliation about how on earth I will be able to tell anyone and hold my head up in public again.

Home is a first-floor flat in a Victorian villa overlooking the park. I bought it for a song because it had been lived in by an elderly lady who hadn't done anything to it for decades. The estate agent got terribly excited about which walls I could knock down and how it would be perfect with a shiny new kitchen and bathroom, but all the time he was talking I kept thinking how wonderful it was that the flat had such a vintage feel to it, and whether I could live there without further modernising and spoiling that.

In the end, I fitted central heating and squeezed a shower cubicle into the bathroom, but I left everything else pretty much as it was, picking up bits of furniture from junk shops and car boot sales and upcycling them so that the flat has a lovely retro feel about it. It's not entirely authentic but I love it.

As soon as I get in, I change into my comfiest pyjamas, because if you can't wear pyjamas when you've just lost your job then I don't know when you can. I make myself a pot of tea and sit at the kitchen table with the manila folder in front of me. I sit like that for a long time.

Once or twice, I pick up my phone to ring Spencer. He's the only one I want to talk to. He'll loyally take my side without question and then make me laugh with his terrible jokes and everything will seem less catastrophic.

Or he would have done before.

But I can't ring Spencer. I've burnt my bridges there.

Who can I tell? The people I spend most of my time with are my colleagues. The thing about a big, exciting job like the one I just lost is that there isn't really much time left over for a social life. And at McDougal & Wright we definitely worked hard and played hard. When you cancel plans at short notice as often as I've done then people stop asking you to things. There have been one too many theatre tickets wasted, one too many dinner reservations missed.

But none of that mattered to me because I had my team. They were always there. They knew not to make arrangements midweek because of the high probability of cancellation. We would get to the end of a particularly challenging campaign and then we'd go to the pub together. The boss would be buying and we'd let our hair down. Work and social life all rolled into one.

8

And what do I have now?

Nothing.

I think about ringing Sal, my closest friend out of work. She'll be sympathetic at least. She won't get it because her job is just something she does to get money to live, but she'll share my huge sense of injustice.

But I can't face it. I can't run the risk of hearing even a tiny hint of the smugness that I suspect will be in her voice when I tell her, because I have definitely gone on about how well I'm doing once too often – not in a mean way but just because I was having such a great time that it slipped out. A lot.

And I certainly can't tell my parents. I know that my mother dines out on stories about me. I know because I've played up to it, feeding her titbits that she can drop into conversations with her friends whose children are doing less well.

I'm the success story of the family. My brothers' lives are chaotic. Xander (short for Alexander) creates performance art and never knows where his next income stream will come from, and Felix (short for pain in the butt) hurtles through his life like a ball in a pinball machine, ricocheting from one disaster to the next without a care in the world. I'm the one with a career and a mortgage. I never run out of loo roll or miss a birthday or fail to save enough holiday days to cover Christmas. And so this is what has become expected of me. I am the model child.

I can't face spoiling that. Mum will be so disappointed in me and then she'll start trying to fix it with her endless suggestions. To be fair, Dad couldn't give two hoots what we do as long as we're happy, but I can't tell him and not Mum, which means I can't tell either of them, or at least not until I've got something else lined up.

Shit.

Elvis wanders into the kitchen. He pauses, fixing me with his almond-shaped amber eyes.

'What are you doing here?' he asks.

'I got sacked,' I tell him.

'Oh,' he replies and then saunters over to his bowl to see if there's anything left from breakfast.

3

The next morning my alarm goes off at seven as usual and I'm about to launch myself into my day when I remember. People with nothing to do have no reason to get up at seven. I can luxuriate in my bed all day long if I choose to. There's no one here to judge me except Elvis but if I get up and feed him first then he can't complain.

I roll on to my back and stare up at the ceiling. This is one of those life-changing moments that people dream of. You know the kind of thing. 'Well, if I hadn't lost my job, I would have never gone on to [add your own extremely exciting opportunity here].'

Just at the moment, however, I can't imagine myself doing anything else. Without my job I genuinely don't know who I am. I feel like I have no identity. What is the point of me? Yesterday, I was the account exec who was going to make our client's fabulous new chocolate truffles the talk of Instagram. Now that will go to someone else, and my amazing ideas will never see the light of day. I pull the duvet over my head and groan.

I contemplate staying in bed all day, which almost feels like something I should be doing just to make a point, but I'm really not that person. I'm more your basic up-and-at-'em kind, whose default setting is doing not resting.

Excavating myself from under the duvet, I reach for a pen and the notebook that lives on my bedside table. I bought it for recording those middle of the night worries or revelations because all the articles I read on improving the quality of your sleep suggest that's what you do. However, I rarely write in it. I sleep quite well as it goes. Or I did.

I open it on a fresh blank page. Very symbolic.

I'm tempted to head the page Plan for the Rest of My Life but that feels a tad melodramatic, so I just write TODAY and underline it twice for emphasis. Then I begin.

1. Get new job.

2. Tell people. (Mum, Dad, Xander, Felix, Sal, Spencer????)

3. Work out finances.

4. Arrange leaving drinks with team??

5. Buy cat food.

Well, it isn't the most comprehensive list I've ever made but it is a start at least.

As it's only 7 a.m. (see earlier point about not remembering to switch off my alarm) I decide to start with the scariest item, which also doesn't involve people who might currently be asleep.

3. Work out finances.

When I open my banking app, my balance is surprisingly healthy – Cheryl must already have arranged for me to be paid what I was owed – and I can't help smiling when I see the total. Then I remember that it has to last me until I find a new job and suddenly it doesn't look that great.

But I have a second account cryptically labelled ICOD, which stands for IN CASE OF DISASTER. As I click that open, silently praising my own foresight, I'm feeling chuffed. When I see what's in there, my head starts to spin. The balance will barely pay for a takeaway. Then I remember that I've already had one disaster this month. My car failed its MOT and I had to fork out for the repairs.

Trying to steady my thumping heart, I tot up all my monthly outgoings and then do the maths. If I'm highly frugal I can eke the money out for maybe five months.

That's okay, I think. Surely I can get a new job in that time, but it doesn't feel like much of a lifeline. And what if I don't find anything? Times are hard, particularly in marketing, and the perfect job might not leap into my lap straight away.

I stop that line of thought before it gets out of hand. Yes, jobs aren't always easy to get but I'm good at what I do. That must count for something. And I do have a bit of time.

Flopping my head back against the pillow, I force myself to think positive and let my imagination roam free for a while. Maybe I could use this unforeseen situation as an opportunity to change everything about my life. I could leave Leeds, go to London, move abroad even. I could rent a shack in a remote corner of a Caribbean island and spend the rest of my life doing hair wraps for tourists or working in a turtle sanctuary or quite possibly both.

It's a fun thought and I indulge it for a good five minutes before I re-engage my practical side. I know I won't do any of that. I love my little flat too much – and Elvis. And even though the weather leaves a lot to be desired, Yorkshire really is a great place to live.

I could tell Spencer that I've changed my mind, follow him up north.

No. I really couldn't. That ship has most definitely sailed and, also, see above about loving my flat, Elvis, etc.

By eight thirty I'm on my third cup of coffee, which has done nothing to reduce my panicky heart rate. I think I should probably tell someone, but who? Not Mum. I can't ring Spencer, so I ring Sal, the only outstanding person on item 2 of my to-do list. Sal and I met a few years back at Zumba. We went to the first class, decided it was harder than it looks and never went back, but we discovered that we got on in the bar afterwards and have stayed friends ever since.

She picks up on the second ring.

'Hi, sweets,' she says. Her voice is breathy like she's running.

'Hi, Sal,' I begin and then swallow hard before I embark on breaking my embarrassing news.

'Can't chat now,' she says. 'Bad time.'

'Sorry,' I say, feeling stupid to have even tried speaking to her before work. 'I'll catch you later.'

'Cool. Have a good day.'

And then she hangs up.

Part of me is relieved. I tried to tell her and it didn't work out. Box ticked. So no one knows about my humiliation yet. Maybe it can stay that way until I've an even better job to tell them about. Keeping it a secret of sorts makes me feel less sick, which has to be a good thing.

I put my coffee cup in the sink and contemplate getting out the vacuum cleaner but decide against it. The flat is clean enough and I don't want to turn into my mother. I start thinking about how else I could usefully use the time I've suddenly been gifted, in between finding a new job, of course.

I could redecorate. Isn't that one of those jobs that people say they'd do if they had more time? But I like my flat the way it is (except maybe the back bedroom, which could use a bit of attention). Perhaps I might learn a language. I could go all *Eat Pray Love* and move to Italy and come back fluent in Italian and fat on all that fabulous food. But what would I do for money?

I could take up drawing. I've always wanted to learn to draw, even though my art teacher at school said I was beyond help. He was probably right.

I could watch all those box sets that I can never bring myself to commit to because, quite frankly, sixty episodes of anything is terrifying.

When I look up at the clock it's not yet nine. How can a day suddenly be so long?

4

For the first two days of my life with no job I behave like a hermit, seeing no one and speaking to no one. I scroll endlessly through all the job sites, applying for anything that looks appropriate. There is nothing even approximately of the quality of the job that I've lost. This isn't surprising. Great jobs like that don't come along all the time. I need to be patient.

I've had no messages from my colleagues and I wonder what Frobisher has said about where I've gone. It would be just like the spineless git to pretend that I've booked a last-minute holiday, just so that we don't bad-mouth him behind his back. I can't risk asking them though, because then I'll have to tell them that I've been sacked and I'm just not ready.

I clean the flat. I talk to Elvis. I talk to myself a fair bit too, geeing myself up with positive affirmations. Time crawls by.

Sal doesn't ring me back. This isn't surprising. She might have been vaguely curious as to why I was ringing before work, but if I'm honest I've let my non-work friendships slip a bit so I doubt I'm at the top of her priority list. That's fine. I'd have ended up lying anyway. I don't try her again.

Also, I don't ring Spencer. I don't text him or FaceTime or WhatsApp. This is seriously impressive and about the only thing I manage to achieve, so I hold on to it grimly like a badge of honour.

Abigail Finch. Loses her fabulous job but resists contacting the man she really likes (yet has just dumped) in the face of serious temptation.

By Wednesday, I'm climbing the walls and need to get out of the flat. So I pack my iPad and my trusty notebook and pen, now no longer relegated to my night-time worries as I have plenty of daytime ones now, and head out.

There's an independent supermarket near where I live. It's the kind of place where everything is more expensive than in the big chains but their suppliers are mainly local so the warmth that comes from knowing you're saving the planet goes some way to reducing the shock of the cost.

The supermarket has a little café attached. Normally, as I race round with my trolley, I cast a wistful glance in its direction, promising myself that one day I will make time to enjoy a nice cup of coffee and maybe even a slice of cake as a reward for working hard all week. But I've never got round to it, so this feels like my perfect opportunity. Instead of turning right into the fruit and veg section I turn left into the café. It's nothing special. Three rows of five Formica tables lead down to the counter. One wall is glass and looks out across the car park. The other is covered with chalkboards setting out the day's specials, and there's a noticeboard where you can post flyers advertising your services or events. I give it a quick glance as I walk past. I would like to spend more time perusing it but the queue is moving too quickly. I make a mental note to look again at a quieter moment – just in case.

As I move slowly forward, I eye the delicious array of cakes on offer. They range from tall moist-looking gateaux adorned with icing and cream swirls, to neat little squares of chewy deliciousness topped with a crisp layer of chocolate, and everything in between. I actually don't have the money for cake, but it's been a tough week so far and I need something to spur me on.

I reach the front of the queue and the woman who is serving stops what she's doing to look at me. Her badge tells me that her name is Liz.

'Ooh, I do love your dress,' she says. 'And your hair. The whole get-up. You look cracking. Give us a twirl, would you?'

I oblige. This is something that happens to me a lot. Today I'm wearing a black shirtwaister dress with big blousy red roses on it and a short driving coat in green tweed. My hair is looped up in curls and I have a headscarf tied like an Alice band holding it in place.

'Ooh, you do look lovely,' Liz says again. 'People these days just don't make an effort like they used to. My mother never left the house without a hat and a pair of gloves. You don't see that any more, do you?'

I have gloves in my handbag. I give her a beaming smile. I'm used to this kind of reaction to my clothes, particularly from the older generation. People my own age just tend to stare, but I don't care. I love how I look.

'Not very often,' I say. 'Please could I have a flat white and a slice of that delicious-looking pear and ginger cake.'

'You can indeed, my love,' she says, grabbing a plate and lifting a slice on to it. 'You've right made my day. You really have.'

I smile again and she busies herself with the coffee machine.

Once I have my order, I find a table next to the window and halfway down the room. I sit facing into the café so I can see the comings and goings, open my iPad and scan through LinkedIn, but there's nothing doing on the job front, and I end up just absorbing my surroundings instead.

The café is busy. Most of the tables are taken up with groups of women of all ages. Some have pushchairs, and I try to ignore the ticking clock that always sounds in my head when I see them. There's one big table to the left of me that has no one sitting at it. There's a handwritten sign in the middle. I assume it will be a reservation notice, but when I look more closely, I see that it says:

COMMUNITY TABLE

A PLACE TO SIT AND MAKE NEW FRIENDS

What's that all about then? Whatever it is, it doesn't seem to be working. I've been here for almost an hour and no one has sat there. Filled with curiosity and in need of a second cup of coffee, I decide to go and ask Liz.

I order another flat white and then say, 'What's the deal with the community table?'

Liz looks across to the empty space. 'Waste of good seats if you ask me,' she says. 'It was the manager, Joel's, idea. He saw it on some fancy-pants website. The idea is if you're lonely then you sit there and other people come and join you. But no one does. Or not many. Sometimes it's empty all day and when we're busy we could really use the space. But Joel's determined. He's giving it six months before he gives up with it.'

'And no one ever sits there?'

Liz pulls a face. 'Well, people do. But it's all the oddballs. The ones who don't spend. That's another thing. Customers can buy a cuppa and put it in the bank, so to speak, and then if people come in and they can't afford a drink we can offer them one. Sit there for hours nursing one cup of tea, some of them. Brings the tone of the place down, that's what I think. I'll be glad when the six months is up and we can break the table back into two and go back to how it was before.'

She hands me my flat white. 'Another bit of cake, my love? You look like you could do with fattening up.'

I know she means well so I don't take offence.

'No thanks, but can I put a drink in the bank for anyone who needs it?'

Liz smiles and charges me for two cups of coffee.

5

Finally it's the weekend, and my friends, who are all still gainfully employed, have time for me. It's Lucy's birthday and Sal arranged months ago for a gang of us to go out to eat at a new Korean place in Leeds. I can't really afford it any more but having spent a whole week in on my own, I am more than ready for some company. Elvis is a great flatmate but his conversational skills are limited.

I'd decided that this is the night I'll share my big news and was almost looking forward to the drama of it all. I'd even rehearsed what I'd say in my head for maximum impact. Silly, I know, but I've been on my own a lot with plenty of time to think. And it's not hard to make Frobisher out to be the devil of the piece because he totally is. None of this would have happened if he hadn't decided he didn't like what I'm all about. I've moaned about him non-stop since he arrived so it won't be a huge surprise to discover that he wasn't that keen on me either.

Now that the evening has arrived, however, I'm feeling less confident. Even with my little speech all prepared, I'm worried about what they'll think. I'm aiming to go all out on the injustice of it, and I hope that my friends will agree that I've been treated really badly, but part of me worries that they might be less supportive in secret. They're bound to question whether I'm as good at my job as I've always said. They've only ever had my word for it, after all.

I try to dismiss these fears as I sit on the bus on the way to town. These are my friends, and even though we might have drifted a bit lately, they'll still have my back. I mean, that's what friends do, isn't it? When the chips are down you all stick together. I'll tell them and I'll explain I didn't do anything wrong and they will see how badly I've been treated. It will all be fine.

But when I arrive, there's only Meena there so I have to hold on to my news for a little longer, not wanting to have to tell the whole sorry tale more than once. Also, Meena is more Lucy's friend than mine so we don't know each other very well.

'Hi. How are you?' I say enthusiastically.

She looks me up and down, as if my dress, tonight a straight, fitted blue shift dress with white trim which I've paired with white lace gloves and a curled-out bob, is somehow not quite right for the occasion. I give my shoulders a little shake. I can style out the judgiest of looks.

'Fine,' she says with an eye roll. 'I'm so ready for this.' She takes a deep gulp of white wine, which she's poured, I assume, from a bottle that's already half drunk. 'How was your week? A car crash like mine, I expect.'

'Aren't they all?' I say with a little flick of my head. Disingenuous I know, but I'm not going to say just how bad my week has been until the others get here.

'Thank God for the weekend after next. Can't come soon enough,' Meena says dramatically.

I have no idea what she's talking about. 'What's that?' I ask.

'The Lake District thing? The spa? You know. The one Sal organised.'

I know literally nothing about it. Has Sal arranged a girls' weekend and not included me? Quickly I try to rearrange my face so I don't look as thrown as I feel.

'Oh that,' I say as if it had momentarily slipped my mind. 'Actually, I can't make it.'

'That's a shame,' says Meena, taking another mouthful of wine which drains her glass. She reaches for the bottle and pours herself some more without offering any to me. 'The spa looks dreamy. I've booked in for back-to-back treatments. If I don't come out like a new woman at the end then I want a refund.' She tips her head back and laughs but it's hollow and fake-sounding.

'I'm sure you'll have a great time,' I say as my mind races over recent conversations with Sal to try and find a trace of this arrangement. I draw a blank. I'm pretty certain she hasn't mentioned it.

The others start to arrive and finally Sal turns up in a flurry of apologies.

'Sorry I'm late. Traffic. Leaves on the line. Taxi drivers' strike. Alien abduction. Take your pick. Happy birthday, Lucy! Have you had a lovely day? I've got a gift.'

She digs round in her bag and extracts a small rectangle chaotically wrapped in green tissue paper which she thrusts at Lucy. Lucy opens it and then stares at the contents quizzically.

'Hopi ear candles,' says Sal. 'Someone used some on me and it was transformative so I thought I'd share. We can do it later if you like, although you'd have to put your head on the table so maybe not here.'

Lucy looks bewildered – Sal has that effect on people regularly – but she rallies and thanks Sal profusely.

The chat around the table is the usual kind of catching up and I half listen as I try to decide what to do. My resolve to share my news has evaporated now that I know about the spa weekend. This is the supportive group of girlfriends that I assumed would have my back when I told them what's happened, but now I learn that they've been busy making plans without me. Suddenly I don't feel nearly as supported as I did. I keep my mouth shut as I try to gauge the situation.

We get the ordering done, and when we're eating our starters and the conversation at the far end of the table is under full sail, I take my chance to ask Sal about the spa.

'You know,' she says as if I must do. 'The one in Grasmere.'

I shake my head.

Colour rises in Sal's cheeks, but she barely misses a beat. 'I must have missed you off the group chat.' There's no apology for that, I notice. 'Maybe I assumed you wouldn't come anyway. You do blow us out quite a lot with work stuff and you've usually got some dinner or other on at the weekends. But I'm sure the Airbnb info mentions a blow-up mattress. You can have that if you like.'

'Thanks,' I reply as brightly as I can, given that I appear to have been entirely forgotten. 'Actually, I do have something on next weekend so it wouldn't have worked for me anyway.'

'I was right then,' says Sal with a little shrug. 'You wouldn't have come. Maybe next time, eh?'

Next time, if you bother to invite me, I think.

The fact that I've been overlooked in the Lake District plan colours my entire evening. I withdraw from the conversation. My 'I've just been unfairly dismissed' story, which I was going to play first for shock value and then for laughs to show that I'm actually okay with it, no longer feels like something I want to share.

I'm almost sure Sal didn't miss me out intentionally. It sounds like she just assumed I wouldn't go, although she could just be saying that to cover the fact that she forgot me. The net result, however, is still that I was excluded. I try to talk myself out of it bothering me. She's right. I have been busy at work recently, ironically, and it's been a while since I've seen them all. I probably haven't been at the forefront of their minds. But still, it hurts.

The meal over, there is talk of a club, but I'm not up for that now. I make my excuses and leave them to it, thinking as I go of how much money I'll save by having an early night to ease the burn of being left out.

'I'll ring you in the week,' Sal calls after me, and I smile and wave but I doubt she will. Sal is too chaotic to keep all the balls in the air. That's what I've always thought, at least. But not so chaotic, I think now. She can organise a weekend away effectively enough.

As I sit on the bus on the way home I try not to dwell on the evening's revelations. It doesn't really mean anything. I'm hardly joined at the hip with them all. We have our own lives. After all, I've lost my job and not told them. Some might see that as a betrayal of friendship, I suppose.

Yet as I let myself into my empty flat I can't help but feel the tiniest bit lonely. Maybe I should have just swallowed my pride and gone on to the club with them. What does the rest of it matter? I know it doesn't, not really. But I go to sleep with a heavy feeling in my heart.

6

In light of the 'not being invited to the spa weekend' revelation of Saturday night, the community table at the supermarket suddenly takes on a different significance for me. I'd thought I had friends and family and former colleagues to support me, that I was surrounded by people who professed to care for me. And yet here we are, a week since I was fired, and I have yet to tell a living soul my bad news, Elvis excluded, and no one has asked.

I'm trying not to examine the reasons for that too closely. I'm a little ashamed of the sense of mortification I'm feeling and how that's keeping my lips tightly closed, but I can't help it. I didn't do anything wrong, but people are bound to wander down the 'no smoke without fire' path, and I don't want to have to deal with the questions they don't like to ask out loud but are clearly thinking. The whole thing makes my guts crunch. It's so humiliating.

Then there are the people I don't want to worry with the news. To be fair, that subset is made up exclusively of my parents. The inevitable daily phone calls from my mother asking if I'm eating properly and if I've got any interviews yet are not something I'd relish. And Xander and Felix will just tell Mum and Dad so they're out too.

And finally there are my friends. This would be the friends that planned a weekend away without inviting me. I wonder why I'm suddenly not so keen on sharing my misfortunes with them.

So that leaves Elvis. He's the only confidant I need at the moment, and he has the huge advantage of always agreeing with me and never putting forward any contradictory views. He might be worth his weight in gold right now.

Monday comes round again and I'm discovering that not working isn't quite as straightforward as I'd assumed. I have all the time in the world but for the life of me I can't bring to mind any of the things I longed to do when I had no time at all, except the ones that cost a fortune. And the things that I do think of would be greatly improved by having a companion to share them with, but everyone is at work. Oh, the irony.

I've only had one message from my erstwhile team and that was from Dan, who is concerned for his own job security rather than my wellbeing. I tell him my leaving was a mutual decision, which is obviously a lie, but as he doesn't message me back, I don't have to defend it.

I don't hear from anyone else. I assume they've been told not to contact me and I keep telling myself that because it hurts a little less than the alternative reason for their silence.

There are still hardly any jobs to apply for, but then again it's only been a week. Amazing jobs in marketing don't come up all the time. I have to be patient and at least my bank account is looking better than it would normally at this time in the month. But of course, that's an illusion. There will be nothing more going in until I get paid again.

Still, I take my job-finding kit (notebook, pen and iPad) and head down to the supermarket café, trying hard not to think of myself as the kind of person who takes comfort from being in a room full of strangers.

The café is busy again. This is something else I'm learning. People sit down in coffee shops all the time. When I had a job, I'd always grabbed a takeaway and fled to my desk, never noticing how many people had china mugs in their hands rather than paper cups.

There's a new notice on the board. Its bright green and blue lettering cheerfully announces a 10K race in aid of a homeless charity. Maybe I could use this time to do Couch to 5K? It takes me less than a second to dismiss that idea!

When I reach the counter, I'm disappointed to see that Liz isn't working today. In her place, there's a girl who looks as though she should still be in school and a guy of around my age. He might be quite good-looking but he's scowling so much it's hard to tell. His name badge says Joel so I assume he must be the boss that Liz mentioned.

Joel is working the coffee machine while the young girl (Bex according to her badge) takes the orders and payment and deals with the food. The atmosphere between them is taut, as if one little yank and something might snap, which is weird because there seemed to be no tension in the team when Liz was here. She and her co-worker were probably dealing with more customers than these two are too, but they just took everything in their stride.

I try not to look at the line-up of delicious cakes and tray bakes. If I select one of those every time I come in here I'll have to start running, and my budget won't stretch to luxuries like that.

When I get to the front of the queue Bex gives me a tight smile.

'What can I get you?' she asks. She sounds nervous even though it's such a simple question.

'Flat white, please,' I reply brightly to encourage her on a bit.

'Anything to eat?'

Tempting, but . . . 'No thanks.'

'One flat white,' she calls back to Joel.

'The ticket,' he hisses at her. 'I need the ticket.'

'Oh yeah, sorry.' Bex fumbles with the receipt and then sticks it to a strip behind her. It's the only ticket on there but I suppose a system is a system.

'It's my first day,' she says to me, her shoulders slumped.

'Well, you seem to be doing really well.'

'Actually she needs to raise her game significantly or it'll be her last,' says Joel, although I'm not sure he intended me to hear. I give Bex a huge and encouraging smile. No one needs a snarky boss.

I wait for my coffee and then carry it back towards my table. For a moment I can't decide whether I like that I think of it as 'my' table but I sit there anyway.

No one is at the community table. When I woke up this morning I had considered the possibility of sitting there myself but I'd rejected the idea pretty quickly. I may be a bit lonely, but I'm not *that* lonely.

Because I don't want to look like I have nothing to do, I browse Instagram without even thinking about it. My feed is full of the kind of things that I usually post. Tempting plates of food in fancy-pants restaurants. Outfits of the day that look like they're straight from London Fashion Week. Complicated latte art. (To be honest, I've never really understood the appeal but I can see that it's a skill.) Story after story informs me what an amazing day people are having. My own feed is looking sadly neglected but what can I post? Here I am in the café of my local supermarket. Again.

I put my phone away and open my iPad instead. Then I get on with the task of trawling through LinkedIn and conclude that maybe I need to look beyond Leeds. I apply for a couple of jobs that aren't really a good match for me, just so I feel like I'm doing something, and finish my coffee.

I'm about to leave when I become aware in my peripheral vision of someone sitting down close to me. I look up and see that they are actually sitting at the community table. It's a man, in his late forties, fifties maybe, with an unkempt beard and greasy hair that curls around the collar of his navy-blue parka. He looks shifty, keeping his eyes low like he's expecting someone to tell him to leave, and he perches on the edge of his chair.

His tray has a stainless-steel teapot for one, a mug and a little jug of milk. I wonder if it's the drink I paid for the other day and immediately feel terrible for having had the thought. I'm sure there are lots of people who pay for drinks for the community table and plenty of people who use them. Just because I haven't seen anyone sitting there means nothing. It's not as if I'm here 24-7. The table might be at maximum capacity for much of the time as far as I know, although from what Liz said it does sound as if it's an underused resource.

I try to glance at the man surreptitiously, hoping that he won't notice. I'm used to people staring at me so I know how disconcerting it can be. But I am curious all the same. He opens the teapot, stirs the bag with a teaspoon and then pours himself a cup. Then he adds the milk. I expect him to put sugar in but he doesn't, leaving me to wonder about why I thought he might. I'm making assumptions that I have no business making, I realise, about who he is and why he looks as he does. The only thing I need to know is that he has decided to sit at that table because he wants someone to talk to or needed a drink he couldn't afford or quite possibly both.

There are a few people in the café on their own. Me for a start, and a woman who is reading a paperback and an elderly chap with the newspaper open in front of him, but only this man chose to sit at the community table. The others are happy in their solitude, possibly sought it out and have come equipped to fully immerse themselves in the peace.

When the table was empty, it was easy to assume that I'd approach if someone ever sat there. Now that they have done, I find that I can't do it. I'm rooted to the spot with my empty flat white cup and my job searching. I just don't fancy talking to a stranger.

Might it have been different if the stranger in question looked a little more approachable? Now there's an uncomfortable question, but as I prod round at it I think that it might. If the woman with the paperback novel had sat down there I can picture myself asking if I could join her, striking up a conversation about what she was reading.

But this is a man who looks almost old enough to be my dad and who is giving me no obvious conversational openers other than 'Are you lonely?' I find that I just don't have it in me.

As my coffee is finished, I have no reason to linger longer in the café so I gather my things together and leave. Walking past the man at the community table, I get a distinct whiff of a sweet, rank body odour and I decide that I've made the right decision. I'm a high-flying account executive, not a social worker. He really isn't my problem.

7

For the rest of the day, I have one of those odd gnawing feelings in the pit of my stomach. I assume to start with that it's the shock of losing my job kicking in, but when I take the lid off and examine it a bit more closely I realise that it's more to do with not going to talk to the man at the community table.

I've always thought of myself as a fundamentally good person. I mean, don't we all? Good, but busy. It's rare that I am faced with such a clear opportunity to put my money where my mouth is. There was nothing stopping me from going to talk to him, and yet I stayed where I was. That behaviour doesn't match the person I think I am. However, the evidence that I might be mistaken about that is staring me in the face.

I'm not sure what was holding me back, but I suspect it was good old-fashioned awkwardness. It's hard enough to start a conversation with someone who seems to be just like me. Faced with the prospect of talking to a homeless-looking, middle-aged man who is sitting at a table specially reserved for those with no one to talk to, I find that all my worthy intentions to be kind just evaporate.

I resolve to do better.

On Tuesday I'm back at the supermarket café. I feel like a regular and I'm gratified when Liz recognises me, even if that's more to do with what I'm wearing today: a full skirt with a poodle on it and a pale lemon turtle-necked sweater.

'Oh, hello again,' she says.

'Hi.' I beam at her and immediately feel self-conscious. She doesn't want to be my friend. She's just doing her job. 'Flat white, please,' I add sheepishly.

'And anything to eat, my love?'

Get behind me, Satan. 'No thanks. Actually,' I continue, trying to make my words light, 'I thought I might sit at the community table today.'

I'm cringing inside. How embarrassing it is to confess that you have no one to talk to. Quickly I try to make it sound like I'm conducting a public service. 'Just in case people are put off sitting down because there's no one there,' I add and immediately hate myself.

'Nice idea, my love,' says Liz, taking my money. 'I'll bring your drink over.'

I know something about feeling self-conscious. I mean, don't we all, but when your parents dress up as Romans in their spare time you get used to people staring. (Have I not mentioned this yet? Well, you're in for a treat.) I sometimes wonder if that's where my love of period clothing came from, but it's not the most flattering connection and I don't like to ponder it too hard.

Even though not one soul is staring or has even noticed that I am going to sit down at the community table, it feels like I have a flashing neon sign above my head: 'This person has no friends. Approach at your own risk.'

Now that I'm standing there, I can see how big it is. As Liz said, it's really two tables pulled together, which feels very indulgent in such a busy café. Ridiculously, I dither over which seat to take. Do I sit at the end, leaving plenty of space for others, or do I plonk myself in the middle and let anyone else work around me? Of course, the question is entirely immaterial as I'm the only one here, but I don't want to put anyone else off by sitting in the wrong place.

I plump for a seat in the middle facing the exit and sit down quickly before I can change my mind. I'm very tempted to hide the community table sign under my chair but I resist. However, I don't think I've ever signalled my social needs quite as loudly as this and it feels all kinds of weird. I'm young and not bad-looking. I have a great job (or I did until a week ago). I have friends and a family who live nearby. Yet I'm sitting at a table designed for the lonely and unloved.

The feeling is horribly familiar but I can't quite put my finger on why. Then I remember school – that horror of coming into class in the morning, seeing that your friend is no longer at the desk next to yours and realising that at some point overnight all the rules have changed and nobody told you.

But I'm not at school. I'm a fully grown adult who until very recently had a busy life stuffed with friends and family and colleagues.

And yet, I find myself here.

Something has gone very awry.

Quickly I leap up and go back to my usual table. No one seems to notice, or if they do they probably think that I sat at the table by mistake and then moved once I realised. Only Liz knows the truth.

She arrives moments later with my coffee which she places on the table in front of me with what I interpret as a knowing look.

'It's not for everyone, my love,' she says and then heads back to her counter.

My head is spinning with conflicting concepts, not least why I feel drawn to sit at the table in the first place. Just how isolated I must be feeling to even consider it is a shock. But then I consider the facts. This enormous, life-changing catastrophe has just befallen me and the only person I've told is Elvis, and he isn't even a person.

I've never thought of myself as unsupported before but maybe that's because nothing like this has ever happened to me. And now I come to think about it, I haven't mentioned the Spencer situation to anyone either. There seems to be an emerging pattern in my life of not having anyone to talk to at crucial moments. Could it be that I only share the fun bits of my life, the parts that match my Insta feed? The idea makes me pause.

On top of that, as if that weren't bad enough on its own, I'm now feeling like a totally inadequate member of society. I've always thought I was a decent human being, but I saw that man sit here yesterday and didn't join him, and now I've managed less than thirty seconds in the hot seat myself.

What does that say about me?

It occurs to me that there's a lot to unpack here. The last week or so has made me confront things about myself that I hadn't been aware of – and it's hard. I don't want people to think that I need to ask for support, even if those people are total strangers, and there is apparently a huge resistance to revealing my vulnerability, right down to taking a seat in a café.

To cover my embarrassment, I dig my phone out and my fingers make their way by muscle memory to Instagram. Until last week, my feed was buzzing with bright images, bubbly captions and excitable emojis. I wasn't over-egging the pudding or making anything up. That was my life, and it was joyful.

I still haven't posted since I lost my job. Part of that's been embarrassment – shame, if you like. And partly it's because I'm not doing anything that feels share-worthy. Yet, I suppose that's the case for lots of people. Why should I be so reluctant to post pictures of my cat or my coffee cup or the rain running down the window?

Of course, I know the answer to that. There's nothing exciting or out of the ordinary about those things. They would lower the high-octane tone and I'm just not quite ready. Actually, at the moment it's hard to imagine that I'll ever be ready.

I take a mouthful of coffee but it's scalding and more bitter than I'm expecting even though every other cup of coffee I've had here has been lovely. I suspect the bitter taste is only in my imagination, but somehow I no longer want it.

Once more I contemplate getting up and going, leaving my coffee undrunk, but I would like to come back here and I'm not sure I will be able to bring myself to do that if I slink away today. My head is a maelstrom of accusations and recriminations and I need to stay where I am until I get myself back under some level of control.

As the minutes tick by and my heart rate slows, I start to feel brave enough to look round the café. I half expect the other patrons to be throwing dagger-like stares at me, the person who isn't quite big enough to offer a hand of support to her fellow citizens, but no one seems bothered. They are all busy with their own business, and me and my fallen principles couldn't be further from their interest.

I get my iPad out of my bag to pull me away from Insta. There's a new email. When I see who's sent it my heart does a little jolt. I let my eyes scan down to read the content, holding my breath. It's very short.

To: Abigail Finch
From: Spencer Mocre
Subject: Last chance

Hi Abbie

Are you sure?

S x

I slam the iPad cover down as if he is actually in there and might slide out and sit next to me. I don't want to think about Spencer and his questions. I have enough on my plate without that on top. But then I think about the way his nose crinkles when he smiles and how he likes it when I do my Frobisher impression and I know that I miss him already.

There's no point wandering down that path, Abbie. You had your chance. You didn't take it and now you have to live with the consequences.

Then out of the corner of my eye I see someone sitting at the community table. I look up and watch. She's an older lady, definitely in her late seventies, maybe eighties. She's slender and very elegant-looking, her soft white hair pulled away from her face in a neat French pleat. She has a pale chiffon scarf twisted artfully around her slender neck.

She has a cup of something clear, mint tea perhaps, and a slice of Madeira cake and she looks as if sitting at the table for people looking for company is the most natural thing in the world. Before I know what I'm doing I'm on my feet and making my way over.

8

'May I join you?' I ask, flashing her my best smile and putting my coffee down on the community table before she has replied.

She cocks her head to one side, chin slightly raised, and takes me in with her pale grey eyes.

'You must do as you see fit,' she replies, which throws me somewhat.

I see fit to sit, but she doesn't move a muscle. No welcoming smile, no 'please be my guest' hand gesture. Nothing.

I pick a chair opposite her and pull it out. It makes one of those ear-piercing screeches that set your teeth on edge as it scrapes across the tiles. I wince.

'Hi. My name is Abigail,' I say. 'Abbie,' I add.

The pause is so long that I wonder if she hasn't heard me. I'm about to repeat myself when she speaks.

'And you're some kind of do-gooder, are you?' she asks, which throws me entirely. What am I supposed to say to that?

'Erm, well . . .' I stumble. 'I do try to do good. In life I mean. Generally. But that's not why I want to sit here.'

The woman's eyes don't let mine go and she sits perfectly still, waiting for me to elaborate. I can feel colour rising up my neck. I haven't blushed in years but there's something about her stare that wobbles me totally off balance.

'I . . . erm . . . well, I lost my job last week. Not my fault, but still. And all my friends are at work and I haven't . . . well. I'm just looking for someone to talk to.'

She nods just once, seemingly satisfied with my credentials.

'My name is Ethel. Pleased to make your acquaintance.'

She holds out her hand but with such a limp wrist that I would have to be a contortionist to shake it. It almost looks as if she expects me to kiss it, like she's an old Russian princess. Actually she looks a lot like I imagine an old Russian princess would look. Ethel isn't Anastasia though. Ethel is a very English name.

I touch the ends of my fingers to hers and that seems to suffice.

We both take a sip of our drinks. For me it's to fill an awkward moment but Ethel looks entirely comfortable, as if sitting at tables designed for sad people with no friends is an everyday occurrence. I'm so tempted to ask if she comes here often but I manage to rein myself in.

Ethel cuts off the smallest square of the Madeira cake and pops it into her mouth. Her nose crinkles and she tuts quietly.

'Yesterday's,' she says. 'I can always tell. Still, it's not bad.'

'I think they do a good cake in here,' I say, trying to get the conversation flowing.

'Do you?' she replies as if I've said something foolish which she is storing in her memory bank for later.

Feeling on the back foot again, I try to justify myself. 'Not that I've tried them all, of course,' I add with a little twitch of my shoulders.

'Then how can you possibly say?' she asks, not unreasonably.

Good God. I'm starting to wish I'd stayed where I was. If this is the way Ethel deals with people, it's no wonder she has to come to the community table to make friends.

But no. That is an uncharitable thought. I have no idea what has brought Ethel to the table and I must leave my assumptions to one side. However, with such a frosty table companion it's a bit hard to know how to strike up a conversation.

'What was the job?' she asks abruptly. 'The one that you so carelessly lost.'

I want to say that there was nothing careless in the losing of it but what would be the point?

'I was an account executive for an ad agency. Quite a good position as it goes. But I didn't see eye to eye with the boss . . .'

Ethel raises one perfectly drawn half-moon eyebrow.

'Well, he didn't see eye to eye with me. I didn't really fit in. So they sacked me and now I come here while I look for something new.'

'Did you like your job?' she asks.

A lump rises in my throat, which is awkward. I don't want to cry. I swallow it back down.

'I did,' I say.

'And were you good at it?'

'Yes.'

'So it feels unjust to you? Being dismissed.'

'Yes. It does,' I agree. 'Very.'

'This is something you can use. Your emotional response to the injustice can be harnessed to create great work in the future,' she says.

I wait for her to elaborate but she returns her focus to her plate, spearing another square of Madeira cake with her knife. She must have been some kind of creative in her former life. A writer maybe, or an actress.

I take a mouthful of coffee, which has cooled a little and no longer tastes bitter now that I'm having an interesting, if not slightly scary, conversation with a stranger. I can't resist asking my question.

'Do you come here often? To sit here, I mean.'

It occurs to me just too late that this might be an insulting question as it presupposes that Ethel has a reason to sit at the Billy No Mates table. But then, she has sat here, so needing company must be implied.

'I come when I can no longer bear the infernal drivel that the television companies put out to entertain the masses during the day. Do they think we have had lobotomies?'

I can't help but smile. I've already made a deal with myself that no matter how bad things get, I refuse to sink to watching daytime TV.

'And do other people sit here? So far I've only seen one man and he sat on his own and then left.'

Ethel thinks about this for a moment. 'Was he wearing a blue coat? Looked like he needed someone to hose him down?'

This is such an inappropriate description that it makes me want to laugh out loud but I try very hard not to. I press my lips together and nod.

'That'll be Bob,' she says. 'He does have a home, despite appearances to the contrary, but I'm not sure he's terribly well acquainted with its bathroom.'

I'm reminded of the hum that came off him as I walked past and I feel ashamed that I made all those assumptions about him simply based on appearances.

'I like your skirt,' Ethel says, squinting at the stitch-work on the appliqué. 'Is it original?'

'No,' I admit. 'It's a replica.'

Ethel lets out a sigh, sitting back in her chair, and I feel like I've disappointed her personally.

'It's from the original pattern, though,' I add. 'I can't sew myself but I know someone who's an amazing dressmaker and she makes most of my clothes for me. That's why I can't eat the cake. She'd kill me if she had to start again!'

And then for the first time Ethel smiles.

A breakthrough of sorts.

'You must show me more of your clothes another day,' she says.

9

By the time I get home I'm actually feeling quite jolly. My encounter with Ethel only lasted as long as it took her to finish her mint tea, at which point she had left without a goodbye or a 'nice to meet you'. I wasn't mid-sentence at the time but I suspect if I had been it wouldn't have made any difference.

But even though the meeting had been brief and I hadn't learned anything except her name and that she detests daytime television, it felt like it had potential. And she had given the smelly man, Bob, a bill of approval, which gives me confidence for any future encounters with him.

A not completely awful day all told.

An uncomfortable question flits across my mind. How come I was happy to go and talk to Ethel, sitting there elegantly in her chiffon, and yet not to Bob in his scruffy parka? Of course, I think I know the answer. Ethel appears to be more my kind of person than Bob. Yet Ethel seems to like Bob.

I'm just working my way round this spiky little thought when I remember Spencer's email and my heart careers back down to my boots again. I've been avoiding the question. I've had other things to think about. But he does deserve an answer.

I open the email on my phone and reread it.

I can't believe he's going so soon. When we first discussed it, I had my big and important job and it was a no-brainer. Give up the flat and the job and my friends and family to chase a barely started relationship dream to the opposite end of the country?

Of course not!

Abigail Finch is not the kind of woman who throws away her life for a man, and on a whim at that, even if she does like him a lot more than she'd care to admit.

But that was before.

Now everything looks very different. I have no job. My friends aren't quite as there for me as I'd assumed and I haven't spoken to my family for over a week, and yet we don't seem to be missing each other. Perhaps I'm not as tied to Leeds as I thought I was.

Am I sure . . . ?

Spencer dropped his bombshell after we'd been for dinner at a Thai street food place in Leeds. I'd just been contemplating whether I wanted a post-dinner cup of coffee or to go to a bar for one last drink when he said, 'I've been offered a job in the Outer Hebrides.'

It was as if he'd said, 'I think I'll get the number 2 bus home instead of the 36.'

I stared at him, not quite sure that I'd heard him properly. 'What?'

'The Outer Hebrides,' he repeated. 'Counting puffins. Well, not just puffins. All the seabirds. And it's more of a volunteer role to start with but you get food and accommodation thrown in.'

'Oh!' I said, delighted for him. 'That sounds fun. How long is it for?'

I assumed he'd say a week or so, maybe a month, and was already thinking how much I'd miss him.

'Six months to start with but it could be a permanent job if it all goes well.'

'Oh,' I said again, hoping that my sudden slump into my chair hadn't been as obvious as it felt to me.

Six months! That's a very long time when you've only been dating for six weeks. And if he did stay on . . . Well, that would be that.

He was looking at me as if he expected a more comprehensive response than I had given up to that point.

'Well, that's great,' I tried, although I'm not sure I was terribly convincing. 'Congratulations. So your job at the call centre . . . ?'

'Resigned. This morning.'

'Oh,' I said for the third time.

I really didn't know what else to say. There was me thinking that finally I'd met someone with potential to be if not 'the one' then at least a long-term thing and suddenly he was telling me that he had other plans.

The shock of it made me dumb as I tried to second-guess his intentions. I assumed this was him letting me down gently, that he saw no future for us. We were relatively new, after all, and it's a very long way to go for a weekend pizza and glass of wine, which was where we'd got so far. But I'd thought our pairing had potential for more. Disappointment must have been dripping off me but also I felt a bit stupid that I'd got us so wrong.

'Goodness,' I said, still feeling floored. 'That's a shame. This has been fun.'

I threw him what I hoped was a quirky 'them's the breaks' kind of smile. It was so awkward. I wished he'd just agree with me and get it over with. My eyes darted around the place for our waiter, so I could order the espresso that I definitely needed, saving myself from the cringeworthy humiliation of the conversation.

'I don't want us to split up,' he said, pulling a confused face that made me want to kiss him. 'Why don't you come with me?'

I turned back to face him, my jaw hanging unattractively.

'What?'

'You could come too. Get work to give you a sabbatical. I'm sure they would if you put together a good enough case.'

'I can't. My boss hates me. There's no way he'd give me an extra day beyond my annual leave, let alone . . .'

I thought about what he was asking. What was he asking? A month off, six months, more? Well, that was unthinkable. It wasn't a lie that I would never have got the time off but also, I didn't want to leave Leeds. There were just too many exciting things going on in my life to step out of it for even a weekend. I wasn't about to give it all up for a man I barely knew. That would be madness.

'Then why don't you resign too,' Spencer said. 'We can go on an adventure together.'

His eyes were shining with the thrill of it all but I could only see practicalities.

'I can't. You know how much I love my job. I can't just give it up. And what would I do for money up there?'

'You're more than just your job, you know, Abbie,' he said. 'I'm sure there's work. Lewis is a big place. Well, not as big as Leeds, obviously, but there must be jobs. And they encourage people to go and live there and work remotely. If Covid has shown us anything it's that we don't have to be in the office every day.'

'But you do have to be there some of the time and it's . . .' I get my phone out and click to Maps. '. . . five hundred miles from here. Not exactly an easy commute.'

'You can fly to Leeds Bradford Airport,' he said, but the sparkle was starting to leave him as it became apparent that I wasn't as into his plan as he was.

'No. I don't think so. Thanks for the offer. I'm touched that you suggested it, but I can't see it working . . .'

'Please think about it,' he said eagerly. 'Don't say no now. Give the idea some proper consideration.'

I shook my head. 'I'm sorry, Spencer. I like you, I *really* do. But I can't just give up my life on a whim like that. I mean, what about Elvis . . .'

He put his hand up to stop me talking.

'Listen, Abbie. This is a shock. I know it is. I probably shouldn't have sprung it on you. But I really think it could be great for us. I don't go for a couple weeks yet. How about you road test the idea, see what you think. And if it's still a no then we can each go our separate ways. But please don't dismiss it out of hand.'

'Okay,' I said. 'I will think about it, but, honestly, I can't see myself changing my mind.'

And I really couldn't, back then.

But now everything has changed.

I search for Lewis and Harris on Google Maps and pull the island around on my finger, exploring all its little nooks and crannies. I move over on to images and the screen fills with photos of beaches that wouldn't look out of place in the Caribbean. Soft white sand and sparkling turquoise sea. I know it doesn't look like that all the time. It's virtually in the Arctic Circle after all, but it is beautiful.

I click on Stornoway, hoping to find an austere town full of rugged uncompromising stone, but the first thing that pops up is the harbour where all the buildings are painted in cheerful pinks, yellows and blues. If Google is to be believed then it's a picture-perfect location.

I shut my phone down. It's stupid to even look. This is not the time to be gallivanting off after a man I barely know even if I do miss him more than I care to admit. I have to sort my life out, get a new job, get things back on track.

And anyway, Elvis hates cars.

10

On Tuesday I make my morning coffee and feed Elvis, who, having mewed relentlessly until I filled his bowl, promptly ignores the food and stalks away. I go through my new morning ritual.

Check my emails for exciting opportunities. Nothing.

Check LinkedIn for new job listings. Nothing that I want to do for a living.

Check my bank balance. Dwindling.

But it's early days. Of course I wasn't going to walk straight into something new. Even the best plans need lead-in times. There is nothing to panic about. All will be well.

I do have to reply to Spencer, though. I can't leave him hanging. He will no doubt have deduced my answer from my silence but still. I wasn't brought up to be rude.

> To: Spencer Moore
> From: Abigail Finch
> Subject: RE: Last chance

I pause, letting the idea of moving to the Outer Hebrides with Spencer, blissfully cut off from everything and everyone I know, dance round my imagination for one more minute, but I can't go with him. It's just not practical. This is precisely the wrong time to leave Leeds when everything is up in the air.

I begin to type, aiming for chatty rather than emotional.

Hi Spencer,

You're going already. I can't believe it's come round so soon.

I have thought about it. I really have, but I can't go with you. It's just not practical. I have too many ties here. But I'll miss you loads. It's been fun.

Love,

Abbie xxx

PS I'll never look at a puffin again without wondering if it's one of yours!

A tear runs down my nose and plops on to the keyboard. It's true. I will miss him. I do miss him. But it's not fair to keep him hanging. I have to cut the thread and move on. Spencer is just one more thing in my life that's broken.

It's starting to look like a long list.

To cheer myself up, I decide to go down to the café today, like it's not something that I've started doing every day anyhow. It was lovely meeting Ethel and I really hope she's there again.

I pick out one of my genuinely vintage frocks – a pale blue tea dress with a tiny floral print and a cream shawl collar – especially for her and hope she'll appreciate it.

When I get to the café Liz greets me with a smile.

'Morning, my love. Flat white is it?'

A warm buzz goes through me – not only am I recognised, but I now have a regular coffee order. That never happened in all the time I was working in the city centre. I beam at Liz. 'Please.'

'Gorgeous dress. My mother is wearing one just like that in a photo somewhere. Well, it's a black and white photo so it's hard to tell exactly, but I'm sure that's what it must have been like.'

I smile my thanks and then Liz cocks her head in the direction of the community table.

'Look who's back.'

I turn, hoping it's Ethel, but in fact it's Bob in his blue parka. His hair is almost shining with what I assume is grease.

'I think he's called Bob,' I reply softly so he can't hear us.

'Is that right?' says Liz, not really interested, and then moves on to the next customer.

I get my coffee and then turn to face the café. I actually have butterflies at the thought of going to talk to Bob, but I'm determined to do it. I stride purposefully in his direction.

'May I join you?' I ask when I reach the table. I can smell him from here.

He starts at my question and then looks to see who has spoken. His soft brown eyes light up when he sees me there.

'Yeah. Deffo. Sit yourself down,' he says, half standing in a gesture of chivalry. 'I'm Bob,' he adds.

'Abbie,' I say. 'Nice to meet you.'

'Likewise. And what brings you here to the table of outcasts?' He winks at me and smiles warmly.

'Much the same as you, I imagine,' I say. 'Bit lonely. In need of company. Bored with the status quo. Take your pick.'

Bob nods and takes a slurp of his tea. Literally a slurp. I try not to flinch but it's an effort.

'So, Abbie. What do you think about this?' He pushes his tabloid newspaper towards me and points at the headline. It's a story about a celebrity who's been caught fiddling her taxes. I wonder if it's a test but there really is only one response.

'We all have to pay tax,' I say. 'Like Oscar Wilde said, nothing is certain except death and taxes,' I say brightly, hoping it's the right response.

'Franklin,' he says.

'Sorry?'

'It was Benjamin Franklin. Not Oscar Wilde.' He corrects me kindly with not a hint of one-upmanship, but I still feel like an idiot.

'God, was it?' I say quickly. 'Shows what I know. He was right though. And just because you're a celebrity doesn't mean the law doesn't apply to you.'

'True enough,' he replies. 'Although it's a bit crap to have your private affairs all over the front pages, even if you are trying to dodge your tax.'

It's an interesting point and one that I've thought about more than once. 'Don't you think, though, that when you sign up to be a celebrity with all the privileges and benefits that come with that, you then have a responsibility to live as blameless a life as you can, and you can't really complain about the press interest if you don't?'

He eyes me thoughtfully, like he's weighing up what I just said. And then he replies. 'Nope. No one deserves to have their dirty laundry washed in the public eye. I don't care who they are or what they've done. It's the papers that should be ashamed, hounding people out of their homes.'

'And us too,' I add. 'I mean, if we didn't buy the papers . . .' I raise an eyebrow at his copy of the *Sun*.

He grins at me. 'You've got me good and proper there,' he says. 'I love a bit of celebrity gossip, me. Me ex-wife, she used to say

"Bob Hoskins. You're worse than a woman." And, yes. That's me name. Bob Hoskins. Me mother was no cinema-goer. Didn't have a clue that she was saddling me with a lifetime of raised eyebrows and bad jokes.'

I try to think of Bob Hoskins films but can't get beyond the cartoon Jessica Rabbit costume that I wore to a fancy dress party once.

'It's getting better as I get older. Most young people have never heard of him,' he adds. He narrows his eyes at me. 'You have though. I can see it in your face.'

'My dad's a film buff,' I say as I wonder exactly what he saw.

'That explains it,' he says.

'Oh, and look who we have here. If it isn't the ice queen herself.'

I follow his line of sight and see Ethel making her sedate way across the café towards us.

11

'Good morning, Robert,' she says as she sets her tray down on our table. 'Abigail.' She nods at us both and I see her eyes linger on my dress.

'Good morning, Ethel,' I say, pleased that she has remembered my name. 'And how are you today?'

Ethel ignores my question and sits herself upwind of Bob.

'Rocky road today, I see,' says Bob, nodding at her tray. 'Plays havoc with the fillings, that stuff.'

The look Ethel gives him could have cut through diamonds, but Bob seems unconcerned.

'I swerve the sweet stuff myself. A moment on the lips, a life-time on the hips. That's what me ex used to say.'

'She must be a very wise woman,' says Ethel, 'apart from her unfortunate taste in husbands.'

These two are comedy gold. I'd got the impression yesterday that Ethel barely knew Bob but it's obvious they have spent plenty of time together and this playful banter is part of their vibe.

Ethel doesn't defend her cake decision but there doesn't appear to be a pound to spare on her narrow frame. Having to watch her weight can't be something that troubles her unduly.

'And you're wearing another interesting garment today, Abigail,' she says to me.

'Yes. This one is original,' I say. 'Or at least I believe it is.'

Ethel reaches out to touch the fabric and pinches it between her fingers. Then she lifts the hem and examines the stitches. 'Yes. I'd say so.'

'Do you sew?' I ask her, not feeling that this question is much of an imposition, given the interest she's shown in my clothes. But again, she ignores my question and turns to Bob.

'Did you get the chisel set?' she asks him.

Bob shakes his head. 'Nah. Got outbid at the last minute. I've seen a nice jig-saw though which is in budget so I'm watching that. Got a good feeling about it.'

I have no idea what's going on, but something tells me that I'll be better watching and learning than asking direct questions. And so in this way I think I gather that Bob lives in a flat with two other men and that Ethel had a dog called Rudolf that died recently – but I might be wrong.

They don't ask anything about me. I wonder if that's a way of deflecting any questions about themselves. In many ways, it's refreshing that the conversation is very much in the here and now without following any of the usual social conventions. But I'm also fiendishly curious about them both and search each sentence for clues. It dawns on me that my friends and former close colleagues all very much fit one mould, so it's interesting to be learning things about people whose lives are so different to mine.

There seems to be an unspoken rule that you only stay at the table for one drink. I'm not sure whether that's to do with budget or a tacit agreement not to let the day run away by spending all their time in a supermarket café. Either way, when Bob gets to the dregs of his tea he makes a move to stand. I get a whiff of him as he moves and his clothing resettles around him.

'Right then. Can't sit round here all day chatting to you two lovely ladies. Places to go, people to see.'

I spot something that looks a lot like sadness flit across his features but it's gone in an instant.

'See you again, maybe.'

Then he raises his arm in salute, something that I suspect both Ethel and I wish he hadn't done judging by the way Ethel's nose crinkles, and then he's gone, out of the door and away. This seems to be another rule of the community table. They don't appear to make a plan to meet here like real friends might. Meetings seem to be based on coincidence.

But they do seem to be friends, of a sort at least. Confused by the dynamic, I say goodbye to Ethel and leave the café as well, wondering as I go how many other regular patrons there might be.

My fridge is looking a little on the sparse side, so I decide to take advantage of being at the supermarket and pick up a few bits and pieces. I'm just in the bakery aisle when I hear a familiar voice.

'Yoo-hoo! Abbie?'

Mum! My heart sinks. I don't feel great about lying to her, which I haven't actually done because I've avoiding speaking to her. Until now.

This isn't her nearest supermarket by a long way, but I know she likes to pop in if she's passing to check out the new chutneys, etc. The place is full of items you can't find anywhere else.

I turn round and see her coming towards me. To be fair, she's easy to spot. Today must be a re-enactment day because she's in full toga and sandals with her hair piled on top of her head in a tumble of artful curls.

My parents like to spend their spare time dressing up and haring round the country to meet other like-minded people. This has been the case for as long as I remember so I'm used to it – they even used to drag us along when we were smaller – but I forget that other people find it surprising, as demonstrated by the public's response to my mother now. Everyone stares at us. I try to ignore it.

I'm pretty sure the re-enactment society has a rule against wearing your get-up to the shops. It messes with the authenticity. But my mum has never thought rules apply to her. 'Oh, it won't matter just this once.' Or, 'Who's going to mind if I just park on this double yellow? I'll only be a minute.' Or my own personal favourite, 'One-way streets are only for people who aren't local.'

I brace myself for the questions. 'Hi, Mum.'

'I thought it was you. But then I thought it couldn't possibly be because you should be at work at this time. Tuesday is a strange day to take off and if you had the week off you'd surely have told us. But, see, it is you after all.'

'Yes, Mum. It's me.' She gives me a 'well, what's the explanation' kind of look, which I attempt to deflect with a question of my own. 'Are you on your way somewhere?' I nod at her toga.

'Oh yes. There's a Daily Life Day near Scarborough. We said we'd show our faces. I shouldn't really be in here dressed like this, but we were driving past, and I just thought I could pop in. No one will notice. Your father's in the car.'

We ignore the fact that every single person in the aisle is craning their neck to stare as they shuffle past us.

'That'll be fun,' I say, although I've never really understood why my parents seem to enjoy dressing up in period clothes and pretending life is different to how it is. The irony of that statement is not lost on me.

'Why don't I pop out and say hello to Dad?' I add, putting my five-seed loaf back on the shelf and heading in the direction of the door. I don't give her an inch to ask a question.

'I'll just have a look at . . .' She waves her arm vaguely in the direction of the international foods aisle, which is surely in need of a rebrand, and I make my way to the car park.

I think about doing a runner at this point. I could say that work rang and I had to leave urgently but then I'd never hear the end of it.

It takes me a while to locate Dad's car. He's sitting in the driver's seat with his coat on but I can see the white of his toga underneath. Arriving in a motor vehicle apparently is fine, vibe-wise.

I knock on his window, and he starts, but when he sees who it is he gives me his big, broad grin. 'Hello!' he mouths through the glass and then messes about with various buttons trying to get the window to go down. 'Fancy seeing you here.'

'Mum sent me. I saw her in the shop.'

'I bet everyone saw her in the shop. Reg will be furious if he gets wind of her being out in costume again.'

'I won't tell if you don't,' I say and wink at him.

'What are you up to?' he asks, and I immediately feel guilty.

'I'm not up to anything,' I reply defensively. 'I'm just . . . picking up some bits for my boss. We've got some customers coming in and he wanted to put on a bit of a spread.'

'I see,' says Dad without even a hint of suspicion. 'Well, we're just on our way out to Scarborough.'

'Yes, Mum said. Nice day for it.'

'It won't be when we get there. Bloody freezing on the east coast this time of year. But all is not lost.'

He lifts his toga and I see a flash of cream Damart thermals.

Mum arrives moments later with a new canvas shopping bag. 'I have hundreds of these things,' she says. 'I always forget to take one with me and then it seems so bad to buy a plastic bag.'

'Well,' I say, looking at my watch in an urgent manner. 'Lovely to see you but I must dash.'

'But . . .' Mum starts but I'm gone.

'I'll ring,' I call over my shoulder. 'Have a great time.'

And then I walk as quickly as I can out of the car park, hoping Dad hasn't noticed that I don't appear to have any shopping.

12

I don't get a reply from Spencer, but I wasn't really expecting to. My answer was unequivocal. But that doesn't stop me jumping every time a message pings though. What with that and the job applications I'm a nervous wreck.

I need a project to take my mind off it all – a cheap one. It's all very well kicking around on my own all day but Elvis is no conversationalist. I'm time rich and motivation poor which is not a space I'm used to occupying.

After a little thought, I settle on decorating my back bedroom. I call it a bedroom but there's no bed in it yet. I've not had cause for many people to stay over since I moved in as my friends and family all live so close. But this might be the perfect time to rectify that.

So I spend the rest of the day on Pinterest coming up with a scheme. When I was working, if someone had said I could spend a day online choosing paint colours and soft furnishings I would have bitten their hand off. Now that I have all the time in the world, the task feels like a chore, something I have to force myself to focus on.

I flick through various screens but my heart isn't really in it. Instead of being a passion project, it feels like another way to pass the time. But then, isn't everything just a way to pass time to some extent?

Oh God. Misery *and* philosophy. Things must be bad!

The only highlight of my days, I realise, is the time spent in the café. In the space of a week I've gone from mild but ever so slightly disdainful curiosity about the community table to actually craving the company it provides for me.

I start thinking about the times I've been there when the others have been too, searching for patterns of behaviour, but I can't find any. I tend to go to the café in the morning. Some days they've been there and on others they haven't.

Maybe Bob and Ethel and whoever else uses the table go in the afternoons as well to mix things up a bit? How will I find out? If I switch to afternoons I might miss them in the morning. The thought that I could just establish myself there all day long feels horribly desperate. I can just picture Liz's face – sympathetic but pitying.

I conclude that I should continue with my morning visits and see what happens. Who knows – maybe *they* are hoping to bump into *me* and have noticed that I'm a morning person?

So the next day, there I am in the café with my flat white and my iPad pretending to be busy with my Pinterest board. I don't sit at the community table unless there's somebody already there. I can't quite identify why that is and I'm not sure I want to unpick it. But I'm close by in case anyone should sit down.

And they do. This one is younger than the others – around my age I'd say. She bustles into the café chatting to herself. I can't hear what she's saying but she seems totally content.

She's dressed eccentrically. I mean, I know I stand out from the crowd, but my style is exactly that – a style. Her outfit is a chaotic and riotous rainbow of colours. Everything is a statement in its own right. Yellow leggings, a bright blue sweater with a pink flamingo on the front, purple Crocs worn with red socks, a green tote bag with 'I love frogs' and a cartoon picture of a smiling frog printed on it. My eye doesn't know where to go first.

She heads for the counter – it's Joel working today – and comes away with a pink milkshake in a sundae glass. It has extra cream and chocolate sprinkles on the top and she carries it carefully, her tongue peeping out of the corner of her mouth.

She passes a table and stops to chat to a couple of women. I can't hear what she says but it's clear from their reactions that they don't know her and don't know what to make of her overt friendliness. They do that terribly British thing of being polite while clearly wishing she would leave them alone.

It's awkward to watch, partly because I know I've done the same thing to odd people myself dozens of times. I wonder how this shunning makes the woman feel, or if she's even noticed. I know I'd have done exactly the same before, felt uncomfortable to have been approached by a slightly peculiar person whose norms were a bit out of kilter with mine. I too would have been coolly polite and dismissive.

But not any more. Almost as soon as the woman sits down at the community table I'm out of my seat and there.

'Hi,' I say before I put my cup down. 'I'm Abbie. Do you mind if I join you?'

She frowns a little as she thinks about it and then smiles. One of her front teeth is missing and the gap makes her look like a little girl.

'No,' she says. 'I don't mind.'

Then she starts rummaging in her bag, ignoring me entirely. I sit down opposite her and wait. She seems to have already forgotten that I'm there and is completely absorbed in her task. As she takes each item out, she places it in a neat row along the edge of the table.

A purse with a cow's face on it. A stapler. A pom-pom made of shiny metallic ribbon. A book (*Harry Potter and the Prisoner of Azkaban*, my personal favourite of the series). A reusable coffee cup. An enormous bunch of keys with a huge cork ball as a key ring. And finally a plastic box of plasters which she lifts in the air triumphantly.

Assuming she has a minor injury, I'm surprised when she opens the box, tips it on one side and slides the contents out. There are no plasters, just an iridescent glass marble which shimmers like the sea on a sunny day.

She examines the marble carefully and then passes it over to me.

'That's pretty.' I sound like I'm talking to a child. It makes me cringe but I'm not sure how else to respond.

'Yeah,' she replies. 'My grandad gave it to me.'

She puts the marble back into the plasters box, closes the lid tightly, gives it a little shake just to be sure and drops it back into her bag, followed by all her other items one at a time. Then she wraps her lips around the straw in her milkshake and takes a long drag, wiping her mouth with the back of her hand when she's finished.

'I'm Dawn,' she says. 'Like when the sun gets up.'

'Hi, Dawn.' I give her my best smile.

13

'I've not seen you before,' says Dawn, eyeing me suspiciously.

'No. I'm new.'

'What's your name again?'

'Abbie. It's short for Abigail.'

Dawn nods, taking this in. 'Dawn isn't short for anything. It's the whole thing on its own.'

'I've met Bob and Ethel. Do you know them?'

She nods again. 'Ethel is a ballet dancer and Bob smells, but Ethel says it's not his fault and I shouldn't pull faces or say "poo" because it might hurt his feelings.'

'That's good advice. I didn't know that Ethel is a ballet dancer.' Although from the way she dresses and carries herself it makes perfect sense.

'She doesn't do ballet dancing any more,' Dawn adds. 'But she used to do it for a job. Do you have a job?'

'Not at the moment,' I say, not wanting to confuse matters by explaining.

'I do. I work as a cleaner but I can only do it when all the people have gone home. I'm a good cleaner. Very thorough.'

She says this as if she's repeating what someone else has told her.

'I love your hair,' she adds.

Today I have it up in a pony tail with the ends curled. 'Thanks!'

'Could you do that to mine?'

Practicalities flood my brain. No because your hair is too thin and anyway where would we do it? I can hardly plug my curling tongs in here.

'Maybe,' I reply vaguely.

'I like your clothes too.'

I'm wearing dark denim jeans with big turn ups and a red checked shirt.

'Do you like mine?'

'I do!' I say, again feeling uncomfortable because I sound a little bit patronising, to my own ears at least. But not, it seems, to Dawn. She beams at me.

'Which is your favourite part?' she asks, standing up and giving me a twirl.

'The flamingo,' I reply with real conviction.

'Mine too. My milkshake is good. Want to try?' She offers me the straw.

'No thanks.'

'What've you got?'

'Coffee.'

She pulls a face. 'Coffee's disgusting,' she says and then finishes her milkshake.

I expect her to make that straw-sucking sound when she reaches the bottom but instead she tips the glass up into her mouth and finishes the drink noiselessly.

'Bob lost his house,' she says. 'And his wife and children. He gets quite sad.'

The switch of direction throws me, and I struggle to keep up as she gives me all this new information.

'Oh dear,' I say, hoping that staying neutral will encourage her to keep talking, but that's all she has to share.

64

'Better go,' she says, standing up. 'I have to buy some baked beans. Nice meeting you.'

And then she's gone.

I sit there processing what I've learned. Dawn must come to the table often as she knows far more about both Ethel and Bob than I've managed to elicit thus far. Or maybe they just don't feel comfortable sharing personal things with me. Perhaps I'm giving off an air that makes people feel cautious of me. I don't think so, but you never know how others perceive you.

It was refreshing, though, to meet someone who is as upfront as Dawn. I bet she wouldn't hide what was going on for her from her friends and family. Even when I wasn't harbouring this huge secret, I can't remember talking to friends and family in as unguarded a way as Dawn just did with me. There is always something to hold back, some mask to hide behind. It's exhausting.

My coffee has gone cold but I drink it anyway and contemplate a second cup. I know the others only seem to stay for one drink, but that's their rule, not mine. And then, from absolutely nowhere, tears come. I feel my throat thicken, the hot pricking at my eyes, and then the corners of my mouth pull down as I start to sob. I try to swallow them back down but now I've started I can't stop.

I put my hand over my mouth to try to stifle the sound. I should leave and go and have my mini breakdown in the ladies. No one relishes public displays of emotion and I'm sitting at the community table. People will assume my life has fallen apart.

But hasn't it?

And who cares if a bunch of strangers do see me cry? We must be entitled to feel upset sometimes, and if that happens when we're away from the privacy of our homes then surely we can just lean into it.

But I find that I do care. I scrabble in my bag for tissues, locate one and try to blow my nose quietly and discreetly when what I really need is a proper blast. I'm aware of one or two people turning to look at me but no one gets up to see if I'm okay – ironic given that I'm sitting at the table specifically designed for people who need help.

I close my eyes and jab my fingernails into my palms to try and regain some control, focusing my attention on that sensation rather than the inconvenient tears, so I don't notice that someone has come to check on me until I feel a light tap on my shoulder.

'Are you okay? Can I get you anything?'

I look up, dabbing at my eyes with the tissue and even in this moment hoping that my waterproof mascara is as good as its name. It's Joel, the manager guy, and the look on his face is one of genuine concern. The last time I saw him he was snapping at that new girl and his expression was all hard lines and irritation, but this is completely different. It doesn't stop me being mortified though.

'How embarrassing,' I mumble through my tissue. 'I'm fine. Honestly. Just having a moment.'

'We all get those,' he says kindly. 'And you met Dawn. She's a character, isn't she?'

Grateful that he's taken the attention away from me I agree enthusiastically.

'Yes. She's great,' I agree. 'I've been coming for a week now and I've met some lovely people. This was your idea, I gather. This table.'

He gives a modest little shrug. 'Well, we're almost never completely full and I just thought it was a nice idea. Mentioned it to head office and they gave me the go-ahead. And it fits with the company ethos. We like to help the community where we can. This year's chosen charity is one that supports the homeless.'

I remember the notice I saw for the 10K. 'Oh, the race?' I say, gesturing at the noticeboard.

'Exactly. Fancy entering?'

I grimace. 'Not really my bag, running.'

'Well, keep your eyes open for other events. Head office is very keen on that kind of thing.' He rolls his eyes and grins conspiratorially. 'It's all about the brand these days, isn't it? Anyway, if you're okay I'll get back to my coffee machine. Sure I can't get you anything?'

I shake my head. 'No thanks.'

I get up to leave, stuffing the soggy tissue into my jeans pocket and making a mental note to take it out before I wash them. As I head for the exit, I think about what Joel just said. 'It's all about the brand.' Is that true? Is the only reason there's the community table because some marketing manager at head office thought it would enhance the supermarket's image?

Given what I do for a living, I know that at least part of that is true but just at the moment it leaves a sour taste.

14

The new day dawns and puffy eyes seem to be all that's left of my little outburst. I do a quick scan to check how I'm feeling and conclude that I'm okay. I suppose it's good that I finally had a proper emotional response to my situation, even if my body didn't choose the most convenient moment to let rip.

And losing your job is a big deal. It's in the top five of life's most stressful events along with financial challenges and relationship break-ups. I know because I googled it when I was feeling particularly miserable. So, it's not surprising that I cried.

But as I'm sitting on my sofa letting breakfast telly wash over me with Elvis asleep on my lap, I start to wonder just how much of my teary outburst was actually prompted by being sacked. Yes, it was a shock, but when I probe a little deeper into the root cause I find that it's more than just that.

I'd thought that I had my life entirely under control, that I was precisely where I needed to be. Yet when I scratch at the shiny surface, that veneer of perfection seems to be coming away under my fingernails. Things really weren't as wonderful as I let myself believe.

No one has been in touch with me. And I mean no one. I try to remember how much day to day contact I had with friends and family when I was busy at work. I suppose days did slip by when I was just too busy to message. But whole weeks?

I've heard next to nothing from my former colleagues. This really hurts but it's like they don't want to be tainted by association. Or, and this is even worse, they weren't really my friends after all. I was part of the team but once I left, I lost my status. I became just someone they used to work with.

My non-work friends have been quiet too. Picking up my phone, I scroll back through my messages to see how long the gaps are. And there's the truth of it staring me in the face. Apart from Spencer, with that thrill of the new relationship, I have barely been in touch with anyone outside work since Christmas. That's months. How had I not noticed?

But it's a two-way street, I tell myself, trying self-righteously to shift the blame on to others. Sal and the others haven't messaged me either. But how often do I initiate a night out or a weekend brunch or even just text to ask how a friend is?

I don't have to look at my phone to know the answer to that one. I'm not a bad person. I haven't ignored my friends on purpose. I was just busy, and my life had fallen into a pattern where the only person I was spending spare time with was Spencer. And now even he's gone.

'What a mess, eh, Elvis,' I say as I run my hand from his ears to the tip of his tail. 'What a bloody mess.'

Well, I can fix that. I start to compose a message to Sal but my fingers hover over the screen. No. Not yet. I still need to regroup, think about what I want and how I want to live going forward. When I've done that, and I have a better idea of what my future looks like, then I can get in touch with people. And in the meantime it can be like a punishment I thoroughly deserve, counting the days when no one checks up on me. How long will it be before anyone does? A couple more weeks?

Months?

Or maybe even not at all.

No. I am not going there. Today I'm going to work on my positivity until I feel more in control. One day at a time is definitely the way to go.

As I eat my breakfast, I realise that I'm looking forward to seeing Ethel and the rest of them, am excited about it even. Partly this must be because I'm lonely here all by myself, but also I'm enjoying their company, their authenticity if you like. There's something so real about them that can be lacking in other people.

But what if our timings don't coincide and I keep missing them? Without a plan of some sort, fate may see to it that our paths never cross again.

This will not do.

I find a piece of A4 card and my pencil case and make a sign.

HI GANG,

I'D LOVE TO SEE YOU ALL MORE REGULARLY. I'LL BE HERE AT TEN

O'CLOCK EACH MORNING.

LOVE ABBIE

Then I doodle some daisies around the border and colour them in. Then I sketch a flamingo standing on one leg. And as a final flourish I add an x after my name.

15

Liz is behind the counter at the café but there's no one sitting at the community table when I arrive just before ten.

'Do you think it would be okay if I left a note on the table?' I ask, my insides clenching at how desperate this makes me look. I'm so tempted to add something about conducting a social experiment on friendship for some paper or other but then I get a grip. Ethel, Bob and Dawn are people, not lab rats. I suck up my embarrassment with a big smile.

'I'm sure that's fine, my love,' she says. 'Flat white, is it?'

'Please.'

I put my notice on the table, drink my coffee and leave but the next day I'm back at two minutes to ten and I'm delighted to see Ethel already sitting there with her mint tea. She is her usual, slightly aloof self so I decide not to mention my sign and just pretend it's a coincidence that we are there at the same time. For all I know it might be.

'Good morning, Ethel,' I say, cheerfully setting my coffee down on the table opposite her.

'Good morning, Abigail,' she replies but then falls silent.

My natural instinct is to chatter through the gap, but I think I might be getting the measure of Ethel, so I decide to hold my tongue and just let the morning evolve. We sit in silence for longer than I've ever done in the company of others since I was sitting exams, but I find that instead of feeling uncomfortable, it's actually completely natural.

After fifteen minutes, Ethel puts down her cup for the last time, the tea all gone.

'Goodbye, Abigail,' she says, and then she sweeps out of the café, her slender frame as erect as a woman's of half her age, her chiffon scarves wafting in her wake.

I sit there, not sure what to do next. I check the time. It's nearly twenty past ten. If the others have seen my message, they don't seem to be responding to it, or not today at least. I get up and follow Ethel out.

The next morning I'm back, and I've no sooner sat down with my coffee than Bob and then Dawn arrive in quick succession. I notice that my sign has gone. I assume that Liz or Joel cleared it away, but it doesn't matter. It seems to have served its purpose.

'Hello, Thingy,' says Dawn, smiling as she approaches me.

She's dressed as if she fell into a rainbow again – a short, tiered skirt in fuchsia pink and a turquoise sweatshirt teamed with the same purple Crocs.

'Her name's Abbie,' says Bob, who is a couple of steps behind her. 'It says so on the note. Great idea that, by the way,' he adds to me, and I smile back modestly.

'I'm rubbish at names,' says Dawn.

Today her milkshake is cream-coloured. Vanilla, I imagine.

'I like your dress,' she says. 'Stand up so I can see it properly.'

I do as I'm asked and give a little twirl. The full skirt splays out from my body as I turn.

Dawn makes appreciative noises. 'Do it again!' she says, and I oblige.

She claps her hands. 'Again!!'

Luckily, Bob comes to my rescue. 'Let Abbie sit down and drink her coffee,' he says with a laugh and a wink in my direction.

Dawn sticks out her tongue and wrinkles her nose in disgust. 'Don't like coffee,' she mutters.

Then she stands up and twirls on the spot. Her skirt also sticks out a little but it's not as spectacular as mine. She gives a little huff and sits down again.

Ethel arrives just as Dawn is picking up her milkshake.

'And we're quorate,' says Bob.

'So, is this everyone?' I ask. 'The regulars at the table, I mean.'

'That's right. Ethel, Dawn and me,' replies Bob. 'And now you, of course.'

He gives me such a sweet smile that I can almost overlook the fact that he smells as if he hasn't showered for a week.

'I wondered,' I say. 'I'm basically nosy.'

'Me too,' agrees Dawn. 'I like to know everything.'

She says this matter-of-factly, as if it's not something to be ashamed of. And why should it be? To be curious is only human.

Now that Bob has started the ball rolling I feel confident to ask a question or two, although nothing too probing. I don't want to scare them all off.

'Have you been friends for long?' I ask, which seems pretty neutral. His reply shows me that I'm right to be cautious.

'A fair while,' he says, but he doesn't look at me when he speaks and so I sense that I'm teetering very close to the line that should not be crossed. I change the subject.

'I'm decorating my back bedroom this week,' I say. 'Well, I haven't started yet. But I'm choosing the colour scheme.'

'I like yellow,' says Dawn. 'I'd paint my whole room yellow if I could but it's not allowed. I can put posters up though, as long as I don't make a mess of the walls. I have lots of posters.'

'What kind of thing?' I ask her.

73

She shrugs. 'Anything I like. I have a poster for Leeds Fest and one for if you feel uncomfortable in a bar. And one for a roller disco. And now I have your poster.'

I draw a blank.

'Your poster,' she insists. 'With the flamingo on.'

Oh! She means the notice I made. So that's where it went. I try to picture her room with its array of artwork that she must have stolen from walls around Leeds.

'It sounds great,' I say.

'What colour have you decided on?' asks Bob, and my mind takes a moment to leap back to where the conversation started.

'For my bedroom you mean? I haven't really. A mint maybe, or a kind of sorbet pink. It's so hard, isn't it? There are so many to choose from.'

And then, just too late, I remember what Dawn told me. Bob lost his house. And now I feel dreadful. Blithely discussing what colour to paint the walls of a very much not lost house is deeply insensitive of me. But I can't backtrack. I'm in too deep. He doesn't look offended though or unduly sad, but I make a mental note to avoid conversations about homes in the future. However, it makes things very tricky if you have to start a conversation with strangers without asking them any questions about themselves. My eyes dart around the café looking for conversational starters but I draw a blank.

Then Ethel saves the day.

16

'When I was dancing in Russia,' she begins, her voice quite ethereal, as if she's speaking in a dream. Immediately she has our attention. Even Dawn, who had been bursting tiny bubbles in her milkshake with her straw, sits still and listens.

'We were not permitted posters of any kind on our walls. Nothing was allowed that might distract us from the purity of the ballet.'

I'm fascinated by this incredible insight both into a world I know nothing about and also into Ethel's past life. And I didn't have to ask a single question, which is a big plus.

'Our lives were dedicated to ballet and ballet alone. We were either in class, on stage or asleep,' she says. 'If we were injured, we still had to go to class so we could learn by watching. It was rather like a boarding school for the corps de ballet dancers. We all lived together in a large institution and we ate together and slept in rooms of six. We were allowed one small cupboard for our clothes and a box under our bed to store our personal possessions. But definitely no posters.'

'That's a shame,' says Bob. He's smiling, which feels a bit off for such a serious conversation. 'I really like some of those old Soviet propaganda ones.'

I'm just wondering what propaganda art has to do with ballet when I see something pass between Bob and Ethel. It's fleeting, a twinkle, nothing more. But it's definitely there. I look from one to the other and narrow my eyes.

'Hang on! Are we having our legs pulled here?'

'Maybe just a little,' she says.

'But you were a ballet dancer, right?'

'I was. But in England not Russia. And I could have whatever posters I liked.'

I'm dying to ask more questions but I need to be led by Ethel and she seems to have stopped talking.

Dawn meanwhile has had her attention caught by something else. 'That man keeps staring at us,' she says.

'Which man?' Bob asks.

'Him!'

Dawn turns round and points at a guy at a nearby table with a glass of cola and a laptop. Seeing that he has been spotted, he immediately looks down and starts typing furiously.

As someone with my own preconceived ideas about the purpose of the community table and what kind of person would sit there a few short days ago, I can understand why he might be curious. Who wouldn't be when a bunch of mismatched oddballs like us all choose to sit in one place? It's hard to think of a different reason why we might all have come together, other than because of the primary purpose of the community table.

But it appears only I am thinking along these lines. It crosses my mind guiltily that perhaps the others don't see themselves as oddballs. I really am no good at this, but I'm trying my hardest.

'Do you think he wants to come over?' asks Dawn in a voice that isn't quite quiet enough for him not to hear. He sinks even further into his laptop.

'I'll go and ask him,' she says, and before anyone can suggest that it might not be a great idea Dawn is on her feet.

'Hello,' she begins when she reaches his table, one just next to ours. 'I'm Dawn. Like when the sun gets up.'

The poor guy adopts that frozen in terror look much favoured by rabbits caught in headlights. Then he seems to rally.

'I'm Viraj,' he replies in a voice so soft that it's hard to catch. He's polite at least.

'These are my friends Ethel and Bob and . . . the other one.'

'Abbie,' prompts Bob.

'Abbie,' continues Dawn. 'We sit at that table at ten o'clock each day because it's a place to make new friends.' She says this as if she's reading the words from the community table sign but she clearly knows them by heart. 'So if you want to make friends with us then you can sit with us too.'

She smiles and almost looks as if she's expecting applause for her speech, but then she turns and comes back to us.

I am mortified for the poor bloke. Truly mortified.

'Well done, Dawn,' says Bob kindly.

Viraj goes back to his laptop, and I wonder if we can restart the very interesting conversation we were having about Ethel's dancing but Bob changes the subject.

'I got that jig-saw, Ethel, and for a good price,' he says.

'That's excellent,' replies Ethel. 'How's the rebuilding coming along?'

Bob's shoulders slump. 'It's slow progress. But I'm getting there.'

'Well, that's the important thing.'

He nods sadly.

Bob's lost house is something else that I'm dying to know about but can't ask. Part of me hopes that the others are as intrigued by what my story might be as I am about theirs.

'Viraj is coming!' says Dawn.

I assume that what's actually happening is that Viraj is leaving, but no. He has put his laptop in his messenger bag, picked up his cola and is heading our way.

'Hi,' says Dawn excitedly, her enthusiasm brimming over.

'Hi, Dawn,' he replies. 'Can I join you?'

'Yes,' says Dawn decisively.

I see Viraj take us all in one by one, making a quick assessment, and I am gratified when he pulls out the seat next to me. In truth, I'd sit next to me too. He's met Dawn, Bob looks like a tramp and Ethel is yet to smile.

'Are you drinking cola?' asks Dawn. 'I don't like cola. Or coffee. But I do like milkshake. And also, I like Thingy's dress because when she spins round it all sticks out. Show him, Thingy.'

I think it's fair to say my mortification levels are currently at an all-time high, but keen to show willing I stand up and give them a twirl.

'That's very nice,' says Viraj politely in his gentle voice. He wears dark-rimmed glasses which he pushes back up his nose with his middle finger.

'Thanks,' I say and sit back down quickly.

I can get a better look at him now he's sitting with us. He's about my age with dark, neatly cut hair and a little moustache that looks like it can't decide if it should be there or not. Perhaps it's experimental. He's wearing black jeans and a black hoody and I'm half expecting Dawn to tell him that she doesn't like black, but she doesn't.

Viraj takes a deep breath and then, as if this is an AA meeting and he has to confess his sins, he begins to speak.

17

Viraj doesn't make eye contact with any of us, focusing on a mark on the Formica to the left of my cup.

'I've just moved to Leeds,' he begins. 'Well, not just. About six months ago. I'm a coder for a start-up.'

Ethel and Dawn exchange bewildered glances.

'He writes computer programs for a new company,' translates Bob. Bob keeps surprising me.

'I fancied a change of scene. Get out of London, you know?'

I don't know but I nod as if I do.

'I like it round here. The countryside is cool and housing is dirt cheap.'

I wince internally, and Viraj quickly adds, 'Compared to prices in London. It's daylight robbery down there,' to which there is a collective nodding of heads. Everyone knows about the London property market.

'But they don't need me in the office much. A post-Covid thing. There aren't even enough desks for us all to be there at once. And that'd be okay except that I don't know anyone up here. All my friends are online. Don't see much of anyone face to face.'

He has my one-hundred-per-cent sympathy on this one. My friends all live here and yet somehow I don't see them either, apart from on Instagram, which isn't the same thing.

'I get that,' I say. 'And do you find that everyone is dead busy? It's super-hard to find a time that everyone can meet up.'

Viraj nods.

'Yes. No time. Everyone is so busy. Quick text here and there, sometimes only emojis. I work weird hours too. I do my best work late at night and I game during the day so that tends to be with people in other time zones. It's a total mind-fuck when you're talking to people in the Philippines and then in LA both at the same time.'

Then, realising what he's said, he grimaces at Ethel. 'Sorry about the bad language.'

'Swear to your heart's content, young man,' she says. 'Not much offends me these days.'

He smiles at her weakly and then glances at me as if he's checking everything's okay. Like that's anything to do with me!

'Anyway, it's all pretty isolating,' he adds.

There's a brief hiatus in conversation and then he says, looking directly at me, 'So, what about you? How come you're here?'

From out of nowhere, a sense of loyalty to Bob, Ethel and Dawn floods through me and I resent his implied suggestion that I am the only other 'normal' one here. Then I realise that's just my take on it. From Viraj's point of view, I might appear as strange as the rest of them did to me. He's probably just started by asking about my story because he's sitting next to me.

'I was sacked completely out of the blue a couple of weeks back,' I begin. 'My job was . . .' I pause as I consider how to describe it. It's not the badge of honour that I thought it was, not to these people at least. '. . . important to me,' I say. 'It was a bit of a shock but I'm slowly getting over it and now I'm trying to find something new. Plus, I discovered that my friends aren't as close as I'd thought they were. And I haven't told my family because I don't want to worry them. Oh, and my boyfriend left me for a job in the Outer Hebrides. So all of a sudden I'm feeling very alone.'

Embarrassingly I can feel my eyes glaze over but I employ the 'nails in palms' trick and manage to fend the tears off.

'First-world problems, I know,' I add sheepishly.

'I never understand that expression,' says Ethel. 'Just because other people have it tougher doesn't make your problems any less valid.'

I smile at her gratefully, but I suspect that in a beauty parade of my setbacks and, say, Bob's, Bob would walk away with the diamond tiara.

'Well, I'm left with plenty of time on my hands, and enough money for now, but none of the things that make life magical,' I say. 'I need to regroup and rebuild. So, that's why I'm here,' I add, smiling at Viraj.

He shrugs in a 'life can be shit' kind of way.

There's a pause and we all play with our drinks, although none of us have much left. Then Bob sucks in a big breath through his nostrils as if he's preparing to dive.

'My story goes back much longer than that,' he says. 'I was a plumber-come-handyman. Had a nice little business, had "Bob'll Fix It!" painted on the side of me van.'

'Like Bob the Builder?' asks Dawn. 'But that's "Can we fix it?" so it's not the same.'

'No,' agrees Bob. 'Not the same. But a little nod in that direction. Like a joke.'

'Okay,' says Dawn slowly. 'But a not very funny one.'

'No.' Bob smiles. 'Not that funny. Anyway, I had a house, a little terrace in Kirkstall, and a wife and two kids, one of each. We weren't loaded or nothing, but we did okay. It was a bit hand to mouth. I didn't have three months' mortgage in the bank like they say you should. But who does, eh?'

He looks around the group and we shake our heads, but I bet Viraj has a nest egg and I would have too if I hadn't had to blow it on my car repairs.

'Then one night some bastard nicks all me tools out of me van. I had one of them stickers, "No Tools Kept in Here Overnight". But it wasn't true. I was knackered. I'd worked a fourteen-hour day and I just couldn't be arsed unloading it all into the house. They must have been watching. Or took a punt on there being tools inside. Either way, I get up the next day and it's all gone, right down to me last screw.'

My heart hurts for him, the injustice of someone just taking what isn't theirs is always hard to process.

'Oh, Bob, that's crap,' I say. 'What about the insurance? Did they pay out?'

He looks at me like I'm an idiot and my cheeks flare.

'So, no tools. No work. No work. No money to buy new tools. A proper vicious circle. I tried to borrow, tools and money. But no one had anything to spare and the banks were . . . Well, let's just say they didn't help. Long story short, I couldn't pay the mortgage, so the building society took the house and then the wife left and took the kids with her.'

Bob sets his jaw and looks towards the queue of people at the counter.

'That was three years ago. Life's been a bit shite since then, but I'm still here.'

He raises an eyebrow and puffs out a sigh, and I imagine there's a whole other story hidden behind that sentence.

This must be what the talk of a jig-saw with Ethel is about. He's trying to rebuild his kit piece by piece.

I feel terrible. There's me moaning about not having any friends and poor Bob has had all this to deal with. And he's still smiling.

I need to take a long hard look at myself.

18

Having been desperate to know the stories of my fellow community tablers, I realise I don't have it in me to listen to any more misery for now, so it's lucky that neither Ethel nor Dawn seems particularly moved by Bob's story. Nor are they showing any inclination to share their own.

I hazard a guess. Ethel is old, so maybe she visits the table because her friends have died. And Dawn. Well, Dawn is just Dawn. She'll chat to anyone.

No one says anything after Bob has finished telling us his story. 'I'm sorry that happened to you' seems so glib.

Then Bob stands up. 'Well, places to go, people to see and all that. Better get off to work.'

This is a surprise. I'd assumed he had no job. God, enough with these assumptions, Abigail!

'Same time tomorrow?' he says with a grin. 'Unless I get a better offer, of course.'

Then he wanders out of the café.

I just sit there, not quite sure what to say next. We can't discuss his story without him being here, so instead I say, 'I didn't realise he had a job.'

'Why should you?' asks Ethel archly. 'You only just met us. And you didn't ask.'

I want to reply that I didn't ask because I was respecting their privacy, but in fact I was only doing that because I'd assumed they had stories they were ashamed of. God, I'm such a cow.

'No,' I say simply.

'He works at a shelter for the homeless in the city centre. Helps out with the people that stay there, does some maintenance work, whatever needs doing really. He lives in a shared house with some other men he met along the way. He's slowly piecing things back together.'

'Wow,' I say, because what else is there?

Ethel stands to leave and as she does so she grimaces.

'Are you okay?'

She wafts a dismissive hand at me. 'I was a ballet dancer. I'm used to pain.'

I'm sure that's true. 'I once read an article about how sore ballerinas' feet get,' I say.

'Your feet are the least of your problems as a dancer,' she says enigmatically.

I've never done ballet. It looks so effortless. I guess it's not.

Dawn goes next, leaving just me and Viraj at the table. I'm so tempted to make some comment to imply that he and I are alike, but if the last week has shown me anything, it's not to second-guess anyone.

'See you again,' I say instead. Nice and neutral.

'Yeah,' he replies and then gets his laptop back out.

I turn and look back as I leave the café and see that he's moved off the community table and back to an ordinary one.

I decide to go into Leeds and have a look at some housey shops for inspiration for my back bedroom plans. Since the pandemic the city centre has been looking sadder with some yawning gaps where familiar high street shops used to be. There are also more people who look like they might have nowhere to sleep. I've never taken much notice before, always rushing by, trying to ignore that they're there, hoping they didn't ask me for anything, not making eye contact.

But today, with Bob's story so fresh in my mind, things look very different. I can see how it only takes one tiny problem for someone's life to change. Something that starts out small, trivial even, can grow into a problem we can no longer find solutions for, and faster than we might believe. Don't they say that we're all just a couple of bad decisions away from catastrophe?

I'm okay though, I tell myself on the bus home. My life is not ideal at the moment, but in the grand scale of things it could be much worse.

This is something I need to keep reminding myself of.

19

I'm almost at the end of my second week with no job, and listening to Bob's story has made me take stock. I think about how it must have felt to see money going out of his bank account day after day with no way of replenishing it, watching his life getting closer and closer to the precipice yet having nothing to grab hold of to stop himself slipping over the edge.

The idea makes me feel sick and I scrabble around to find the differences between his story and my own. I'm only just unemployed. I don't need tools to work. I can get any job – it doesn't have to be in marketing. Do I really need the kudos that comes with a high-status job? This is hard to answer. If I'm honest then I think I probably do. It's how I am, how I define myself. But I have no job, high status or otherwise. Ultimately Bob and I are the same. I'm just a little bit behind him.

I have to take some seriously deep breaths to hold myself together. This is proper scary grown- up stuff and I'm dealing with it solo. I check my bank balance. Things are still okay there. I've been frugal so far, buying only the absolute necessities, assuming you include my new flat white coffee habit in that category. A bit of cheap paint for the back bedroom isn't going to bankrupt me. And if I end up selling the flat then having decorated it will be a good thing, I think fatalistically.

But I do need a job.

I get the iPad out and begin scrolling through the same vacancies that I saw yesterday, scrutinising them for an angle I might have missed.

A message pops up on my screen.

It's Spencer!

My heart leaps. I can't help it! A bit slow off the mark, my head sends a message to my heart to get its act together, but I've clicked before my head has delivered its message. It's a photograph of the harbour of brightly coloured houses that I'd seen on Google.

'I am here!' the message says with a smiley-face emoji, the one wearing sunglasses.

My first reaction is sheer joy to have heard from him. My second is to wonder why he's sent the photo when I thought we were clear that things were over between us. Maybe he's going to offer me a running commentary on his new life. I'm so delighted to have a message from him that I don't want to think that one through.

I suppose that how we move forward from here will depend partly on how I react to this first communication. Ignore it and he might get the hint that I'm not interested. Reply and he could take that as a green flag to send more.

And then there's the job thing. I used to regale him with funny stories about work. I'd been so buzzy and animated about pretty much everything. I don't think Spencer was the kind to only be with me because I had a glamorous job, but what if that sparkle was the thing he really liked about me? I can't help but think that my sparkle has almost gone out now and so I might be considerably less attractive to him.

I close that thought down. I'm almost certain that Spencer likes me for me . . . almost.

I ponder this as I sit on my sofa in my very familiar sitting room. My world, once full of exciting and interesting people and places, is exceedingly small, made up mainly of my flat and the café in my local supermarket. Seeing photos from somewhere new, even if I'm unlikely to ever visit there myself, especially in my reduced financial circumstances, has to be a good thing right now.

Stacked against that is how alone I'm feeling. My head is telling me that it won't be good for me to invest any more emotional energy in Spencer. I simply don't have enough to spare.

I go with my heart before my head can overrule me.

'Looks gorgeous,' I reply and pointedly don't attach a kiss to the end of the message nor ask any questions to open up a dialogue.

That's okay, isn't it?

I tell myself it is.

Next, I open Instagram and tumble down a rabbit hole of interior design and fifties fashion, finally watching someone crochet a tiny little frog complete with jacket and trousers. Time gets away from me and when I look up again, I'm late for the tablers.

I rush and get to the café around ten fifteen. They are all there, laughing at something that Bob has just said. Dawn looks up when she sees me coming.

'Hi, Thingy,' she calls. 'We're coming to your house.'

This almost stops me in my tracks but I keep smiling.

'Oh yes?' I reply, hoping my face isn't saying the direct opposite.

'Don't panic,' says Bob, whose intuition I'm coming to respect. 'We're not moving in, and you can say no if you like, but we thought we could help you with your home improvements. I can turn my hand to painting and decorating and Ethel is a dab hand with a sewing machine so she can run you up some curtains in a jiffy.'

'And I can clean up the mess,' says Dawn. 'I'm very good at cleaning.'

She says this with her head held high and I can't help but smile at her.

Viraj clears his throat. 'I make a mean cup of tea,' he says and then apologetically adds, 'Not that practical, actually.'

To say this is a bit of an ambush would be to understate it, but I find myself agreeing before I have time to overthink it. Inviting my new friends to see my home is a natural thing to do and if they want to help with my decorating project then so much the better.

'Great!' I say. 'When can you start?'

'Today!' shouts Dawn with indubitable enthusiasm. 'Now!'

I put my hand up. 'Hang on. I haven't picked the colour yet and I haven't even started looking at fabrics. But,' I add, 'knowing that the dream team is booked in will give me the boost I need, otherwise I'll just dither forever.'

Bob winks at me. 'That's the spirit.'

'Tomorrow then,' says Dawn.

'Give the poor woman a chance, Dawn,' says Bob. 'You just let us know when you're ready, Abbie.'

'Okay! And I'll provide the tea and biscuits.'

'Which I can make,' adds Viraj.

We spend some time on my iPad and I show them my Pinterest board, which they all peer at and pass around. Dawn isn't that impressed with some of my colour ideas, mainly because they aren't yellow.

'So your place is like you, then?' asks Viraj. 'With the vintage thing, I mean,' he adds, looking a little bit awkward that he has made such a personal observation on such a short acquaintance. But I don't mind.

'Yes,' I say. 'When I bought the flat the thing that really spoke to me was that it hadn't been touched in decades. I've done a few things to modernise it, but other than that I'm trying to stay firmly mid-twentieth century.'

'Sounds cool,' says Viraj. 'I'm strictly a blond wood and chrome person. Clean lines. No crap. I bought a flat overlooking the river.

One of those new builds. It's nice but I haven't spoken to a living soul since I moved in.'

I roll my eyes at him sympathetically but my gut tightens. I'm conscious that we're sailing into tricky waters again, talking about our living accommodation, but my fear proves ungrounded.

'I'm living in a house that the shelter owns,' chips in Bob without a hint of awkwardness. 'It's a halfway house to give us an address and a bit of stability while we get ourselves back on our feet. It's a bit like the place the building society stole off me,' he adds. 'But not as nicely done out.'

'How about you, Dawn?' I ask, feeling braver.

'I live in a big house with my friends,' she says proudly. 'We do cooking and cleaning and Bev comes in every day to check we've opened the curtains and washed up. And sometimes it's Dougie that comes.'

'That sounds perfect and good fun too,' I say. 'And how about you, Ethel?'

Ethel stares at me with that icy gaze that she used so often when we first met. I worry that I have overstepped some invisible line, but then she says, 'I live alone.'

We wait but she gives us nothing else. That is to be our lot, it appears. But that's okay. Receiving all this information at once is overwhelming enough. Ethel can keep her air of mystery as far as I'm concerned.

'Like me then.'

'And me,' says Viraj.

'Great, isn't it?' I add.

Ethel nods tightly but I'm rewarded for my restraint with a tiny smile.

20

On Friday night I get a text from Sal. Seeing her name on my phone screen is a shock, like I've been pulled out of my pretend little world back into the real one, and it takes me a moment to realise that this is a good thing.

Hi. Just checking in. Coffee tomorrow a.m.? Ten-ish?

This feels odd until I realise that tomorrow is Saturday. All my days just run into each other at the moment because there's nothing to distinguish one from the next.

What I do know, however, is that my mornings at ten are already spoken for. We haven't yet hit a weekend on our new fixed time arrangement, but I'm almost certain that the others will be at the community table waiting. And with a jolting realisation it comes to me that I can't let them down. Sal is an old friend, but where has she been over the last couple of weeks? Okay, I didn't tell her I might need some support, but isn't she supposed to be able to intuit that by friends' Spidey sense? And the lack of an invitation to the spa weekend thing is still smarting a little.

Well, my priorities have changed.

Busy at ten, I type back. *Afternoon instead?*

The three little dots appear at once and I wait for the reply to land.

No can do. Catch up next week.

And so, with those five little words, I appear to have blown my chance of a meet-up.

Great. Speak soon x I write.

There's no reply.

I suppose I can no longer say that my friends are ignoring me. In fact, they can now complain that I'm keeping them, or at least one of them, at arm's length. But oddly, I find that I don't really mind. The tablers aren't friends per se, but it seems I would rather spend time with them than with Sal right now. And I have made a commitment of sorts to them, which is more than Sal has done for me recently.

I get dressed with care, choosing one of my favourite dresses in a bright floral print with a nipped-in waist and a full skirt, and I curl my hair and pin it up in rolls. Can't have standards slipping.

But when I get to the café there's no sign of the rest of them. The table with its cheery little notice is like the *Mary Celeste*, not a soul in sight. My heart sinks like a stone. I hadn't realised how much I'd been looking forward to seeing them. Our meetings have become the highlight of my day.

On top of that, I've blown Sal out for no reason. I could just text her back – *Hi, my plan fell through and I'm around after all* – but what would that look like? That she came second. No, it's my own fault. I gambled and I lost and now I have to deal with the consequences of being on my own.

Well, I'm here now and I have my trusty iPad so I might as well use the time fruitfully. I join the queue to get myself a drink. It's Joel working with another young girl I don't recognise. They certainly get through them here. This one looks a little more promising than the last, or at least Joel is shouting at her less.

As I approach the front of the queue, it dawns on me that I haven't seen Joel since I burst into tears in front of him. I'm hoping he won't recognise me or will have forgotten the incident entirely but when he sees it's me, he smiles kindly, and I know that he remembers both me and my outburst.

'Hi. All okay?' he asks, injecting his words with enough meaning that I can hear a subtext.

'I'm fine, thanks,' I say. 'And thanks for the other day.'

'De nada,' he says with a little flick of his hand. 'What can I get you?'

I order my coffee and a piece of millionaire's shortbread because it's the weekend so what the hell. As he sorts my order, I watch him. He's quite good-looking when he's not scowling. In fact, there's something quite attractive about him, especially now that he's been kind to me and because I know the community table was his idea. I'm definitely not in the market for romance. God, my life is in a big enough mess already, but if I were I could do worse.

'Your friends not in today?' he asks as he hands me a steaming cup of coffee.

I like that he calls them my friends. I wouldn't have done a week ago.

'No. They must have had a better offer,' I reply, laughing to make it clear that I'm a go-with-the-flow kind of girl and it doesn't worry me being here on my own. (I'm not sure a laugh can convey all that, but still . . .)

'I find that hard to believe,' he says as he passes me the plate with my chocolatey loveliness on it.

Is he flirting with me? I think it unlikely, but it throws me nonetheless. I give him a little smile and then go and sit down, opening my laptop and continuing my endless hunt for the perfect paint colour. I should just go to the DIY shop and be done with it. You can't get a proper idea online anyway.

As I try to spot the difference between Calamine Pink and Powder Puff, I remember what they all said yesterday about coming to my place to help me decorate. If it were anyone else I'd probably think it was more of a gesture than a genuine offer, that they said they'd be happy to help but then no date would ever be fixed for the work to be done.

Suddenly I'm desperate to message Spencer. I don't know if it's having Joel flirt with me or because I'm excited about having some new friends, but I want to share these tiny snippets of news with him. I imagine us out for a drink, me describing the quirks of each of the tablers, Bob's kindness, Ethel's ability to stand back and yet still be involved. I picture Spencer laughing at my stories, my hand brushing his as I reach for my glass.

I stop. That is just a story I'm telling myself. It's not real. Spencer is gone. It was the right decision to finish things with him and it still is.

I pull my mind back to the offer to help me decorate. One thing I think I know about my new friends, even from our short acquaintance, is that if they say something then they mean it. They have taken enough crap. I very much doubt they are the sort to make empty gestures.

I probe around in my head to find out what I feel. It would definitely move the relationships on a fair few steps. Sitting around in a café swapping life stories is one thing, but opening up my private world to them, effectively a bunch of strangers, is a horse of a very different colour.

Then I remember that I've already agreed to the venture even though it's most unlike me to say yes to a plan on the spot without leaving myself an escape route. It'll be fine, I tell myself. It might even be fun.

21

When we all reconvene the following week, however, something other than my decorating steals the limelight. We settle down, making general enquiries into each other's weekends. I don't tell them I turned up on Saturday in case I come across as a bit desperate. I also know that none of the others did the same because I was there and they were not, but I do tell them I've finally settled on a colour scheme and I'm ready to crack on with the decorating whenever they are.

There's a brief discussion around Bob's shifts and how little work Viraj can get away with before someone notices he's not where he should be. Dawn is yet to arrive, but she said that she cleans offices in the evenings so I assume she will be relatively free during the days.

And then Dawn appears wearing the most striking outfit yet. There's a kind of corset affair in black with a blue T-shirt underneath and an enormous skirt with enough fabric for ten more. It is, of course, canary yellow and in some kind of synthetic satin that looks like it could start a fire all on its own.

Reactions around the table differ widely. There's a sharp, and I want to say horrified, intake of breath from Ethel and Bob claps his hands together, delighted.

'Oh, now aren't you as pretty as a picture today.'

Dawn beams at him. 'Do you like my skirt? I made it myself.'

To give Bob his due, he makes a pretty good stab at looking surprised.

'I'd never have known. You're wasted as a cleaner, Dawn. You should have been a fashion designer.'

This is bordering on teasing and makes me feel a bit defensive, but his smile is so broad that it's clear he's doing no such thing. Dawn beams at him again, but then her face slips a bit.

'The only trouble is,' she says, twisting round to fiddle with the waistband, 'it scratches me.'

'Let me have a look,' I say. 'Maybe there's a little flaw in the fabric or something.'

I stand up and go to examine the skirt, but as I put my hand into the waistband to investigate something sharp slices into my finger.

'Ow! Did you leave a pin in there by mistake?' I ask, sticking my sore finger into my mouth before I bleed on the nasty yellow material.

Dawn looks confused. 'I didn't use pins,' she says. 'Don't have any.'

I'm wondering how on earth she's managed to control the slippery fabric to run it through the sewing machine without any pins when something occurs to me.

'How is it all held together, Dawn?' I ask her. 'Did you sew it by hand?'

Dawn looks very pleased with herself. 'I didn't sew at all,' she says. 'I used Sellotape and staples.'

'Oh good Lord,' mutters Ethel.

'Staples!' I say. 'No wonder it's scratching you. I'm surprised you're not torn to ribbons under there.'

'And it fell to bits a bit on the way,' continues Dawn. She's looking pretty forlorn now, all the excitement brought by her new skirt gone. 'I wanted a skirt like yours that sticks out when I twirl. But this one . . .'

She performs a little pirouette, but instead of floating out around her like my skirt does, it twists and wraps itself around her legs so she looks like she's been caught up by a huge yellow bed sheet.

Dawn's face falls into an expression of such disappointment that I want to throw my arms around her and give her a huge hug. She drops into the nearest chair and then leaps up again as another staple digs into her flesh.

'Ow!! That hurts!'

'It's all in the cutting-out,' says Ethel. 'If you want to get a skirt to flare then you have to cut the fabric in the right way.'

'I didn't really know about cutting,' says Dawn. 'I just scrunched it all together at the top and then fastened it with tape. It doesn't do the swirly thing though. And it cost loads of money. I bought all the yellow they had so there'd be enough.'

'You certainly have plenty of fabric,' I say, hoping this one positive fact will cheer her up. It doesn't. She looks more despondent with each passing second.

'How did you make yours do that?' she asks me.

'I bought mine,' I say. 'Ready-made. And it just did it. I can't sew for toffee.'

After a moment's pause Ethel says, 'I can sew.'

Her expression suggests that she wishes she hadn't said that out loud but it's too late now. Dawn pounces on it.

'Can you sew a skirt like hers?' She points at me like she's accusing me of something.

'Quite probably,' says Ethel. 'Although I'd need to see the skirt.'

'Can you go get it, Thingy? So Ethel can make me one.'

I'm thinking fast. 'I could,' I say. 'But how about this. Why don't you all come to my place tomorrow? I can show Ethel the skirt and we can look at the decorating situation. I assume you still want to help with that?'

Bob, Dawn and Viraj nod enthusiastically. Ethel sits perfectly still, but she can sew rather than paint if she prefers.

'And I've got a sewing machine, I don't know if it's any good. My mum bought it for me. I think she thought I might get the sewing bug but I never did. So maybe Ethel can have a go at making the skirt and we can work out what we need for the back bedroom.'

'Great plan,' says Bob.

So that's how I end up giving a bunch of virtual strangers my address.

22

I'm unfeasibly nervous about the masses descending on my little flat. I want the place to look its best because I am really proud of it, but a tiny part of me doesn't want them to judge me. I know how ridiculous this sounds and I genuinely can't think of four people less likely to do that, but I suppose I'm used to it happening and old habits are hard to shake.

This makes me work out just how long it is since I had *anybody* over. It's been a seriously long time. My workmates and I used to go out straight from the office and I generally meet Sal and the others at a restaurant or the cinema. There's an intimacy to opening your home up to other people, even if you know them well, so it's no wonder I'm nervous.

I try to balance out my anxiety by not vacuuming in a 'they can take me as they find me' kind of way. A silly thing, I know, but it makes me feel a little bit better.

The doorbell rings at ten o'clock. They're so punctual that I wonder if they've been camped out on the doorstep waiting for the clock to tick over the hour. After a quick glance round to check that everything is in its place, I open the door and run down the stairs to let them in.

'Hi, everyone. Welcome. Come in,' I say, my words all tumbling over one another.

And in they troop: Dawn first, then Ethel and Bob, who seems, from the lack of odour, to have had a shower in honour of the occasion, and finally Viraj, who steps over the threshold like a cat, curious but ready to flee should there be any danger inside.

Dawn sets off to explore without waiting to be invited. The flat isn't very big so it doesn't take her very long.

'It's old-fashioned,' she says when she gets back.

'A bit like me then,' I reply, smiling at her.

She eyes me oddly, like she's not sure that's a good thing.

'Please,' I say to the others. 'Make yourself at home.'

I gesture at the lounge but they stand there looking like they aren't for budging. It's not a huge hall so we're standing very close to one another.

'Who'd like tea? Or coffee?' I ask brightly, trying to move things along. 'I should know all your orders by now, shouldn't I? Mint tea, Ethel?'

She gives me a single and very decisive nod. 'That would be most pleasant,' she says, and then, thankfully, she leads the others through to the lounge.

I go to the kitchen, put the kettle on and fire up the coffee machine. Bob joins me and starts opening my cupboards until he finds my mugs. He takes out five.

'Great place,' he says, genuine admiration in his voice. 'I see what you mean about it having been untouched for a while. That fireplace is a beaut. And is the panelling original seventies?'

'I imagine so, I didn't put it up. I know it's not quite my period but I'm a bit nervous about what I'll find behind it if I take it down.'

'I could take a look for you,' he says. 'If you like.'

He sounds as if he's feeling his way, trying not to overstep a boundary that he can't see, but I'm delighted. Trying to get hold of any kind of tradesperson is nigh on impossible and here's one who can, by all accounts, turn his hand to most things.

'That would be amazing. I'd pay you of course.'

I could kick myself as soon as the words are out of my mouth but I don't seem to have caused any offence.

'Mates' rates,' he says.

The kettle boils and he helps me to set a tray with everyone's drinks and a plate of flapjacks that I rustled up earlier. Then we head back into the lounge. Dawn and Viraj are on the sofa, Dawn almost on top of Viraj, who seems to be trying to push himself as snugly into the armrest as he can. Ethel has chosen one of my dining chairs and sits, back straight, waiting silently.

I hand the drinks around and position some coasters at strategic places on my Ercol coffee table (a junk shop find of which I'm particularly proud). Dawn immediately puts her drink down directly on to the table and I wince internally. The need to pick it up and reposition it is overwhelming but it would make me look so fussy. But there's no need to fret. Ethel has my back.

'Please use the coaster, Dawn,' she says in her clear, frosty voice. 'One should never put a vessel down on a wooden surface.'

'What's a vessel?' Dawn asks, picking her cup back up and putting it on the coaster.

'Anything that holds liquid,' replies Ethel. 'It can damage the wood.'

'I did not know that,' says Dawn, but she isn't in the least upset by it. 'Can we make my skirt now?' she asks.

The pace of life in Dawn's world can take your breath away but I'm still a little bit on edge so instead of relaxing over the drinks I leap into action.

'Yes! Good idea. Just let me get the sewing machine.'

I haven't used it since I moved in, and I have to wipe a layer of dust off the case before I take it back into the lounge. I set it down on my tiny dining table and plug it in. It buzzes into life. I also fetch my sewing box, which Ethel, having cast an appraising eye over the contents, nods her approval of.

'Over to you, I think, Ethel,' I say with a smile that isn't returned.

Dawn passes Ethel a bag for life stuffed to the top with the nasty yellow fabric and soon the two of them are busy.

'Want to see the room I need to paint?' I ask the others.

Bob gets up immediately. Viraj, who has spread himself into the space that Dawn has vacated, looks less keen to move. I'm not sure how much assistance he is going to offer in this endeavour but it doesn't matter. It's just nice that he's here.

Bob and I head into the back bedroom. There's not much in there, just a couple of boxes of stuff I've collected from car boot sales and which I've been waiting to display.

'North facing,' he says. 'And two outside walls. Does it get chilly in here?'

I have no idea as I've never really used the room.

'I suppose so,' I say.

'We'll bleed the radiator,' he says. 'I can have a quick look at your boiler while we're at it. Make sure it's okay. I'm not a registered gas engineer,' he adds, looking slightly awkward. 'But I know what I'm doing. I won't blow the place up.'

I don't doubt it.

'You're a godsend, Bob,' I reply and I mean it.

'We'll have this place knocked into shape in no time,' he says, smiling like a man in his element might. 'Now, what are you thinking for the walls?'

23

We spend most of the day at my place. Bob and I rub down the walls and sand the paintwork. Every time I try to cut a corner, he's on to me.

'I'm normally a paint-over-the-cobwebs kind of decorator,' I confess and he rolls his eyes.

'If you want a decent finish then you need to do your prep,' he says, and of course I know he's right.

We work side by side and I find it's much easier to talk when I'm not looking directly into his eyes.

'So, will you go back to what you were doing before?' I ask. 'When you have your tools back.'

'I doubt I'll ever replace them all,' he says. 'It was a lifetime's collection. And some of them belonged to me dad. They don't even make them tools any more. And do you know the worst of it?'

I shake my head.

'The little bastards will have chucked the lot. They're only interested in the power tools. They can shift them quick, no questions asked. But I bet they dumped the rest in a skip somewhere. Such a bloody waste.'

I have to agree.

'I'm happy enough doing what I'm doing at the moment,' he adds. 'You know, helping out at the shelter. It doesn't pay much but when you've been to the depths yourself you can offer a bit of hope to them that's there now.'

'So, things are a bit better for you than they were?' I ask, not wanting to pry but sensing that he's willing to open up a little.

'Some stuff is. I'm not living on the streets any more. Not that I did that for long, but, believe me, Abbie, one night is more than enough. Scariest time of me life, having to work out who you can trust and who is too out of it to know what they're doing. Mind you, most homeless people are too busy surviving to do you any harm.'

I nod like I understand but actually I haven't a clue. I can barely imagine it, let alone empathise.

'But I'd like to get back on an even footing with me kids. Don't see nearly enough of them.'

'A boy and a girl, you said?'

'Yeah. Chloe. That's me daughter. She's fourteen and Jake is twelve.'

I smile encouragingly.

'They're a handful at the moment. Chloe's fourteen going on twenty-four. You know what girls are like at that age.'

'Well, I was one,' I say, that being my total experience of teenagers.

'But their mum – Sonia. I don't think she wants them to see me. I reckon she's ashamed of me.'

I can't see his face but I can feel his dejection from the tone of his voice.

'Can't blame her really. I'm a shit role model for them.'

I want to leap in and defend him but what do I know really? So I bite my tongue.

'And it was dead hard to keep up with seeing them when I was in the hostel. I didn't have my own room and they didn't like it, being around all the other men in there. I couldn't blame them. I didn't like it either. I used to try and take them to McDonald's but I never had enough cash for everything they wanted. In the end they just stopped coming. Sonia told me they were too embarrassed to have a dad who was homeless.'

I've seen men with small kids in McDonald's at the weekend. I always assumed they just lacked imagination. It never crossed my mind that it might be the only place they had to go.

'Oh, Bob, I'm so sorry,' I say weakly.

'What've you got to be sorry for? Did you nick my tools?'

'Well, no . . .' I begin.

'Well, save your pity for someone who needs it,' he snaps and for a minute or two we just rub down in silence but then he adds, 'Sorry, Abbie. Didn't mean to bite your head off. Bit touchy.'

'No need to apologise.'

It feels like I should reciprocate with something personal of my own but then there's a whoop of laughter from the lounge. We look at each other and then down tools to see what's going on.

Dawn is in the middle of the lounge wearing the bare bones of a dress very similar to mine although it's currently inside out and held together with pins. Ethel is on the floor at her feet pinning up the hem and Viraj is passing her pins, although I see from Ethel's expression that it would possibly be easier if she did it herself.

'That looks amazing already,' I say.

Dawn gives us a twirl, sending Ethel flying. She laughs wildly, delighted with the way the skirt spreads as she spins.

'Stay still,' complains Ethel, 'or we'll never get this pinned up.'

'Look, Thingy,' Dawn says. 'It's just like yours. But mine is better because it's yellow.'

'It is,' I agree, and, actually, despite the nasty fabric, you can tell it's going to be glorious. 'You're very talented, Ethel.'

She gives me a kind of harumph by way of reply.

By the mid-afternoon the back bedroom is all prepped and ready to go and Dawn has half a new dress. She is beside herself with impatience and keeps asking when it will be done.

'Faster if you stop asking me every two minutes,' says Ethel, her head bowed over my machine.

I'm not sure what Viraj is doing, but he has his laptop so maybe he's busy programming something.

I hadn't anticipated them still being here, so I haven't got anything for us to eat. It all feels a little bit awkward. Wouldn't it be perfect if Viraj chose this moment to reveal that he actually qualified as a chef before he went into software design?

'Shall I nip down to Greggs and get us some sausage rolls or something?' is what he actually says, which is almost as good.

We give him our orders – everyone has a favourite item, don't they? Viraj is dispatched to pick it all up and Bob and I nip to B&Q to get the paint and more decorating paraphernalia. As we all sit round my tiny dining table chomping away, I realise that I haven't been this content for ages.

'Would you teach me to sew?' I ask Ethel as I polish off my tuna roll. 'I'm always having to take stuff to a friend of mine to take things in, or let them out,' I add, cocking my head in the direction of the Bavarian slice with my name on it. 'It would be much better if I could do it myself.'

Ethel considers this for a moment and I genuinely think she's going to say no, but then she surprises me.

'Yes. I could teach both of you if we had two machines.'

'Ooh, yes,' says Dawn, clapping her hands together.

'I wouldn't mind learning that stuff,' says Bob. 'Might come in handy.'

I throw him a 'how and when exactly' kind of look and he shrugs and adds, 'Well, you never know.'

'You never do,' I agree. 'Viraj?'

Viraj raises one side of his nose as if this idea is doing nothing for him but then he sees us all staring at him expectantly.

'Oh God . . .' He pauses and then seems to come to a decision. 'In for a penny, in for a pound.'

'That's agreed then,' I say.

'And this is finished,' says Ethel, pulling the dress out from under the foot of the machine and holding it up by the shoulder seams.

Dawn whoops and snatches it, pressing it against her body and twirling on the spot. Then she starts to strip off her clothing.

'Dawn,' I say quickly, 'do you want to use my bedroom for that. There's a mirror in there.'

She sees the benefit of this and returns a minute or two later with the dress on. It fits her perfectly, skimming her curves in all the right places. When she spins, it flares out just like my dress does. Judging by the smile on Dawn's face she is delighted.

'Thanks, Ethel,' she says and then rushes over and gives Ethel such a huge hug that I genuinely worry that she will flatten her. Ethel strains her neck to escape.

'You're welcome,' she says in strangulated tones but her eyes are sparkling.

24

The idea of sewing lessons really grabs the tablers, especially Dawn and Bob who mention it again before they leave my house and yet again the following morning when they turn up at mine to continue with the painting and dressmaking. And I have news on that front.

'I spoke to my friend,' I tell them. 'The one who does my alterations. She teaches sewing and she says she'll lend us her studio as long as I can vouch for the competency of our tutor . . .'

Ethel lets out a snort.

'Which I can of course,' I add quickly. 'She has eight machines so that will be great. And she says we can use the studio in the mornings as she has groups in the afternoons and evenings. So that couldn't have worked out better.'

'Sun shines on the righteous,' says Bob.

'Who are they?' asks Dawn.

'Us,' I tell her, my brain running ahead as I try to work out how I'll explain the expression, but it seems that no further explanation is necessary.

'When can we start?' she asks instead.

'I reckon we'll have finished the painting the day after tomorrow,' replies Bob, 'so any time after that.'

'Glad to see you're not the kind of workman who leaves one job unfinished to start on the next.' I laugh.

'As if!'

So it's all agreed. Ethel says she has more fabric than she will ever use in her flat (which is another mystery that I'd like to get to the bottom of) and so agrees to donate what we'll need and in the meantime Bob and I get on with the painting.

He makes a great director of works. He gives nice clear instructions to each of us and then watches like a hawk to make sure we do a proper job. The bedroom isn't big and Ethel and Viraj are less interested in helping, so that leaves the three of us wielding paintbrushes of various sizes while the other two keep us going with cups of tea and custard creams.

From time to time, we hear squawks of laughter coming from the lounge. Ethel and Viraj seem like an unlikely friendship but, I reflect, I could say that about all of us.

We also have to work round other commitments. Bob has his shifts at the shelter and Dawn appears to have an enviable social diary and slopes off from time to time to meet some friend or other, but I am happy to continue on my own and the room is finished as Bob predicted except for the blind, which Ethel promises to run up as soon as I choose the fabric.

'You'll be able to make it yourself,' says Dawn. 'When Ethel has told us how to sew.'

I want to tell her that we're unlikely to learn much in a few short sessions but there's no need to burst her bubble.

The room looks fabulous and immeasurably better than if I'd done it on my own.

'Looks right good, that,' Bob says. 'But do you know what it needs?'

I scan the room, trying to see whatever is missing, but apart from the blind I draw a blank.

'A toast. So we can launch the good ship back bedroom.'

'Definitely,' I agree. 'I've got some prosecco.'

Bob rolls his eyes at me.

'Prosecco? Prosecco?! You're way too posh for me, Abbie. Have you not got any cans in your fridge like a normal person?'

My mind is already working out how quickly I can get to the corner shop when I see that he's grinning at me.

'Prosecco'd be great,' he says with a wink.

So, we toast my new room with a quick glass of fizz before Dawn has to rush off and clean.

'Will they see that I'm drunk?' she asks. I can't decide if it's concern or mischief in her expression.

'Drunk? On one glass!' scoffs Bob kind-heartedly. 'I doubt anyone will even notice.'

And so week three of my life with no job sails by and, quite unexpectedly, I'm having a remarkably good time. I'd thought I needed the buzz of an opening night or a great PR party to be living my best life but it turns out I was wrong. Each new day has a focus, I have people, I might even call them friends and I don't think they'd object, who are pleased to see me, and I never feel like I'm letting anyone down. I'm having just as much fun with the tablers as I do with my friends.

Of course, it's not all flowers and dancing unicorns. I don't have a job and I still haven't told anyone from my old life about that. But I'm coming round to the opinion that it's really not important. I'll tell them when the time is right. And that's not yet.

I get another message from Spencer. I have totally resisted messaging him myself, which has felt like one of the labours of Hercules at times, but if he wants to contact me, who am I to stop him?

This time he attaches a few photos. One is of where he's staying. It looks like a youth hostel but he seems to have his own room, which must be a blessing. I'm thinking that we're far too old to share with strangers when I remember Bob's story and I reframe the thought. If sharing with strangers were required then I could do that. I should just be grateful that I don't have to. The hostel looks nice. It's on the edge of a bay, and I wonder if he has a sea view from his room, but asking that feels like too intimate a question in the circumstances so I don't.

The final photo shows a smiling group of people all in outdoor wear. I assume they are Spencer's fellow puffin counters. Most of the group are men but there are one or two women. One in particular catches my attention. She's pretty and blonde with twinkly eyes and a snub nose and she's sitting very close to Spencer with an arm thrown casually around his shoulder. I feel my lips purse as I stare at the photo, scrutinising it hard to see if any parts of their bodies are touching. Having stared at it for more time than is necessary I conclude that it reveals no kind of relationship between the two of them. Then I give myself a talking-to. What business is it of mine if Spencer does want to find himself a perky little love interest up there in Scotland? I almost delete the photo to stop me looking at it again, but I decide to hold on to it for now. If I delete it I'll only end up recovering it later.

I reply keeping my response chirpy and neutral. Then I make a copy of the group photo and crop it so that I can only see Spencer. Blown up like that the image loses its definition but it's still recognisably him. I know I shouldn't have done that but I don't delete it.

Now that the painting at my place is finished, we drift back to meeting in the café as before. Liz raises an eyebrow when she sees me in her queue.

'Hello, stranger. We thought you'd all found somewhere better to go. Joel's been quite out of sorts. He's been taking it as a personal slight against his community table.'

'As if we'd switch allegiance,' I say brightly. 'We've just been otherwise engaged for a couple of days, but we're back now.'

For a moment, my mind skips to Joel's kind face, how thoughtful he'd been, but I drag it quickly back to the here and now. I don't need any complications of that kind in my life. Things are quite complicated enough.

I keep quiet about where we have been, not giving Liz any clues, but I can see her trying to work out what we could possibly have been doing together. My role as international woman of mystery continues.

I quite like it.

25

'We shall make pyjamas,' says Ethel. 'The bottom half at least.'

She says this in a way that makes it clear she'll have no truck with objections.

'I shall bring a selection of fabrics and you can all choose.'

'Ooh. Just like *Sewing Bee*,' I say. 'Is there a haberdashery?'

I look round the table for signs of recognition, but apparently the other tablers don't watch *The Great British Sewing Bee*, except, rather surprisingly, Bob.

'Can I be Patrick if I grow a little moustache?' he says with that trademark grin.

That man continues to confound me.

'Absolutely,' I reply.

Claire's studio isn't far from my place, which in turn isn't far from the café, and we arrange to meet there at ten the next day for a two-hour lesson. Claire talks Ethel through the machines.

Ethel seems enthralled by the automatic needle threader. 'So useful when your eyesight starts to go,' she says cheerfully, as if this is nothing to be worried about. 'And this really cuts your thread for you? Just by pushing this button. How things move on. I learned on an old Singer. It had a treadle.'

'What's that?' asks Dawn.

'Instead of using electricity you had to make it work with your feet,' said Bob.

'Like a car?'

'A bit,' replies Bob patiently.

Having satisfied herself about Ethel's competency, Claire leaves us to it and the lesson commences. Ethel has already run up a pair of pyjama bottoms so we can see what we're aiming for.

'They're one size,' she says. 'You just have to alter the waist with the drawstring and roll up the legs as required.'

'Clever,' says Viraj.

'I'm not just a pretty face, young man,' she says sniffily, and Viraj mutters an apology but then they exchange knowing smiles. They really did seem to bond the other day.

That aside though, I'm surprised that Viraj has stuck around. Dawn pretty much bullied him into joining us in the first place, so I would have expected him to slink off at the first opportunity, and yet he's still here. And now he's going to be sewing pyjamas. I suppose it takes all sorts.

A comic ten minutes follow as we all try the pyjamas on. Dawn and I are both wearing dresses. Mine is a shirtwaister with rich crimson polka dots and Dawn is in her new yellow one which she's worn each time I've seen her since it was finished. This means that we can try the pyjamas on without getting changed. It's more complicated for Bob and Viraj, who traipse off to the loos in turn but both declare the sizing to be fine. Clever Ethel indeed.

She tries to teach us how to thread the machines but after several failed attempts she gives up and does it for us. I'm not sure she's the most patient of teachers.

We cut out our pattern pieces and Ethel explains about notches, the small triangle shapes that act as markers, which you have to cut round.

'I haven't got any notches on mine,' says Dawn as she cuts feverishly.

'They all have notches,' replies Ethel archly. 'These are yours.' She holds up the ribbon of fabric that Dawn has snipped off.

'Oops,' says Viraj sarcastically. 'I've cut round mine, Miss.'

Ethel throws him a look that would curdle milk and Viraj looks down at his work, but not before giving me a cheeky grin that I can't help but return.

With the pattern pieces cut and the machines threaded, there is nothing stopping us from getting started. I begin cautiously, the needle crawling up and down, but as my confidence grows, I press down harder with my foot. The machine runs away from me and I squeal, but after a moment or two of experimentation, I find a speed that suits.

Dawn is on the machine next to mine and when I hear its motor racing I fear the worst. Yet when I look up Dawn is completely in control. She feeds the fabric under the foot like a pro and when she takes her work out at the other end, the seam is dead straight and very neat.

'Someone's got hidden talents,' says Bob.

'Who?' asks Dawn, spinning round in her seat.

'You! You're a natural.'

And she is. She is the first to finish and her pyjamas are by far the neatest. Even Ethel seems impressed.

'Very nice, Dawn,' she says. 'Very nice indeed.'

'What can we make next?' asks Dawn.

'Hang on, Speedy Gonzales. Some of us have a way to go.'

Bob holds up his work. He has joined the wrong edges together and instead of a pair of pyjama bottoms he seems to have a very narrow skirt.

'Oh shit,' he says when he realises. 'That's not right. What have I done?'

'You sewed the wrong bits together,' says Dawn. 'That's why it isn't like trousers.'

'Damn,' says Bob. He holds the tube in front of himself and tries to step into it. 'I hear skirts for men are in fashion.' Then he loses his balance and topples over with a crash.

'You like tools, don't you, Bob,' says Ethel coolly. 'Let me introduce you to this one.' She holds up a small piece of plastic. 'The quick unpick.'

By the end of the morning only Dawn has her pyjamas complete but Viraj and I aren't that far off with only a bit of finishing to do on the drawstring.

Dawn puts hers on and struts up and down the room like a supermodel. We cheer her on which makes her performance all the more flamboyant. She waves her arms over her head and twirls.

It's very impressive. 'You make an excellent model,' I say.

The rest of us try ours on too. Viraj has to hold his bottoms up to stop them falling down around his knees and, after Bob's false start, he's quite a long way behind. Mine fit fine but I have far less confidence than Dawn. Even though there are only the five of us there, I'm too self-conscious to perform like she does and I'm relieved when we've finished modelling and I can take them off.

We start tidying up. Leaving the studio as we found it is a condition of use.

When everything is as it should be, Ethel says, 'I think that was reasonably successful. For a first attempt.'

'Same time next week?' I ask, not really sure of what the response will be, apart from Dawn of course. I can't decide if I'm surprised when the answer comes back as a resounding 'yes'.

26

On Sunday I'm summoned home for a family lunch. These are held sporadically. We're not the kind of family that meets up around the dining table every week come what may. But when an invitation is issued it's a three-line whip on attendance. Partners are also invited, but I'm yet to have a boyfriend that I dislike enough to inflict my family on. Only joking, but a relationship needs to be fairly serious for me to bother with all the questions. I suppose if Spencer had stuck around, he might have been the first.

My brothers have to attend as well. Felix has no regular girl-friend although he has dragged a couple of them along over the years. I think that was more because it was free food they didn't have to cook, and they are generally so hungover from their Saturday night with him that they contribute little to the con-versation. Xander is different. He's been going out with Lou since they were at school, so we all know her pretty well, although she's terribly shy. She doesn't speak unless you ask her a direct question and even then she looks as if she'd rather you hadn't. I think she finds us a bit much when we're all together. She's an only child and if her parents aren't librarians then they're in the wrong job.

I pick out a straight black skirt and a cashmere twinset in a rich emerald green and turn up with a bottle of wine and a mid-range bunch of flowers that I picked up in Marks & Sparks.

As I drive over there, I practise deflecting questions about work. I formulate vague answers in my head that will hopefully put them off the scent. Work is bound to crop up. It's one of those conversational starters for ten, and that's multiplied for me because, as I now realise, I might have gone on about my job a bit too much in the past.

I hope I can get away with wishy-washy responses and don't have to lie outright to Mum and Dad. That doesn't mean that I'm ready to confess the truth, but the thought of actually lying gives me a heavy feeling in my stomach which I really don't like.

'Hello, love,' says Dad as he opens the door. He pulls me in and gives me a quick squeeze. 'Your mother has a new stola and she's not happy with it. Just tell her it's perfect, would you. Give us all a break.'

'What's wrong with it?' I ask, genuinely curious.

'I haven't a clue. Something about the colour, I think. Now, go on through. No sign of Felix yet but Xander and Lou are in the lounge.'

He takes the wine and flowers from me and I do as directed. Xander and Lou are indeed sitting on the sofa deep in conversation, which they pause when I appear.

'Hi, sis,' says Xander, dropping an arm casually around Lou's shoulder in case, I assume, she needs some moral support.

'Whatcha,' I reply, dropping into a chair. 'All good?'

They both nod. As you've probably gathered, my siblings and I don't live in each other's pockets and I don't see much of them beyond these Sunday lunches so the swapping of news should really be happening now. I'm ready with my rehearsed replies but it will be easier if I bat the attention away from me from the off.

'How's work going, Lou?' I ask because it's an easy way to engage with her, and then I could immediately kick myself because it's obviously going to lead to a reciprocal question about my job.

But Lou can be relied on to say the least possible. She just says that it's fine and doesn't ask about mine, so I dodge that bullet.

I sense that Xander is going to ask though, but fate intervenes in the shape of Mum. She bustles into the room wearing a stola and making tutting noises. For those not as familiar with ancient Roman clothing as I am, the stola is the garment that married women apparently wore. It looks a lot like a toga to the uninitiated but it's basically more of an over-dress. This one is just like all the others she has except that it's yellow. I wonder if, as Dad suggested, it's the colour that's bothering her but I assume that she requested it when she ordered it.

'Hi, Mum.' Then, mindful of Dad's comment, I add, 'That looks nice. Is it new?'

'Yes, but I'm not sure about it at all. The pleats are all wrong.'

I'm really not sure that anyone is going to pull her up on the pleats on her stola but I try to look sympathetic.

'From my research there should be more of them and they should be far more delicate.'

'I like the colour,' I say, trying to distract her from the incorrect pleating. 'I have a new friend who loves yellow. In fact, another friend has just made her a yellow dress based on one of mine. She's teaching a group of us to sew. We've already made some pyjama bottoms.'

It all comes out before I have time to think about the consequences. Fortunately, my mother is too distracted by her unsatisfactory stola.

'The colour isn't right either,' she moans. 'The Romans had saffron, of course, but that made more of an orange. This is far too buttercup.'

A narrow escape. Mum isn't listening and so hasn't heard what I said. I'm about to add that I'm sure the Romans could create different shades of yellow and orange by using more or less pigment when Lou pipes up and utters what I swear is the longest sentence I've ever heard her say.

'I've always wanted to learn to sew. Do you think I could come along to the classes? Is there a website or something to sign up at?'

How do I answer that without explaining exactly who Ethel and Dawn are and how we ended up in my flat copying a dress? And before I've had time to think it all through, I say, 'It's more of a private arrangement but I'm sure you could come along. I'll need to check.'

That'll be okay, I think. I can pretend to check and then just tell her there isn't room.

The fact that Lou has spoken is enough to drag Mum from her clothing dilemma. It appears that she was listening. Very little gets past my mum.

'Now wouldn't that be lovely,' she says, 'if Lou could come and join your class, Abbie. Who did you say was running it? Someone you've met through work?'

Mum knows that I had no life outside McDougal & Wright.

'Er . . . She's called Ethel and she's, like, a friend of a friend.'

'Ethel. That's a name you don't hear every day. Is she an older lady? Although they call children the strangest things these days, strange to my mind at least. All those old people's names on brand-new babies.'

'Yes. Ethel is a bit older than most of my friends. She used to be a ballet dancer.'

This detail slips out, I realise, because I'm proud to have a friend who had such an interesting job.

'I wonder if she can sew stolas,' says Mum, ignoring the reference to ballet and fiddling with the layers of fabric.

'I'll tell you what,' I say. 'When I've learned how to do it then I can make your stolas exactly how you'd like them. Now, is there anything I can help with in the kitchen? You go and get changed and I'll put the carrots on.'

And with that we move on from my friends from the community table.

Dad wanders in with a round of drinks which he distributes. 'How's work, Abbie?' he asks when we're all settled.

My flush is instant and all-consuming and I thank my stars that Mum is in the kitchen because there's no way she would have missed it. Dad, on the other hand, seems oblivious to my discomfort. I have a split second to decide what to do. Tell him and ruin a perfectly pleasant Sunday lunch with Mum going into full-on panic mode and me then having to face her questions about why I've waited so long to mention such an important development in my life. Or lie.

'It's great, thanks, Dad. And how was that thing in Scarborough?'

27

Felix finally arrives for lunch with our parents an hour late. I was all for just plating his up but Mum was having none of it. She claims she doesn't have a favourite, but if there were only one place left on the life raft, Xander and I would be getting wet.

He blusters in, kisses Mum, says hello to Dad and then announces that he's starving and when's lunch. Xander and I exchange glances but I know better than to point out the obvious. So we all troop through to the dining room and I help Mum to put the dried-up chicken and seriously over-crispy roast potatoes, which would all have been perfect an hour ago, on to plates.

'How's it going being the world's greatest marketer?' he asks me through a mouthful of carrots. 'Made a million yet this year?'

I squirm in my chair and hope no one notices my cheeks flare. Luckily everyone is intent on their food.

'It's fine,' I say briefly.

'Don't tease your sister,' says Mum. 'Abbie's job is very demanding and she deserves to be paid well for what she does.'

'So do I!' replies Felix indignantly. 'But I was robbed of a promotion last week by some bird who flashed her tits at the boss.'

'I'm sure that's not right,' says Mum. 'Not in this day and age.'

'Well, all I'm saying is that I was the best man for the job but she got it,' replies Felix with a twisted eyebrow raise designed to convey something suspicious.

I know I should speak up to defend the poor woman who isn't here to defend herself and who I don't doubt got the job on merit alone, but I don't want to open the conversation up into the realms of work. So instead I ask him about his latest money-making scheme which he'd been full of the last time we were round the table.

'How's it going with the camper vans? Have you bought your first one yet?'

The idea, not a bad one for Felix, was to buy old camper vans, do them up for the glamping market and then hire them out. It's hardly an original scheme but no less sound for that.

Felix drains his red wine and pours himself some more. 'Nah. Have you seen how much those things go for?'

I haven't, it not being something I'm interested in. I would have thought he would have though, and would then have factored the cost into his budget when testing out his concept. But it appears not.

'Pricey?' I ask vaguely.

'Like you wouldn't believe. And the stuff to tart them up! I looked at cushions and shit online. Some of them are like sixty quid each! For a cushion!'

Setting up a luxury glamping van will take more than a couple of cushions, I think, and not least a serviceable camper van engine, but again, I keep my unpopular views to myself.

'You could get Abbie to make your cushions,' says Xander. 'She's going on a sewing course with Lou. She could do it at a discount.'

'I'm sure she'd make them for nothing to help her brother out,' says Mum.

She's wrong.

But Felix is no longer interested in tarting up camper vans.

'Dropped the idea,' he says. 'No, now I'm writing a novel, a thriller. I saw a thing on YouTube. There's a fortune to be made, apparently. You just publish it yourself and then watch the cash roll in.'

I know nothing about being an author but I'm pretty certain there's more to it than that.

'I always fancied writing a book,' says Dad wistfully but no one takes any notice.

'How far have you got?' I ask Felix, but I already know the answer.

'Not started yet,' says Felix predictably. 'I'm letting my ideas percolate. I've been sitting in that trendy espresso bar near the station, people watching and making notes.'

'À la J. K. Rowling,' says Xander, rolling his eyes in Lou's direction. 'Worked out okay for her.'

'Yeah. Exactly,' says Felix, Xander's gentle teasing passing him by entirely. 'I was in there the other day and the barista asked me if I wanted to buy a coffee for a stranger. They run this ridiculous scheme where you pay for not just your own drink but for any old randomer who might want a coffee for free. I said no but if he wanted to give me mine for nothing then that would be great.'

This I can't ignore. 'I think buying a drink for a stranger is a great idea. Putting something back, passing on your good fortune. And you never know who might benefit. They might be really desperate.'

'I was really desperate! It was my first caffeine shot of the day.'

He grins and looks around at us so we can all laugh at his comment. I want to smack him.

'Seriously though,' he continues before the rest of us have a chance to express a view. 'It's all going a bit too far, don't you think?

If you want a drink from an expensive espresso bar then get a job and buy one yourself. Don't rely on someone else to do it for you.'

He says this as if he pulled himself up by his own boot straps rather than having a privileged start in life and then taking regular handouts from Mum and Dad.

'But what about random acts of kindness?' asks Xander. 'Paying for someone's drink is just a kind thing to do. I read a book once where the guy paid for the car behind him at a toll booth.'

'That's just stupid,' says Felix dismissively. 'Why would you even do that?'

'Because it's nice. What if you were the guy in the car behind? Wouldn't that make your day?'

'It's, like, five quid. It's hardly going to break the bank.'

'It might for someone. It might be the difference between them eating that night and not. You just don't know.'

They don't know just how close I am to being broke, and the thought that I might have to make choices like this makes me feel queasy.

'They say that, don't they?' says Dad. 'You shouldn't judge someone until you've walked a mile in his shoes.'

Dad often says fairly profound things like this and is generally ignored.

'Well, I don't go round asking for charity,' says Felix, 'so I don't see why other people should.'

I can't stand any more.

'That's the whole point, Felix, you moron,' I snap at him. 'They don't ask for help. It's the kindness of strangers.'

'You'll be saying next that people who end up begging on the street don't deserve to be there. If you make shit decisions it has consequences.'

'What? Like they end up on the streets on purpose?'

Felix puts his hands up and shrugs. 'Don't they?'

'Of course not. And, anyway, you have no idea what has happened to anyone, good or bad. Who are you to judge? You should just treat everyone fairly and with kindness.'

My stomach squirms a little as I remember how I thought a few short weeks ago, how nervous I was of actually talking to anyone at the community table. Had my views really been so far from my brother's? But whatever I thought then, now I know better.

'You're such a dick.'

'Abbie. Not at the table,' says Mum.

'I'm sorry but he is. And I can't listen to any more of his crap.'

I get up and start clearing the plates. Lou leaps to her feet and helps me.

'I think your dad's right,' she says in a voice so quiet I can barely hear it. 'You shouldn't judge anyone until you know their story.'

Righteous indignation courses through me. Of course we shouldn't, and I'm really annoyed with Felix for judging Bob and Ethel and the others without even meeting them. I know that I too had been worried about how people would see me now that I don't have the enviable job, but I'm still the same person I was. I'm learning that I am more than just my job, and the tablers most definitely are. But I can't defend them without fessing up to my secret, and, even though I've come a long way, I'm not quite ready for that, it seems. Felix, meanwhile, is still going on about how hard he's worked to get where he is and how other people should do the same, and doesn't seem to hear her.

28

Monday again! The pace with which my life is flying by is frankly terrifying. I'd assumed I'd have a job by now, or at least a couple of interviews, but there's nothing out there. Each day I scour the internet for suitable openings, looking further and further afield, but no one is hiring people at my level. I could take a huge pay cut and apply for something much more junior but then I'll never be able to keep up with my outgoings. Disaster will still arrive – it will just take a little longer.

I sit at my kitchen table with my notebook in front of me and try to work out where I can make cutbacks. I could sell the car, but that might reduce the number of jobs I can apply for and there are few enough of those as it is.

I could take a lodger into my newly decorated back bedroom. I think quite hard about this option before rejecting it for now. I may yet get to that. Unpalatable as it is, it's definitely preferable to losing the flat.

It crosses my mind that I could cut out my daily trips to the supermarket café. Even if I only buy coffee and no cake, it still adds up. But I dismiss this idea. If Bob can afford to buy coffee then I'm damned sure I can. At least Bob has a job, which is more than I do at the moment. I keep telling myself that this is a temporary state of affairs, but the longer things go on the harder it is to stay calm.

To take my mind off my dire situation, I fill my days with all the things I've never had time for before. I make photo books for every holiday I've ever had and then one for each year, even though I can't afford to get them printed. I tidy my wardrobe, washing and mending everything so that I have the full range of my clothes available to me again. I think I must have lost some weight since I was sacked as a couple of items that were quite snug now seem to fit. Every cloud, I think bitterly.

I sort out my kitchen cupboards and am horrified by the out-of-date items I find loitering in them, which I promptly chuck. I binge-watch the box sets that I've always meant to see and make playlists on Spotify for every occasion.

For a chunk of most days I sit, phone in hand, almost messaging people. I don't know how many messages I start to Sal. Chirpy bouncy messages:

> *Sorry I've been so quiet but you'll never guess what's happened to me.*

Or

> *Meet me for a drink tonight and I will tell you something seriously juicy!*

But the thought of explaining about the job and how I feel about it feels like a huge mountain that I have to climb. I'm curled up at the very bottom and I can't imagine ever having the energy to begin, and that was before I learned that I'm not as important to her as I'd thought.

The longer my silence goes on the stronger my reluctance to get in touch grows. I can even feel myself retreating like a snail pulling back into my shell.

And then there's Spencer. It would be the work of a moment to type out a quick question to him. He's messaged me a couple of times so I know he wouldn't mind. But I was the one who said we should split up. It's not fair if I start sending out confusing mixed signals to him now, especially if he's embarking on something with that pretty woman from the photograph. Look at me being all open and reasonable!

Sometimes when I'm feeling super-low, I pull the photo of him up and just look at his smiling face. We were so new in our relationship that we hadn't got as far as taking photos of each other, and his social media profile picture is an orange sock. So this solitary image is all I have and I torment myself with it, thinking about what might have been.

But even if life is a bit grim, all is not entirely lost. I have the tablers.

Every weekday at ten I make my way to the supermarket café to meet up with whoever is there. The routine of it has become the backbone of my day. I'm the only one who always goes. There are a couple of ways of looking at this, but I prefer to see myself as lynchpin of the team, the one consistent member who can be guaranteed to be there for anyone who turns up. I hope that's how they see me too. That's definitely easier than the other interpretation – that I am so alone that without them I'm struggling to find a reason to get up in the morning.

Occasionally someone new will sit at the community table and I am now happy to chat to them, but no one else joins us as a regular member. And, actually, I don't really want anyone new. It would spoil the group dynamic. I'm tempted to remove Joel's sign altogether but I know that's not really in the spirit of the community table, so I resist.

This morning only Bob and I are there by ten past ten. I take the opportunity to pick up the conversation we had when we were painting my bedroom.

'How's it going with the family?' I ask him. 'Have you seen them?'

His shoulders droop and all the sunshine goes out of his face.

'Nah. I thought it was hard when the kids were smaller but now that they're old enough to make their own decisions it's really crap. Jake'll say he's coming but then he doesn't show up. He's always got some excuse, summat he's forgotten he was doing. He just doesn't want to see me.' He stares into his cooling cup of tea. 'And Chloe doesn't even pretend to want to come.'

'Oh, Bob, I'm so sorry.'

'Not your fault.'

'Well, no. But it's still shit.'

He shrugs. 'Yeah. I'm hoping they'll come round in time. It'll be easier when I have me own place.'

We both know that's unlikely to happen any time soon but it doesn't need saying.

'How about you?' he asks, and I can see how hard he's trying to be positive. 'Any jobs on the horizon?'

I force a smile. 'Yes! There are one or two things that look really very promising,' I lie.

He nods. 'Makes sense. A bright capable girl like you is bound to get snapped up sooner rather than later. And that'll be our loss,' he adds with such a genuine smile that it brings a lump to my throat both for how lovely he's being and because I'm being so dishonest about everything.

We both sip our drinks. I feel awful for lying but Bob is quieter than usual too. I know there's the stuff with his kids but it seems like there's something else on his mind as well.

'Are you sure you're okay?'

'Yeah,' he says, but I'm not convinced.

I wait.

'There's this lad turned up at the shelter. Not been homeless long. You can always tell, see it in their eyes. That fear, not knowing what's going to happen to them. Something about him reminded me of our Jake and it's thrown me a bit. I mean, no matter what's happened to him, this boy is someone's son and now he's sleeping rough without anyone looking out for him.'

I've seen kids on the streets of Leeds too, so young they look like they should be at school. I'd assumed they were just playing truant, had somewhere to go back to at the end of the day. I wonder now whether I only thought that because it was easier for me to process.

'He came in too late in the day, though. No beds left. We gave him the name of another hostel to try but I bet they were full too. There are never enough beds. But I can't stop thinking about him and wondering where he ended up.'

'Maybe he'll show up again.'

'I wish there was more money in the system,' Bob says, 'to help the young 'uns. I reckon if we caught them early enough they'd have a much better chance of turning themselves around. But there's nothing. No slack anywhere. Not that I can help. I barely have enough for me sen as it is.' He sighs deeply. 'Sorry, Abbie. Didn't mean to bring the mood down with my doom and gloom stuff.'

'You haven't,' I say, trying to sound like I mean it. 'I can see how hard it is. And it's lovely that you care enough to want to help.'

He gives me the sharp look I get when I've been too middle class. 'Just because I've got no cash doesn't mean I don't care. See you tomorrow.'

Then he gets up and leaves.

The shame I feel runs all the way down to my toes.

29

When Dawn walks into the café the next day wearing her newly sewn pyjama bottoms, heads turn. It's actually one of her more conservative outfits, but the supermarket has a 'No pyjamas' rule and it's her flagrant breach of that that appears to be causing the consternation. I see women at other tables cocking their heads discreetly in her direction and signalling their disapproval with their eyes.

Dawn is, of course, totally oblivious to the ripples she's making. She heads straight for the counter.

'Hey, Liz. Like my bottoms? I made them. Ethel showed me. I'm going to make some in all the colours.'

Liz looks up from serving her customer to take in Dawn's new look and then nods approvingly.

'They're great, Dawn. I wouldn't mind some of those myself. I bet they're dead comfy. Just the thing for relaxing at home.'

Liz catches my eye and winks.

'Not just at home,' says Dawn. 'I wore them all day yesterday too. I can make you some if you want. I'm really good at sewing. Ethel said.'

'I wouldn't mind a pair, as it goes,' says Liz. 'How much are they?'

Dawn is thrown by the question. She frowns and then shrugs.

'Well, why don't you have a think?' says Liz. 'And in the meantime, what flavour is it to be today, my love?'

'Chocolate. With sprinkles. And squirty cream.'

Dawn brings her drink over to the table where Ethel, Bob and I are already sitting.

'Loads of people like my bottoms,' she says as she sits down.

'I'm not surprised,' I say. 'They're great. Will you make some for Liz?'

Dawn nods as she sucks some milkshake up through the stripy paper straw.

'Got no more material though,' she says.

'I have plenty of fabric,' says Ethel. 'I could bring some here and Liz could choose which she liked. How much do you want to charge?'

Dawn shrugs and we scratch our heads. I daren't admit to how much the loungewear I bought just before I lost my job set me back, so I keep quiet.

'Well,' said Bob. 'Let's cost it out like a proper job. First there's materials.'

'She can have the fabric for nothing,' says Ethel. 'She'll be doing me a favour getting it out of my apartment.'

'Then there's time. Dawn worked fast – two hours? Probably less. But we can't charge at trades' hourly rates. That would make them too pricey for anyone to buy. And then there's the electric. We didn't pay to borrow the studio. Do you think she'll lend it again, Abbie?'

'Yes, but I think she might charge us if we start using it a lot,' I say.

Bob nods again, frowns and then licks his finger and sticks it in the air. 'Haven't got a clue what to charge,' he admits.

'I'll ask Liz,' says Dawn, and without getting up she shouts across the café. 'What would you pay for some of my bottoms?' she asks.

'Come over here. Let me have a proper shufti,' says Liz more quietly.

Dawn scampers across and does one of her trademark twirls in front of the counter.

'Lift your top up. Let me look at the waist.'

Dawn does and Liz makes appreciative noises at the drawstring fastening. 'Twenty-five quid?' she says.

Dawn's eyes open wide which Liz interprets as her opening offer being too low. 'Okay, thirty-five but I can't go any higher than that.'

Dawn, who is for once lost for words, nods quickly and comes back to join us. Her mouth is wide open now too. 'Did you hear what she said?' she whispers.

We all did.

Dawn just sits there with her chin virtually on her chest. 'Thirty-five pounds for something I made!'

An idea is starting to form in my head but I'm not quite sure how it will go down. I decide to keep it to myself for now.

Ethel picks the ball up. 'How about when we next go to the studio I bring all the fabric I have? You might have to collect me in your car, Abigail. And then we can make some pairs in various colours and Liz can choose which she likes best.'

'Not sure anyone would want to buy what I make,' says Bob with a laugh.

'You will improve,' replies Ethel sternly. 'It just takes focus and practice.'

Bob adopts a serious face and salutes obediently at Ethel.

I decide now is the moment to put my idea forward.

'What about this?' I start. 'And say no if you think it's ridiculous. Yesterday Bob was saying how the hostel needs more funding for extra beds. What if we said that for each pair we sold we'd make a donation to the hostel?'

They think about it for a second.

'That's not a bad idea,' says Bob. 'If everyone agrees.'

A deep line appears between Dawn's eyebrows. 'What would we do with the rest of the money?'

'Well, you'd keep it,' he says. 'Like a kind of wage for the work you did sewing the bottoms.'

Dawn thinks about this for a moment. 'So how much for us and how much for the hostel?'

This is another of those questions that I don't feel qualified to answer, but Bob has it covered.

'So, if we sell them for thirty-five pounds a pop. I think that's a bit steep me sen but let's work with that for now. And say we split that sixty/forty. That would be . . .' He does the maths in his head. 'Twenty-one pounds per pair for the sewer and fourteen for the hostel.'

Everyone is quiet for a moment.

Then Dawn pipes up. 'I think twenty-one for the hostel. They need beds for all those people.'

Bob nods. 'They do, Dawn,' he says.

'Hey, Liz,' shouts Dawn across the café so that all the other patrons stop talking and turn to look. 'Is it okay if we give some of the money you pay for your bottoms to Bob's hostel?'

'Of course it is, my love,' replies Liz. 'That's a brilliant idea. Joel'll like it too, what with our charity of the year being that one for the homeless.'

I see the other customers in the café nodding approvingly to one another.

30

The four of us sit back in our seats, grinning at each other like cats with the proverbial cream.

'Genius!' says Bob. 'Well done, Abbie.'

Over the last few weeks I've put my foot in it many times with Bob but this finally feels like I've got something right. There's a warm glow in the pit of my stomach, the kind that comes with praise from someone whose view is important.

'Can I point out that we have precisely one order,' says Ethel, bringing me right back to earth. 'This is hardly the makings of a business empire.'

'Maybe not,' Bob concedes. 'But assuming Dawn makes the goods . . .'

'Which I will,' chips in Dawn.

'And Liz parts with the readies, which I don't doubt that she will, then that's one bed for one homeless person for a night. Bloody brilliant.'

Ethel nods grudgingly.

'And if we sell another pair then that'll be two nights,' says Dawn. 'And if we sell another pair that'll be three nights.'

This could go on all day. Bob touches Dawn gently on the arm. 'You've got it, Dawn.'

'We'll need to see if Viraj is up for it,' I say. 'What do you think?'

We all agree that he probably will be. I pick my phone up to message him as if he's a regular friend and then I remember that I don't have his number. Almost immediately a message lands with a photo attached. A close-up of a very cute-looking puffin fills my screen. Dawn sees it and picks up my phone to examine it more closely.

'Dawn! You can't go looking at other people's phones like that,' reprimands Bob.

'Thingy doesn't mind, do you, Thingy?'

I shake my head, because what alternative do I have, but my stomach does a little flip because there's only one person who could be sending me pictures of sea birds. I have to try really hard not to grin like that cat from Cheshire.

'Oh, it's gone,' she says because the preview of the message has disappeared. 'Show me again.'

She hands me the phone and I click into Spencer's message, desperate to savour it but unable to do so without looking rude. I hand it back.

'That's a funny-looking bird,' Dawn says, peering at the screen, and I have to agree with her.

'It's a puffin,' I tell her. 'From Scotland.'

'Why did someone send you a puffin?'

And before I have time to reply she's reading Spencer's message out loud.

'*Thought this might make you smile. Plenty more where he came from. Come for a visit and I'll show you. S x,*' she reads and then, 'Who is S x?'

'For the love of God, Dawn, give the woman some privacy!' says Bob.

But I don't mind, not really. 'S is short for Spencer,' I say. 'And he was my boyfriend until quite recently. But then he got a job in Scotland and we decided to split up.'

'Did you love him?' Dawn asks.

She really takes not one single prisoner.

I swallow hard. 'No, I don't think so. It was a new thing, so we hadn't got that far. But I did like him quite a lot.'

Dawn nods thoughtfully. I don't look at Bob and Ethel but I sense their interest being piqued by this new detail of my life beyond the café.

'Where is Scotland?' asks Dawn.

'A long way north. Here' – I reach for my phone – 'I'll show you.' I open Maps and search for Stornoway. 'Here.'

'And where are we?'

I scroll the map all the way down to Leeds.

'Well, that's not very far,' says Dawn dismissively. 'You should go.'

'There speaks your social secretary,' says Bob. 'And you thought your life was your own.'

'Stornoway. That's on the Isle of Lewis, isn't it?' asks Ethel. 'Very beautiful up there, or so I'm told.'

'I don't know,' I reply. 'I've never been further north than Edinburgh.'

'I think I danced in Edinburgh,' muses Ethel. 'It's all so long ago. The theatres rather blend into one another.'

'That must have been wonderful . . .' I begin, trying to shift the focus away from Spencer and his puffins, but Dawn is having none of it.

'So, will you go? Shall we text him back now and tell him you will? I'll do it.'

She starts typing and Bob snatches the phone away from her.

'No,' he says simply and hands me the phone back, but as I look down at the screen I see that Dawn's managed to type two letters – *OK*. And beneath them in smaller type it says 'Delivered.'

I could be angry but what would be the point? I'll just message Spencer later and explain what happened. He'll probably see the funny side. I mean, it is kind of funny.

But I suppose I could go. I have all the time in the world and I could probably find a cheap train, or even a bus! And I would like to see where he's living and what he's doing. The pretty woman with the wide smile pops into my head before I can stop her. I can't be jealous of something that might only be real in my imagination, can I?

Then again, we have quite emphatically and determinedly split up. Wouldn't it be a bit weird if I went to visit?

'Will we meet at the sewing studio tomorrow?' asks Ethel. 'I can look out the fabric this afternoon and then you can pick me up, Abigail.'

She says this as if it's already decided and for a moment I lose the thread of the conversation, my head being full of Spencer and puffins.

'Er, yes. Making the PJ bottoms. Got you. I'll just check with Claire that we can have the studio but hopefully that'll be fine. You'll just have to let me have your address.'

Ethel gives it to me and I make a note in my phone. I don't recognise the road but I'm excited to find out a little more about her. She gives me a landline telephone number too, just in case.

When I get back home, I reflect on the morning's activities. We have set up a charitable enterprise and I seem to be accidentally going to the Outer Hebrides.

Not a bad return for one cup of coffee.

31

I explain to Claire about the fundraising for the homeless shelter and she says that we can use the studio for free for three months. 'It can be my contribution to a worthy cause,' she says.

The next day, I arrive at Ethel's place at around nine thirty to pick up her and her fabric stash. I'd put the address in my sat nav but when I pull up I'm certain I must have made a mistake. I check the postcode, assuming that I've typed it in wrongly, but no. This does appear to be the place.

It's an old mill conversion, the kind that cities in the north of England are littered with, relics of a once thriving industry. This one is a beautiful example and seems to have been converted sympathetically and not on the cheap. The Yorkshire stone hasn't been sandblasted to within an inch of its life but left with blooms of centuries-old soot here and there, so that the place looks authentic and intriguing. The window frames are thin and painted black, giving it a sleek, understated look, and some of the apartments have balconies with planters and bistro tables and chairs on them rather than drying laundry and old bikes.

This is not where I expected Ethel to live. In my head she had a bungalow or a tidy little end terrace. Once again, my expectations have been confounded. I think I should probably give up second-guessing people.

There is a large entrance foyer which I enter tentatively, still not entirely convinced that I'm in the right place. It's high and airy and the exposed heavy stonework shows how solid the building is. It will no doubt stand here for centuries to come.

I check my notes and press the appropriate bell. Almost at once I hear Ethel's voice on the intercom.

'Who is it?' she asks crisply even though I assume she knows already.

'It's me, Abbie.'

'I thought so. Come upstairs. The lift is behind you. I'm on the third floor.'

Ethel is standing at her front door as I step out of the lift, looking as elegant and serene as ever. I wonder briefly if she would ever wear a pair of the pyjamas she's taught us to sew but I doubt it. Ethel is not a loungewear kind of woman.

'Come in,' she says. 'I think we may have to make more than one trip. I hope your car isn't full.'

The apartment is breathtaking. I don't know where to look first. The main living space is all open plan with what looks like the original wooden floorboards, dotted with Persian-style rugs. The walls have been plastered and are painted a pale duck-egg blue. There are heavy-duty steel beams cutting across the ceiling, painted cream with luscious trailing plants dangling in various places. Her furniture is sparse: a large corner-unit sofa and coffee table, a dining table and chairs, an oversized bookcase neatly stacked. At one end the wall is covered by a huge mirror with a ballet barre attached. I imagine from her shape and the way she carries herself that Ethel still uses this most days.

'Wow! This is a beautiful apartment,' I say.

'Thank you.' Her response is gracious but doesn't encourage any questions. 'The fabric is through here.'

She leads me to what I imagine was a bedroom but is set up as a workroom. There's a long countertop into which her sewing machine has been sunk so that it's flush. She has a mini haberdashery on one side, threads in every colour all laid out on a peg board and what looks like an old pharmacist's cabinet with glass drawer fronts that contain trims, buttons and the like.

Laid across a large cutting table are many bolts of fabric.

'I have chosen traditional cottons in the main,' she says. 'But also some more unusual choices for our more quirky customers.'

Dawn pops into my head and from the way Ethel's lips are turning slightly upwards I imagine she is thinking the same.

'Put your arms out.'

I do as I'm told and she layers bolt after bolt of fabric on to me until I am almost staggering under the weight. It takes us three runs to get it all into the car and at no point do I ask why on earth she has so much fabric.

However, as I drive I can't resist asking her about her amazing home. 'How long have you lived there?'

Ethel shrugs as if such details are of no interest to her. 'I bought it when I retired,' she says. 'Not as a dancer. That was a very long time ago. As a ballet mistress. I taught in ballet companies, after I finished dancing myself. But eventually even that became too hard and so I settled here in Leeds.'

'Why Leeds?'

Ethel goes very still next to me. I keep my eyes on the road but I can sense that she's barely even breathing. 'I had a friend here,' she says. 'A very special friend. She died.'

'I'm sorry.'

'Thank you.'

We don't speak after that, both lost in our own thoughts and the traffic.

Maybe that's why she found the community table. The loneliness. I think about her, sitting all alone in that huge apartment with her ballet barre and her sewing and no one to speak to, day in day out. Of course, I could be completely wrong about this. Let's face it, I've been wrong about pretty much everyone else. But something tells me that in Ethel's case I'm not that far from the mark.

Bob and Viraj are on the doorstep when we get to the studio and they help me in with the fabric. Dawn arrives just after all the fetching and carrying has been done, and the bolts of fabric are strewn across the cutting table just waiting for our attention. Unsurprisingly her eye seems drawn to the brightest colours and patterns.

'Liz would love this,' she says, picking up the corner of material dotted with eggs and feathers in peacock blues and purples.

This may be true – I don't know Liz well and it's hard to guess at her style choices when I've only ever seen her in her café uniform – but just in case . . .

'How about we all pick something different and then we'll have five different pairs for her to choose from,' I suggest.

'I'm not sure anyone's going to pick my pair,' says Bob, and we remember the disaster that was his first attempt.

'Yeah. Yours were rubbish,' says Dawn.

'Only a fool repeats their mistakes,' says Ethel, eyeing him coolly.

'That's me told, then,' he says before picking up a checked flannel and taking it back to his workstation.

32

It's much easier to sew the pyjamas second time around. Because I have a better idea of what I'm doing, I can concentrate on making the finished product neat and tidy. By the time I hold the bottoms in my hands the idea that someone might part with good money for them doesn't feel completely ridiculous.

I show Ethel shyly and she examines my seams and then nods her head in approval.

'Good. Very good, Abigail.'

It's like being at school having your work checked by a particularly terrifying teacher.

In fact, everyone produces a decent pair, even Bob, who keeps checking what he's doing with Dawn as he goes along and consequently manages to sew the right bits together in the right places.

We lay the five pairs out on the cutting table and stand back to admire our work. It's taken us just under two hours.

Dawn walks the line examining them. 'I like mine best,' she says. 'Then Thingy's. I like the dots on hers.'

'What's wrong with mine?' asks Bob in mock indignation.

Dawn considers them. 'Nothing. But checks are a bit boring.'

'Fair enough,' says Bob.

'So that's five beds we've made,' says Dawn, and as we realise what we're looking at a hush falls over us. She's right. These simple garments represent a bed for the night for five rough sleepers.

'Assuming we can sell them,' says Viraj.

He's got a point. It's all very well Liz saying she'll take one pair but that's a long way from having them all sold.

At once my mind flicks into Abigail account executive mode. I haven't thought about work for weeks but now ideas start popping in my head like the bubbles in a glass of fizz. I go from nought to one hundred at warp speed and already I'm envisaging a social media campaign, a website with full merchandising capability and at least one appearance on prime-time TV.

I rein myself back in.

'Shall we ask Joel if we can put them out for sale on our table?' I ask. 'It fits with the supermarket's charity of the year, after all?'

'Good idea,' says Bob. 'Maybe we can shift a pair or two.'

'I can make a sign,' says Dawn. 'With the price on. And say that we made them and that the money is going to buy beds for people who have nowhere to sleep.'

That's a lot of information for one sign, but I don't want to be bossy so I keep my mouth shut.

'I can set up an app on my phone so that people can pay by card,' Viraj says. 'Who carries cash these days?'

Well, Bob and Dawn for a start, I think, but he's right. We're far more likely to get some impulse purchases if we lower the resistance to buying by letting people just tap and go.

'That's a great idea,' I say.

'I can set up a separate account for the money,' he adds. 'So we know exactly where we are.'

He is a virtual stranger but I have absolutely no concerns about him doing a runner with our cash.

'Shall we make some more?' asks Dawn, already picking up a new bolt of fabric and heading back to her machine.

'Not today,' I say. 'We have to tidy up and leave. But maybe the next lot will be quicker. Assuming we sell this first batch, that is.'

Of course there is a possibility that Liz was just being polite and that no one else will be interested in our pyjamas. This really might be a one-off.

But something deep in my gut tells me that we're on to something. Pyjamas are associated with feeling warm and safe and that makes them the perfect way to draw attention to those people who don't have that simple luxury.

Back at my flat, I sit with Elvis on my lap and my iPad on the table in front of me. I google how to get to the Outer Hebrides. It's not like I'm really going to go but it's good to know what my options are.

A veritable plethora of alternatives pop up, from walking (six days) to driving (around eleven hours) to a flight from Manchester. If I get the train up to Edinburgh it's just a quick hour's hop and that's barely any time at all. I'm not sure why I thought the place was so inaccessible.

I let my hand wander across the screen, clicking on links to see the costs. It's not cheap but it's not impossible, especially if I can stay with Spencer. I bite my lip. We were so new that we hadn't even got that far yet. Of course, I'd thought about it – the first time. I have to say that in my imagination I didn't picture us in a hostel in Scotland with a whole bunch of hairy twitchers on the other side of the wall but I could live with that.

Maybe I could go, just for a couple of days. The idea starts to settle itself, like when Elvis sits on my knee, turning round and round until he finds the perfect spot.

Then I go to the message thread between me and Spencer. The last message was Dawn's cheeky 'OK'. He hasn't replied, not even with a shocked-face emoji. What does that mean? Is he sitting up there thinking 'Shit! Did she mean it?'

Well, there's only one way to find out.

Are you serious about me coming to visit? I type and send before I can overthink the message.

I stare at the screen, see the message delivered and wait. Then the dots appear. Spencer is typing.

Yes!

Why is my heart beating so hard?

Okay, I type. *Then I'll come.*

I hit send before I have time to think better of it.

33

Viraj offered to take the pyjamas home with him from the studio, so I'm pleased to see that he's first at the table the following day, our little stash in a bag for life at his feet. He is clearly waiting for some direction on display tactics, which is good. We need this to look as professional as we can from the outset rather than looking like Scouts selling home-made buns.

'Morning,' I say, putting my coffee cup down carefully.

'I've got the online shop all done,' he replies, straight to business. 'I know we were only talking about having a tap and go payment system but I got carried away.'

He pulls a face that makes him look all geeky and sweet.

'That's great,' I reply, genuinely in awe of someone who could do something so seemingly complicated with such apparent ease.

'Selling online is more efficient than selling from a table in a café,' he adds, 'and less embarrassing.'

Right on cue Dawn arrives with a sign made out of the inside of a cardboard box which is almost as big as her. She's wearing her own pair of the bottoms. Viraj and I exchange 'now that's a great idea, why didn't I think of that?' looks.

'We missed a trick there,' I say, looking down at my checked capri pants dolefully. I may be the one with a marketing background but I'm not so experienced that I can't be taught a thing or two by a total beginner.

Dawn leans the sail-like sign against the table and a little shower of silver glitter flutters to the floor.

'Hello. I made the sign. It says everything on it.'

'So it does,' I reply. I might have thought her proposed wording was too detailed for a sign but I hadn't reckoned on the sign being so big.

She does indeed have all the details covered.

'Where are they?' she asks, looking around for the pyjamas.

Viraj passes her the bag and she tips the contents out over the table. Our lovely hand-sewn garments land in an undignified heap, looking very much like the wherewithal for a jumble sale. My inner saleswoman is struggling to maintain her composure.

'Shall we tidy them up a bit?' I suggest. 'So it looks more like a shop.'

I fold each pair neatly and then put them into a small pile which takes up about the same amount of space as one of the café's trays. We don't yet have permission from Joel to sell here but we will surely stand a better chance of getting him to agree if we don't make his café look a mess.

Liz comes over, grinning at us all. 'You made them then.'

This is the moment of truth. Will she honour her offer to buy a pair or was she only joking?

Dawn is straight on it. 'We did. I made these ones for you.' She pulls her peacock-blue pair out, destroying my tidy pile. 'Do you like them?' She thrusts them at Liz.

'But you can choose any of them,' I add, not wanting to pressure her into buying something she doesn't want. I don't give the option to change her mind, though.

'Let me see . . .' says Liz as she takes in the options. 'And are they all the same size?'

'Yep. One size fits all,' says Viraj.

'Very good. I think I'll choose . . .' It's like waiting for Patrick and Esme to pass judgement on *The Great British Sewing Bee*! I'm quite nervous. '. . . The ones you made for me, Dawn.'

She lets the legs hang and holds them up against her body. 'What do you reckon? Do they suit me?' She looks at Dawn, who nods enthusiastically.

'Yes, I knew they would. I picked the colours specially.'

'Well, you have a good eye. Now, my love, how do I pay you? How much did we say?'

I swallow. It's one thing to agree a price in theory. It's quite another to extract the readies when the product is in front of us. I'm expecting some objections or a degree of haggling at the very least.

Dawn has no such qualms. 'You said thirty-five pounds which means that twenty-one pounds will go to the hostel where Bob works,' she says, giving Liz precisely no wriggle room.

'Let me get my purse.'

Liz has cash so we don't have to test out Viraj's new system and then we sit there, bathing in the glory of our first sale until Bob and Ethel arrive.

'Sold out, have we?' asks Bob as he sits down.

'No!' Dawn's voice is petulant. 'Only Liz has bought some so far. Shall I go and ask everyone at the tables if they want any?'

She goes to stand up as we all say 'No' simultaneously.

'I think we need to wait for the customers to come to us,' I say gently.

Dawn looks like she doesn't agree but she sits back down and takes to staring intensely at the other patrons, willing them to look our way. When one or two of them, sensing that they are being watched, do look over, Dawn points at her sign and at the small pile of pyjama bottoms but they look away again pronto. No one wants to be forced to engage with the oddballs at the community table.

By the time I get to the bottom of my cup of coffee, which I eke out longer than usual, we have still sold exactly one pair.

'This isn't working,' says Dawn. 'No one is buying. And they have to because we need to give the money to Bob to pay for the beds.'

'We can't force people to buy,' says Ethel.

Dawn looks at her as if that is exactly what we should be doing.

'I think we need to rethink our marketing strategy,' I say. 'We're in the wrong place. People come in here for a drink. They're not expecting to buy anything else and they're confused by our offer. We need to be somewhere where people go with the intention to shop.'

'Like the market!' says Dawn.

'Well, yes. But not there. We don't have a stand and we only have four pairs to sell.'

We fall silent as we try to think of somewhere that's not the market but like the market, but we draw a blank.

'Let's have a think overnight,' says Bob. 'We must know someone between us.'

'I don't know a soul in Leeds,' says Viraj. 'That's kind of why I'm here in the first place.'

'Well, you can still have ideas,' says Ethel sniffily.

'And what you've done so far is fab,' I add, not wanting him to take his bat home. His online set-up and Dawn's cardboard sign are all we have on the marketing front. 'I think that's a good idea, Bob. Let's meet back here tomorrow and pool our ideas.'

And so we leave, with four pairs of pyjama bottoms in our bag.

34

I have a few ideas overnight but nothing earth-shattering. We are trying to sell four pairs of pyjama bottoms so we don't need much of a marketing strategy. The obvious thing would be to put a post on Facebook. If I got the wording right, I'm sure I could get them sold without too much effort.

My thumb hovers. This will be my first post since life changed and the contrast with what I was sharing before couldn't be more stark. I've gone from photo shoots and glitzy parties to home-made pyjama bottoms. There will be questions and then I'll have to go public about losing my job. Playing fast and loose with how I answer questions from my parents in private is bad enough, but lying in public? I'm not up for that.

But anyway, me selling our wares is not in the spirit of a team venture. I shouldn't just hijack matters and I doubt the others have much access to a computer let alone an active social media presence, apart from Viraj of course, but despite his prowess on a keyboard he doesn't strike me as a big user of Instagram and the like.

Viraj is definitely the dark horse of the group. So far, I have learned why he's in Leeds but next to nothing about him as a person. It crosses my mind that he doesn't quite fit in, but this thought makes me smile. None of us fits in, which is really the point.

But fitting in or not, he's the first at the café when I arrive and is looking decidedly smug.

'Where's the merch?' I ask him, noticing that the bag isn't with him. 'Couldn't you stomach the humiliation of another day like yesterday?'

I'm joking of course and I can see in his face that he gets that. But he has news.

'Sold them,' he replies with a little upward rise of his eyebrows. 'I took them into the office yesterday, explained about Bob's shelter and then my colleagues were falling over themselves to buy a pair.'

'Nice! Well done you.'

Viraj rolls his eyes at me. 'Literally no effort required,' he says dryly. 'And I doubt any of them will ever be worn. It was all about virtue signalling. They're not interested in actually helping. They just want everyone else to see them being a kind person. Actually,' he adds, 'they probably will wear them just so they can post and tell even more people about this "really cool cause they supported".' He makes sarcastic air quotes.

'But does it matter?' I ask. 'The net result is the same. The product is sold, the money is in the bank and we will have provided beds for five people. It's not a bad start.'

I smile but then I think it through.

'It's not really sustainable as a business model, though, is it? Making stuff is fun but we're not a factory. We can't produce nearly enough to provide a consistent stream of income. For that we'd need to take it all much more seriously and I'm not sure that's practical.'

'No,' agrees Viraj. 'We all have jobs for a start. Except you and Ethel.'

The fact that I have no job makes my heart jolt. I manage to forget about it for some of the time but each time I remember it gets worse.

Viraj considers me thoughtfully. 'It's okay, isn't it? You not having a job at the moment.'

I swallow.

'Shit, it's not, is it? Sorry. In my world people are between contracts all the time but we get paid such stupid money that it's never a problem.'

'It's okay just now,' I say, adding what I hope is a convincing smile. It's apparent that I missed my mark.

'Ah,' he says. His gaze drops to his feet then up at the ceiling. He taps his fingernail against his teeth. 'Look. I can lend you some. If you're short.'

The lump that rises up my throat makes it hard to breathe. I don't know this guy from Adam but he's offering me the kind of help that I wouldn't even ask my own family for, given that they think I'm the responsible child who stands on her own two feet.

'Thank you,' I stutter, genuinely touched. 'That's so kind. But I'll be fine.' I smile and then am horrified that this releases a single tear. I brush it away quickly, hoping he hasn't noticed.

He nods. 'Well, the offer's there if you need it.'

I mumble my thanks and rush to the ladies to pull myself together. It takes more than a minute.

When Dawn and Bob turn up you can almost touch their delight.

'So we made . . .' Dawn begins. The tip of her tongue peeps out as she tries to do the maths, but she gives up pretty quickly.

'One hundred and five pounds,' supplies Bob. 'For a little under two hours' work.' He pauses. 'Which would be a great return if there weren't five of us. So that's actually ten hours' work. Which is round about the minimum wage.'

'Time freely given though,' I say, and Bob agrees.

'Can we do that every week though?' he wonders out loud.

'We were just thinking that very thing.' I nod at Viraj because I can't quite look at him.

'And even if we could, can we find someone to buy the blessed things?'

This is another issue, although I'm sure I could have a pretty good stab at it.

'Rather than trying to provide a constant stream of cash, maybe we could hold a one-off event?' As I say this, I get a little buzz of excitement. This is what I do – organise events. Ad shoots, product launches, press nights, they all come as easily to me as breathing, and I know I could do something here too. A glitzy party in a place-to-be restaurant is very different to raising money for a homeless shelter, but an event is an event. I'd be playing to my strengths, which, after my enforced period of inactivity, feels good.

Bob nods enthusiastically but Dawn doesn't look best pleased.

'I like sewing things,' she says petulantly.

'Perhaps we can come up with something that has some sewing in it?' I say, although nothing is leaping to mind. 'And in the meantime, we can keep on with making the pyjama bottoms. We have plenty of fabric.'

Dawn's smile returns. 'Good.' And then with the startling change of conversational direction that I now expect from her she adds, 'Did you go and see the puffins?'

I am momentarily thrown but Bob comes to my rescue. 'We saw Abbie yesterday, Dawn.'

Dawn looks like the significance of this isn't making much impact. She shrugs in an 'And? Your point is?' kind of way.

'It's a long way,' clarifies Bob. 'You can't just go after tea. A trip like that needs a bit of planning.'

'Oh,' says Dawn. 'So no puffins.'

'No puffins yet,' says Bob.

I shuffle in my seat, not that keen on them talking about me as if I'm not there.

'I'm not sure when I'll go,' I say. 'If at all. I've got a fundraising event to plan first!'

Why does that feel like such a cop-out?

35

The next morning I'm sitting at the breakfast table telling Elvis about my plans for the day when the doorbell rings. I'm wearing my prototype pyjama bottoms and a T-shirt I've used to decorate in. My hair is a bird's nest and my face is scrubbed clean of any feature-enhancing make-up. I am definitely not visitor-ready.

It'll probably be the postman or someone trying to deliver something to one of my neighbours, and I decide to brazen it out. After all, if I choose not to get dressed until after eight thirty then that is my prerogative.

But it's not a delivery person. It's Dawn.

She looks dreadful, her eyes puffy and her clothing choices even more random than usual. I don't bother with pleasantries. It's obvious something is badly wrong.

'Dawn! What's the matter? Come in!'

I stand aside to let her past and she heads straight for my lounge and flops down into my sofa, head in her hands.

'I don't know what to do,' she says. 'It's all gone bad.'

Then she starts to cry. I might have expected her to cry as she does most other things – dramatically and with great gusto – but she is very contained as she sits there, the rising and falling of her shoulders the only outward sign of her distress.

'Oh, Dawn,' I say, sitting next to her and putting my hand on hers tentatively because I'm not certain what she wants from me. 'I'm sure that whatever it is we can sort it out. Why don't you start at the beginning and tell me all about it.'

She gulps a little, swallowing down her tears. 'I've killed someone,' she says.

I definitely didn't see that coming.

'You've done what?'

'I've killed Precious. Well, she's not dead yet but she will be soon and it's all my fault.'

'I think that's unlikely, Dawn,' I say in as calming a voice as I can manage. I have no idea if this is true. I barely know Dawn. Maybe she has a violent streak that I haven't seen yet.

But my head is running through the possibilities and I'm sure she can't really have hurt someone. She isn't the type. This will be a misunderstanding, a confusion of some kind. My eyes flick to the clock on the wall just in case I have to give the police a statement. I really hope this isn't going to be a genuine confession to murder.

'Just tell me what happened.'

Dawn looks up at me then, her round face so innocent. Because she's generally so animated, I have never really looked at her features before but now I see that she has tiny gold flecks in her blue-grey eyes and a smattering of freckles across her cheeks. That and her missing front tooth all add to the air of guilelessness. Dawn is no murderer. Of that I'm certain.

'It was my turn to make tea last night,' she says. 'And we were having chicken nuggets and rice and baked beans, with yoghurt for pudding. I like those ones that are shaped like strawberries but they're a bit pricey, so I buy the big tubs instead and then put some in everyone's bowl. It tastes the same but it's not as good as the squeezy strawberries.'

It's obvious that she's going to take a while to get to the nub of the story, so I nod encouragingly.

'I made the nuggets in the oven. I did what it says on the bag. I put the oven at the right temperature and cooked them until they were hot all the way through. I cut one in half to check.'

'That's good.'

'But the rice.' Her breath catches as she sobs again.

'What about the rice?' I ask gently.

'There was rice in the fridge from Frankie's takeaway. And I couldn't be bothered to cook more so I just used that.'

I'm not really sure how this story is going to end in murder. 'Well, that's good too.'

She raises her chin and looks right at me, her pale eyes brimming with glistening tears. 'No. No it's not. I did it in the microwave. And then we ate it. And then in the night Precious started puking. And it's all my fault.'

I'm losing the thread here and Dawn must see the confusion on my face. Her eyes narrow and I wonder if I really have misread her after all.

'You're supposed to be clever,' she says accusingly. 'But you're stupid. It's obvious. I've poisoned her. They taught us at college that you shouldn't eat rice that's been cooked before. It has food poisoning in it. And I did and now Precious is going to die and I'll go to prison.'

Her head drops into her hands again and she starts to shake.

I relax. Did I not know there would be a simple explanation? Well, ninety-nine per cent of me did anyway.

I put my arm around her shoulder and pull her towards me. 'No she's not, Dawn.'

'How do you know?' she asks without lifting her head.

'Well, for a start it's very unlikely that the rice was bad if it had been in the fridge and was only a day old.'

'But they said at college . . .'

'Yes. I know and they're right. You do need to be careful. But I've heated up lots of rice and eaten it and I'm not dead, am I?'

Dawn raises her eyes and stares at me as if she's actually considering this.

'No,' she concedes reluctantly.

'And,' I continue, 'more importantly, did you eat the chicken nuggets and rice and beans?'

Dawn nods sadly.

'Just the same as Precious did.'

She nods again.

'And this other girl, Frankie. Did she eat it too?'

'We all did. It was my turn to make tea and we all ate what I made. There wasn't any other tea.'

'And you're fine?'

Dawn thinks about this for a moment and then nods.

'And Frankie is fine?'

More nodding.

'Then it isn't what you cooked that made Precious ill. It could be anything. Something she ate during the day or a bug she's picked up. If it was the rice then you'd all be ill.'

I can see the relief wash over Dawn's face as the logic of this hits her. 'She said it was my fault. She said I'd killed her.'

'Well, I'm not a doctor but I think she's wrong about that.'

'So I won't go to prison?'

I shake my head. 'No.'

'And she won't die?'

'I can't say that for definite, but I very much doubt it.'

And then Dawn's huge open smile is back. 'That's good,' she says. 'I was scared.'

'You did the right thing coming here,' I say. 'Friends are always great in a crisis.'

'And you're my friend, aren't you, Thingy?'

'I definitely am. Now would you like something to drink? I can make a milkshake if you like.'

'Yes,' she says. 'I would.'

36

After Dawn has finished her milkshake and I've got dressed we head off to the café to meet the others. Now she no longer thinks she's going to prison, Dawn is back to her normal chatty self. She talks ten to the dozen so that I can barely get a word in, but I don't mind. She carries an infectious energy that I enjoy. Being with her is like standing in a room full of lightbulbs on a cloudy day.

As we walk, I think about how unwilling I was to engage with her at the start, worried in case she overstepped some social norm and embarrassed me into a place that I didn't dare venture into. How ridiculous that feels now. She's just Dawn. There's nothing at all to be anxious about.

'I watched *The Great British Sewing Bee* last night,' she says. 'Bev told me about it. She's our helper. It's on catch-up.'

'Did you like it?'

'Yeah. I like the middle part best.'

I try to remember the different rounds they have on the pro-gramme each week. 'Is that the bit when they have to make some-thing new out of something old?'

'Yeah. I reckon I'd be dead good at that. I'm dead good at sewing.'

'You are! Maybe we could call into a charity shop on the way and you could pick up something to transform.'

Dawn thinks about this briefly. 'Yeah,' she says.

The nearest such shop to the café is one for a homeless charity, which seems very appropriate. Dawn chooses a striped man's shirt and a floral summer skirt, both a riot of colour.

'What will you make with them?' I ask as we walk along.

Dawn pulls the clothes out of her bag and the shirt billows like a sail in the breeze. 'Don't know yet. Maybe add some bits of the shirt into the skirt?'

I can't quite see how that might work. The fabrics are very different weights and don't sit naturally together, but I'm no expert. Then again, neither is Dawn. She sees things differently to me. Where I spy potential pitfalls, she sees only possibilities. It's very refreshing.

When we get to the table Ethel is the only one there.

'I nearly murdered Precious,' Dawn tells her cheerfully. 'But Thingy says I didn't. So I'm okay now.'

You would imagine that this statement would need some serious unpicking but Ethel seems happy to take it at face value.

'And we bought some clothes to turn into other clothes like I saw on the telly,' she says.

'Show me,' says Ethel, more interested in this than the untimely death of Precious.

I go to the counter to order my coffee and leave them to it. Joel gives me a little nod when he sees me.

'Morning. Flat white?'

'Please,' I reply. 'How are you?'

'Can't get any staff,' he says with an exaggerated sigh.

'What happened to the last one?'

'Stopped turning up.'

'Something you said?' I ask him cheekily, but he doesn't look very amused.

'You don't want a job, do you?'

164

I actually consider this for longer than I'd have thought likely a month ago, but then I shake my head. I can't drink coffee with my friends if I'm working. 'No thanks.'

'See!' he says as if his point is proven. 'Can't get the staff.'

He busies himself with the coffee machine, banging out the grinds and cleaning the steam jet.

'Did Liz tell you about our business venture?' I ask him lightly, but watching him closely for any clues to his attitude.

'Selling those clothes you've made? Yes. She showed me what she bought. Not bad. Did Dawn really make them?' He throws me a look that is pure scepticism with a dose of incredulity.

'She did!' I confirm. 'That woman has hidden talents.'

'Have you got any left?' he asks.

His back is to me so I can't read his expression, but I very much doubt he wants a pair himself.

'No. All sold. Why?'

'I was just thinking, if you had any more, we could take a photo of you all and I could send it to head office, a kind of update on my community table idea.'

He does, at least, have the grace to look slightly uncomfortable about this suggestion. Selling the pyjamas is supposed to be about Bob's shelter, not Joel's career. But don't they say that all publicity is good publicity?

'Well, we need to make a new batch,' I say. 'So, we can bring them in here before we sell them if you like? Maybe we could set up a stall and you could get some footage of us in the act of making money for the shelter.'

A tiny tell-tale crinkle in Joel's nose tells me that this is going further than he intended, but that just serves him right for trying to use us for his own ends. I'll shame him into helping if it kills me. I feel my opinion of Joel starting to shift to a slightly less glowing place.

'Yes,' he says with unconvincing enthusiasm. 'Great idea.'

Bob and Viraj have arrived by the time I get back and once they all have drinks and Dawn has explained how she didn't actually murder her housemate, I share the news.

'Joel wants to take some photos of us selling our PJs in here,' I say. 'So he can send them to head office.'

Ethel and Bob exchange wry glances, Viraj tries his best to look excited and Dawn is the genuine article.

'That's fab,' she says. 'But we don't have any left.'

'We'll just have to make some more.'

Dawn pulls a face. 'But what about my transformation?' she asks, pulling the shirt and skirt out of their bag and flapping them so violently that I fear for our drinks.

'You sew so fast, Dawn. I bet you can do both.'

So, it's agreed we will convene at the sewing studio to rustle up the next batch.

As I walk home, I realise that I couldn't go to the Outer Hebrides now anyway. I have an exciting event to organise and so I simply don't have time to go gallivanting off.

This is good. It means that I can push the whole idea out of my mind. I keep reminding myself that I finished things with Spencer for a reason. With us living five hundred miles apart, our relationship just can't have a future. It's not practical, and it will do my poor little bruised heart no good at all to keep thinking about him all the time, let alone to go up there and see him in his new life with his new friends and, possibly, his new love interest. For my own self-preservation, I need to cut loose.

I'll message Spencer and tell him and then that'll be one thing fewer to have to worry about.

37

We are on a roll!

We all arrive at the studio on time and are at our machines and ready to sew by ten past ten. It's definitely getting easier to make the pyjamas now that we have a couple of pairs under our belts, so to speak. Dawn has taken to it like a duck to water and works at almost twice the speed of the rest of us. When I stop to get teas and coffees I see that she's branching out, making a pair using two different fabrics, the front in one design and the back in another. She's chosen fabrics that clash violently but I can see that might appeal to a certain kind of customer.

'They look great, Dawn,' I say as I pass her. 'You could do a pair with different legs too.'

'Doing that next,' she says, without looking up from the seam she's sewing.

The rest of us are being more traditional with our fabric choices but I imagine there's a bigger market for that type of thing. Or maybe not. In looking for our unique selling point maybe we should all be more like Dawn and go for the more eye-catching ideas. There would certainly be less competition.

'I've had a thought,' I say over the buzzing machines. The sound stops, except for Dawn's. She stops for no one. 'I'm wondering if a way to distinguish our product from all the others is to be more creative in our designs.'

Viraj throws me a horrified look, like I've just suggested he paint the ceiling of the Sistine Chapel.

'Nothing too ambitious,' I reassure him. 'But we could use more unusual fabric choices and combinations. Really make a statement.'

'Not a bad idea,' says Bob. 'It's not like anyone is going to wear them out of the house . . .'

Dawn coughs.

'Except you, Dawn,' he adds. 'So they could be pretty outlandish.'

'Exactly!' I say, delighted that he's got my point. 'And that could be what sets us apart.'

'When we've run out of Ethel's material, which will be soon, we can go to charity shops and buy stuff to recycle into more, like on *Sewing Bee*,' says Dawn without looking up.

She's right. My imagination is running wild as I see a whole clothing empire based on recycled items. I see myself pitching the account to a keen team of advertising execs, and briefly my head is full of the possibility of being the client for once. I imagine letting Frobisher give me his best shot and then just turning him down because I can.

But I think I may be getting ahead of myself. This is just a few pairs of PJs.

'We need to think about our overheads,' says Bob. 'Ethel's donated her fabric very generously for nowt . . .' He smiles at Ethel and she rewards him with a very gracious nod back. 'But if we're having to buy the fabric then we'll need to either make less profit or put the price up.'

Or take less of a cut for our time, I think, but I can't suggest that. I feel that's something that needs to come from Dawn or

Bob, for whom time is money. Maybe it is for Ethel too, although I suspect she has enough for her needs.

It is for me as well, I realise with a jolt. My notice money won't last forever. Also, all the time I'm spending sewing means there's less available for job hunting. That ought to be my priority, but this feels more important.

All this aside, I can't be the one who suggests we sew for nothing.

'Or we just don't take anything out for ourselves,' says Bob as if he was just inside my head. 'Put all the profits towards the shelter.'

There's a beat. I don't want to be the first to agree with him and I can see from Viraj's face that he is thinking the same.

Dawn wrinkles her nose. 'Don't get it,' she says.

'Right,' begins Bob. 'You know we said at the start that we'd give some of the money to the shelter and keep some for ourselves.'

Dawn nods slowly.

'So, I'm saying we could just give all the money to the shelter instead.'

Dawn processes this. 'So we wouldn't get any money?'

Bob shakes his head.

'But the shelter would get more.'

'Yup.'

Dawn looks up at the ceiling as she thinks about this. She's quiet for a long time, for her at least, and we all just sit there, watching her.

'Okay,' she says. 'I'll sew and not get paid. But I have to do my cleaning job or Bev will be cross with me. We have to have a job. It's one of the rules.'

'It won't get in the way of your cleaning job,' says Bob. 'We can sew instead of going to the café if you like.'

Dawn pulls a face. 'Can't do that,' she says. 'Liz'll miss me. And what about my milkshakes?'

'Okay. Then we'll do both,' says Bob, grinning at her. 'Milkshake one day. Sewing the next.'

He might smell a bit, but he really is the kindest bloke I've ever met.

'Is that okay with you too, Ethel?' he asks, but I get the impression that he already knows it will be.

'It is,' replies Ethel.

'Great!'

'We need a name,' says Viraj. 'Something catchy for the website.'

'We have a website?' asks Ethel.

'We do. I set it up before. With full online trading capability. But it's a bit short on eye appeal.' Viraj gives us a modest smile. 'Design's not really my department.'

'I can pull together some ideas for how it could look,' I say. 'I'll do it this afternoon. We do need a name though.'

There's a pause while we all think.

'How about Pyjamas for Beds?' I suggest.

Dawn looks nonplussed.

'That's a bit rubbish,' says Bob. 'And it won't work if we branch out into anything else.'

I might have taken offence in a previous life but now I just laugh. And anyway, he's right. 'Go on then! What's your genius suggestion?'

Bob stares at the ceiling, lips pursed. 'Nothing springs to mind right this second but give me time.'

'How about "Time for Beds"?' says Viraj.

'That is not bad,' replies Bob. He says it out loud a couple more times, trying the name on for size. 'Yes. I reckon that'd work.'

'Why don't we ponder as we sew?' suggests Ethel and the hum of the machines starts up once more.

By the end of the session, we have seven more pairs ready to sell, one each from me, Bob and Viraj and two from Ethel and Dawn. They are a mixture of the traditional and the more unusual designs, and when I've ironed them I think they will make a nice little stack for Joel and his photo opportunity.

We're just sweeping up the stray threads and fabric scraps when Dawn makes an announcement. 'I like Time for Beds. That's what we're called.'

And so it is decided.

38

I miss a call from my mum. In fact, I miss several. I'd turned the ringer off on my phone when I was in the bath reading and forgot to turn it back on. I suppose it shows how few people are trying to get hold of me that the calls are almost a day old by the time I find them.

Despite indications to the contrary, I'm not a very good liar and if Mum probes just a little bit she'll see straight through me. I ring her back with my heart in my throat, ready to gush about whatever new account I've been working on.

'Hi, Mum,' I say brightly.

'Oh, Abbie. There you are,' she says, sounding more irritated than concerned.

'Sorry. I had my phone on silent.'

As I say this, I realise that if I were still working this wouldn't have happened, or not for as long. I panic and start to craft what I hope is a convincing lie. (See above point about being no good at lying.) 'We had an important pitch meeting at work and I turned it on to silent for that but then I must have forgotten to switch it back.'

There's a pause at the other end of the line. 'This would be a meeting at McDougal & Wright?' she asks.

'That's right?' I reply. My voice appears to have put an inconvenient question mark at the end of my sentence.

'It's just that Audrey Smith, who lives at the end of the road, said her daughter-in-law has just started working there and I told her all about you, and told her she should get in touch so you could fill her in over coffee . . .'

Shit. I can see exactly where this is going.

'But when she asked about you, they said you'd left.'

I have less than a second to think of an explanation and my brain doesn't work that fast, so I opt for the truth.

'No. I left about a month ago,' I say vaguely, knowing as the words come out of my mouth that they aren't going to satisfy my mother.

'You never said,' is her response. Not 'Oh dear, how awful for you', or 'Oh dear, are you all right?'

'Didn't I?' I reply, because two can play at that game. 'I was sure I had.' I screw my face up at this blatant lie. There is no way that Mum would have forgotten me casually mentioning that I was without gainful employment.

'I see,' Mum replies. The bristles in her tone virtually reach out of the phone and scratch my cheek.

'I was going to tell you . . .' I add, abandoning my lie to die in the water. 'I just didn't want to worry you.'

This is good, making it more about Mum than me. She makes an approving little sound down the line.

'I don't know what your father will make of it.'

I doubt very much whether Dad will make anything of it at all. His main concern in life is that his children are healthy and happy and I am clearly both.

'Is that what those sewing lessons are about?' she asks. 'Do you want to be a fashion designer?'

The ludicrousness of this statement is my mother all over. It's all about extremes with her, there are no half measures.

'No. I just have some unexpected free time and I've always wanted to learn.'

'Save you spending money on all those clothes alterations, I suppose,' she concedes.

'Exactly. And how are you? And Dad?'

This diversion tactic will never work but it's worth a shot. Mum ignores the questions entirely.

'So, what will you do?' she asks. 'I assume you're looking for a job. They aren't that easy to come by and you're not getting any younger.'

'I'm thirty-one, Mum! Hardly on the career scrap heap just yet.'

'Time marches on, Abigail.'

'Well, I'm taking some time to have a think,' I say. 'I will probably stay in marketing and I don't want to leave Leeds but other than that I'm pretty open.' As I say this I realise that it actually sounds pretty closed, but I press on regardless. 'And at the moment I'm doing some decorating and some sewing, and I might go and visit Spencer on Lewis.'

'I thought you two had split up.'

She doesn't miss a thing.

'We have,' I say, smiling down the phone inanely, 'but he's invited me up anyway.'

'I see,' she says, and I assume she now thinks that I'm chasing after him.

This is precisely why I didn't tell her any of it in the first place.

'It's all okay, Mum,' I say more gently. 'I have everything under control.'

'Hmmm,' she says, sounding less than convinced.

Part of me feels that I should be apologising for letting her down. I've blown any bragging rights she had with her friends by

174

losing my fancy-pants job and probably spoiled her self-image as mother of a successful child. If we'd been having this conversation a few weeks ago, I would probably have fallen on my sword and made promises about getting an even bigger job so she can be prouder still.

But I'm actually feeling quite excited about what I'm working on with Bob and the others. No, it doesn't come with all the trappings of the account exec and it definitely isn't paying the mortgage, but it's fun and even though I haven't known my new friends from the community table for long, they are already people I don't want to let down.

'And I suppose the freebies will stop,' she adds. 'That's a shame. We loved those truffles.'

And I immediately stop feeling bad. Before I get a chance to explain any of this or comment on the lack of freebies going forward, Mum has moved the subject away from my many failings and back on to herself.

'Well, we're going to Cirencester this coming weekend.'

'That'll be fun. Will you wear the new yellow stola?'

'No. I sent that back. The colour was all wrong.'

I'm just wondering whether there is much of a market for saffron-dyed stolas when I realise that she's ending the call.

'We'll be back on Monday,' she says. 'Take care.'

And then she's gone.

Well, at least everything is out in the open now. That feels better even if my mother's response was as unsupportive as I expected.

Sitting at the kitchen table with my iPad and a notebook, I start to make a few notes about Time for Beds, coming up with taglines and possible logo ideas, and before I know it Elvis is rubbing at my ankles wanting his tea. I show him what I've done and he purrs appreciatively. He really is a most discerning cat. I'm quite pleased with it too. The design builds around a cartoonish pair of pyjama bottoms which I've coloured in various stripes and checks and then dotted around the mock-up page.

I find an image of a bed in the same kind of style and make the duvet match the vibe of the pyjamas. Then I add a couple of round clock faces for the 'time' part. The overall effect is very bright and cheerful.

I pause. Homelessness is a serious business and I don't want the website to make light of that. But at the same time the community tablers radiate positivity despite having come through some challenging times themselves, and this is what we need to be reflecting.

I add some copy explaining what we're doing.

'Our pyjama bottoms are handmade in Leeds. One hundred per cent of the money we raise goes to help provide beds for people who find themselves with nowhere to sleep.'

I choose a bold serious-looking font which contrasts nicely with the cheerful images and then I add a banner with 'Time for Beds' across the top. By the time I've finished I think it looks pretty good.

I'm sure Elvis also approves by the way he coils himself around my shins.

39

When we show Joel what we've made he is obviously delighted but won't let us sell any until his photographer friend can take the pictures. Yet again, I can't help thinking that Joel has his priorities a little bit off here, but we want the publicity so I don't challenge him. This takes him a couple of days, by which time we've been back into the studio and made another batch.

I'm having so much fun. It's wonderful to have a sense of purpose again. We have a job to do and we are all pulling together to get it done. The banter in the sewing room is hilarious, second to none, in fact. Mainly it flies between Bob and Dawn with the occasional interjection from me. Ethel, with her keen moral compass and sharp tongue, keeps things appropriate and Viraj mainly laughs at everything.

It reminds me of being in the office, but without the pressure and the underlying sense that you might be stabbed in the back at any moment. I'm not sure how aware I was of the competition between my colleagues and me, but now I notice how much more supportive the atmosphere in the sewing room is.

In fact, I'm having such a lovely time that I forget to check my inbox and see that I've missed a possible interview. My heart is in my throat immediately and I feel light-headed with panic. Abigail Finch never misses an email, let alone one that might have led to a new job. But as my breathing returns to normal and I am able to think objectively again, I wonder if I would have gone to the interview anyway? The job – a high-flying account executive for an advertising agency – wasn't entirely what I'm looking for and I'm having so much fun sewing. Having fun has to count for something, right?

Now we are starting to look like we mean business. Dawn has continued with her more quirky designs and I have experimented using two different complementary fabrics. Bob put some glittery ribbon as the drawstring in his. We truly have something in stock for pretty much everyone.

I show the tablers my proposals for the website. Designing by committee is never a great idea, and we all have very different ideas about style, but eventually we settle on a look that everyone is happy with.

It's just missing one thing.

'Can we take some pictures of the shelter itself?' I ask Bob tentatively. 'To put on the page. And maybe speak to some of the people staying there? Then we can demonstrate where the money is being spent?'

I half expect him to kibosh that idea but he does the complete opposite.

'Yeah. Deffo,' he says, enthused by the concept. 'I'll have a word with the woman in charge and maybe a couple of the blokes I know well. They won't mind. Maybe we can give them a page on the site?'

'Rather like testimonials,' says Ethel.

'Exactly,' I agree, pleased that she's understood my idea. 'They can say how the shelter helped them turn their lives around. Just like it did for you, Bob.'

Bob's face changes instantly. 'I'm not going on it,' he says darkly.

178

'I wasn't suggesting . . .' I splutter.

'Good,' he replies, his tone crisp. 'That's okay then.' Then his voice softens a little. 'I don't want my kids having to see that. They've been through enough.'

I nod, remembering how cruel school kids were when I was young. Things must have got much easier for bullies now they have the entire internet at their disposal to hide behind.

'I totally understand. I just meant it would be nice to speak to some people who have managed to get off the streets, like you have. But not actually you,' I add for clarity.

This seems to bring him back on board.

'Not sure it's a great idea for us all to go, though,' he adds. 'It's not a zoo.'

'Do you want to do it on your own?' I ask. 'You can borrow my camera. Or phone photos would be fine.'

I look at Viraj for confirmation of this and he nods. 'Phone photos are high res enough.'

'I think you should come too, Abbie,' Bob says. 'So they can see that it's not something I've dreamed up on my own, or a scam. We can take a couple of pairs with us to show them too.'

'I'm not wearing them,' I say, eyebrows raised.

'Wouldn't dream of asking.' Bob's grin is back in situ. 'And anyway, seeing what you're wearing is one of the highlights of my day,' he adds. From any other man this might have been a really cheesy pick-up line, but from Bob it's just a straightforward comment with no seedy undertones.

Today it's a tea dress with a kitten print.

Dawn clears her throat. She's wearing her twirly yellow dress again, teamed with her purple Crocs and a blue mohair sweater over the top.

'And you as well, Dawn,' he adds.

'Good. I dress just as good as Thingy,' she says sulkily.

'Better, I'd say,' I tell her. 'Because you have your own style and I'm just copying what other people used to wear.'

This obviously pleases Dawn as she grins and nods wildly. I've never thought of my style in those terms before. Just because barely anyone else dresses like me these days doesn't make it original. My style is like my clothes – acquired from someone else.

'When shall we go?' he asks. 'This aft?'

'It's as good a time as any,' I say and immediately feel my nerves rising. I know it sounds dreadful but other than dropping money into paper cups and buying the odd copy of *The Big Issue* I have never engaged with anyone living on the streets before. I've barely even made eye contact. Will they see that in me, think I'm just a do-gooder?

Am I just a do-gooder?

I have no idea.

Bob gives me the address of the shelter where he works and we arrange to meet there in the afternoon.

'Not too late, mind you,' he says. 'Things tend to get a bit busy around teatime.'

I think about getting changed. I don't want to look too . . . I don't know what. But then I decide that is who I am and I have no reason to hide that or pretend to be someone else. I am one of the fortunate people in life, but I'm also very aware of that fact. I hope that comes across.

The shelter is out in the suburbs of the city centre and from the outside it looks like any other building. Nothing about it screams homelessness, but then why would it?

Bob ushers me along. When we are in the café Bob sometimes seems anxious, as if he's expecting someone to have a go at him at any moment. Now we are on familiar ground for him he is more relaxed. He opens the door for me, and I ignore the smell that hits me when he lifts his arm. Briefly I wonder if I will ever be in a position to mention it to him. It's such a personal issue, but I'm sure he would have a better reaction from other people if it wasn't the first thing you noticed about him. Anyway, that is not for today.

'I'll take you to meet Bernie. She's the boss. Well, she's not actually, but she's the one that makes everything run smoothly.'

I can feel how nervous my smile is. He must see it too.

'Don't worry,' he adds more quietly. 'She's right nice. Nowt to worry about.'

We walk down a long corridor and I get glimpses of the various rooms as we go past. A couple are offices, desks and shelves stacked with paperwork. One is filled with piles of clean bedding, another with stacks of toiletries and what looks like donations of everything you can imagine needing if you found yourself with nothing. Finally, we pass a huge kitchen, the scent of frying onions and bolognaise sauce wafting through the air.

'Smells good.'

'Yeah. The chefs do a great job. And it's all cooked from scratch. None of your processed muck.'

We reach a door and Bob taps on it lightly. 'Knock, knock,' he says.

There's a woman sitting at the desk. She's about my mum's age with silver hair cropped to her head and very high cheekbones. She's not wearing any make-up but her eyes are huge and bright blue behind her heavy-framed glasses.

'Hello there, Bob. How the devil are you?'

'All good.'

'Grand,' she replies. Then she spots me. 'And who's this?'

'This is my friend Abbie.'

I give her my most winning smile.

'Hello, Abbie,' says Bernie and then looks back to Bob for an explanation.

'Now then, Bernie,' he says. 'We have a proposition for you.'

40

Bernie pushes her glasses up on top of her head and considers us curiously with her huge blue eyes. 'Now what kind of proposal could you want to be making to me, Bob Hoskins? Should I be worried?'

She has a lovely soft Irish burr to her voice.

'No!' he says and then turns to me. 'She shouldn't be worried, should she, Abbie?'

I feel about six years old. Where is the confident account exec that I was a month ago, the one who presented ideas to her team with self-assurance and authority? Here, among real people working with real issues that actually matter, I feel small and insignificant. But not out of place, exactly.

'I don't think so,' I say.

Bob picks up the reins. 'We've come up with a fundraising idea and I wanted to take a few snaps to put on the website.'

'Sounds intriguing. And this would be for the shelter, would it?' asks Bernie.

'Yeah. A group of us have been sewing these pyjama bottom things,' Bob begins. I hand him a pair and he passes them over to Bernie, who examines them and makes an impressed sort of sound.

Then she raises a hand. 'Stop right there. You made these? You? Sewing?'

Bob affects a hurt expression. 'Yes! I'm a tradesman, you know. I can turn my hand to most things.'

Bernie smiles. 'So you can. Carry on.'

'Anyway, the fabric has been donated up 'til now but when that runs out we're going to pick up old clothes from charity shops to transform into new stuff.'

Bernie nods slowly like she approves of the scheme so far.

'And we've agreed that we'll give our time for free. We can borrow a sewing studio which is also free, for now at least. So that means we can give pretty much one hundred per cent of what we make direct to the shelter.'

'Interesting idea,' says Bernie, although she doesn't seem to be as blown away by it as I'd like. I suppose she hears a lot of fundraising ideas and is naturally sceptical.

'How will you sell them?' she asks, homing straight into the obvious Achilles heel of our idea.

I feel like this is more my field than Bob's so I gird my loins and chirp up.

'We've built a website with e-commerce capability,' I say. 'We have a link in a local supermarket . . .' This is a bit of a stretch but it's not a lie. 'I have a background in marketing so I know how we can use social media to increase visibility. We don't have a huge production capacity so there will be an element of "word of mouth" locally as well.'

It's a weak plan but it is at least a plan. I pull my best hopeful face. Bernadette contemplates us thoughtfully, weighing up what we've told her so far.

'I have to be careful what I let the shelter put its name to,' she says. 'It's serious work we do here and I don't want it trivialising in any way.'

There's a pause and then she looks at Bob warmly and adds, 'But as I know Bob and as it's not a totally bonkers idea, I'm happy for you to use a few photos on your site.'

'And we were wondering about talking to some of your clients, to get some real-life stories.'

I know at once from her expression that I've overstepped the mark.

'No,' she says firmly. 'Things are often on a very delicate balance here. I can't have unqualified people trampling all over the work that we do.'

As she says this, I realise just how naive my idea was and I can feel my cheeks flush.

'But what you could do,' continues Bernie, 'is link to the stories that we have on our site. Then if people are genuinely interested they can click through.'

'Great idea,' says Bob, and I agree too.

'What were you thinking, Bob? For the photos?'

Bob considers. 'A bedroom. Obviously. The kitchen. Maybe a meal if it's a long shot and you can't identify anyone. Would that work?'

'Yes. I'd say so. Grand.'

Then she gives us a smile that says, 'I'm very busy and you've had your allocated time slot', and Bob and I reverse out of the tiny office.

'Right. Let's crack on,' says Bob. 'Shame about not using some real stories but I get what she's saying.'

'Me too. Where shall we start?'

He takes me through to the bedrooms and we stand at the door of a dorm room with eight single beds in two neat rows. A girl is changing the bedding, working her way methodically through each one.

'Hi, Stace,' Bob says. 'This is Abbie.'

Stace says hello, pulling on pillowcases with a practised ease.

'We're just going to take a photo when you're done,' says Bob.

'Want me in it?' she asks, bobbing her hair, pouting and pushing a shoulder forward provocatively.

'Not this time,' says Bob and I'm gratified to see that he doesn't return her flirty tone, even in jest.

When the beds are made we take a few shots, moving around to get the light just right. Shafts and shadows slice across the room, and I can already see the shot in arty black and white on the website. Then we head on to the kitchen. It's a hive of activity in there and no one breaks off from what they're doing to chat. Bob snaps a couple more images and then thanks the chefs as we leave.

'It'll be a while until they serve the food,' he says to me without meeting my eyes. 'You might as well get off. I can take the rest.'

I'm being dismissed. For whatever reason Bob doesn't want me here any longer. I don't unpick that.

'Okay,' I say. 'If you're sure.'

He nods. 'Yeah. No point you being stuck here all afternoon. And I'm supposed to be working.'

Maybe it's as simple as that. He doesn't want to be seen hanging around when he should be doing something useful.

I hope it's that.

I'd hate to think that he was ashamed of me.

41

And so the website goes live. We take some photos of our product, laying a pair out flat on the cutting table in the studio and then standing on a chair so that we can get the shot from above. It doesn't look quite like what you'd see on a real clothing site but it's good enough.

'We probably need some pictures of us wearing them as well,' I say.

Everyone looks at their feet except Dawn, who waves her arm around like a super-keen primary school child desperate to answer a question.

'That's great, thanks, Dawn,' I say and snap a couple of images of her front and back.

'Shall we do one of me walking in them?' she asks as she begins a very convincing model strut.

'Surely just photos is enough,' says Ethel and I agree but gently, so as not to burst Dawn's bubble.

'Although . . .' I begin slowly, knowing they won't be that keen on where I'm going next. 'We say they are one size. It might be good to show how that works.'

I run my eyes across the group. We are all different shapes and sizes. Ethel is tiny in every way, barely five feet three in her stocking feet with a frame like a child. I'm a few inches taller and your typical straight up and down. Dawn is much curvier than me but around the same height. Bob is a bit taller and has a bit of middle-aged spread and Viraj is built like a beanpole. We couldn't have chosen five more different body shapes if we'd picked them out of a catalogue.

Viraj shuffles from foot to foot, obviously uncomfortable with the idea but not wanting to say so.

'How about we make it a group shot?' I suggest. 'Rather than us each posing individually. That should make the point about the sizing and also shows off the team.'

So I deploy the timer on my phone and, after balancing it precariously on a box on the windowsill, we manage to get a decent photo of the bottoms fitting our different body shapes with us gathered in a *Friends*-style gang that doesn't focus on anyone individually.

We upload the pictures along with the ones that Bob and I took at the shelter and I tweak the copy, the others sewing more stock as I work. By the end of the morning, we have a functioning shopfront and a few more pairs to sell.

Ethel clears her throat. 'I would just like to say,' she begins portentously, 'that I am remarkably proud of all your efforts. Taking into consideration that none of you could sew a couple of weeks ago, I think our products are of a very good standard, although some of our purchasers might be luckier than others in what they receive.'

She doesn't look at anyone in particular but Bob objects.

'I take offence at that,' he says, grinning broadly. 'I know my first attempt wasn't brilliant' – he cocks an eyebrow – 'but I reckon mine are as good as anyone's now.'

'I agree, Robert. You've done very well.'

'And now we just need to sell them,' I say. I thought I'd just said this in my head but somehow I manage to say it out loud and it comes out more sceptically than I intend.

Viraj agrees with me. 'Yep. Not much point to all this if we don't make any money.'

'So, what's the plan?' Bob asks, rubbing his hands together like he's ready for anything.

'We need visibility,' I say. 'We could approach the *Yorkshire Post* for a feature but I think we should see how well we can do on our own first. That'll give us more clout when we do approach them.'

'Well, I think that might be over to you,' says Bob. 'None of my mates have that kind of money to drop on anything, let alone a pair of kecks for lounging about in.'

I don't give Ethel and Dawn time to say something similar, although I'm sure they would have similar concerns about not having access to our target market.

'I think this next part is up to me and Viraj,' I say without explanation.

Viraj nods, seeming to sense the truth in my words. The ease with which he cleared the first batch is proof, and he lives his life online so he must be drowning in potential purchasers. And when he's worked his way through all the people he knows then there are all the gamers or whoever he spends his time with. I bet they don't get dressed for days on end and could really use some funky leisurewear that comes with added warmth from knowing that you did some good when you bought them.

It's much the same for me. At the last count I had at least two thousand followers on my social media accounts. Some of them are bound to be happy to put their hands in their pockets for a good cause.

'Dead right,' says Viraj. 'You three sew and me and Abbie can sell.'

He sounds so confident that I can feel a bit of it rubbing off on me.

'We can sew too, though,' I add. 'I like the sewing part.'

As the machines hum and the banter flies around the studio I set up an Insta account for Time for Beds using one of the cartoon PJ images as the profile picture. I write a bio explaining what we're about and add a link to the website.

'Does anyone object to me posting the picture of us all online?' I ask. 'I won't tag anyone.'

The group exchange questioning looks and Bob shrugs.

'Okay by me,' he says, and so I do and add a caption about us being the team behind the product. I include what I hope are appropriate hashtags and post it.

'While we're here, I'll take a few more photos of us in action at our machines,' I say. 'We'll need stuff to keep the Insta feed satisfied.'

'You make it sound like a monster,' says Ethel.

'You're not far off there, Ethel,' I say. 'Social media is a fierce taskmaster.'

She turns her attention back to her seams and I type a post on my own account to announce the arrival of Time for Beds. I have it all set up and ready to go.

Then I pause as I think whose accounts this post will go to and how it will be received. I've hardly posted anything since I lost my job. To start with I was too embarrassed about my fall from grace to draw any kind of attention to myself. I just pretended that I was on a digital detox without actually announcing that.

But now being seen to be living 'my best life' on social media no longer feels relevant. Part of me even wants to start sharing the fun I'm having in the café and in the sewing room. Not only would those kinds of images be honest but they would also feel authentic in a way that my previous posts didn't. Yes, I was in all those fabulous places and doing all those enviable things, but wasn't that just a case of right place right time rather than a real reflection of me? The fact that tumbleweed has been rolling through my direct messages suggests that maybe honesty and authenticity might have been conspicuous by their absence.

I scroll through my recent pictures, mainly of shenanigans in the sewing room and Elvis being cute, but I don't post any of them. I think there's still a little bit of me that isn't quite ready to disclose how much things have altered in my world.

Needs must on the marketing front, though. There's the greater good to be considered here and I have to get the word out about Time for Beds. Everyone is counting on me for that.

But I can't get away from the fact that this will be the first time most people will have heard from me in over a month. I brace myself for all the questions that are bound to ping into my inbox about this apparent change of direction. People will want to know what I'm up to and might even think this is part of a new job.

And there's Sal and my other friends. Surely they are going to wonder why I haven't mentioned my change in circumstances until now.

I explore my feelings on this point and discover that I can live with that. I have no reason to be embarrassed. I am a person beyond the job I used to have. There is more to me than that, even if I am only now starting to appreciate it. I've swapped delicious chocolate truffles being promoted by beautiful models in to-die-for apartments for home-made pyjama bottoms and Bob! People will just have to deal.

I hit post and it's gone.

Time for Beds is out in the wild.

42

As I predicted, the direct messages and comments start dropping almost as soon as I post. I suppose that me popping up out of the blue waving a shiny new account fuels the fire.

The messages range from the polite to the intrigued to the downright nosy, but they all want to know the same thing. Where have I been and why am I suddenly selling handmade leisurewear for a homeless charity? Not many seem that interested in *how* I am. I park that.

After typing much the same message out several times, I craft a round robin reply that I can tailor for different people.

> *Hi. Sorry about the radio silence. I left my job and I'm taking some time out while I decide what's next. A group of friends and I are working on a new project to help support a homeless charity in Leeds, so if you are interested in buying a pair of our handmade super-cool PJ bottoms then that would be fantastic. Only one of us could sew before we started so it's all been a huge adventure so far. Hope all is good with you. Abbie x*

I send this message, or a version of it, to every comment and DM that I receive but I don't make the connection between the beeps coming from Viraj's side of the room and my messaging until he fishes his phone out, looks at the screen and swears.

'Whatever you're doing, Abbie, keep doing it. It's working.'

It dawns on me what he's saying. 'Are all those beeps . . . ?'

'Sales? Yeah.'

He flicks to another screen.

'That's eight so far, no, nine. Ten.'

'How much stock do we have?' I ask slightly frantically.

'A bit more than that but not much. If we carry on at this rate we'll be sold out in the next half an hour.'

'Bloody hell, Abbie!' says Bob. 'That's fantastic.'

'That's the power of social media,' says Viraj with a nonchalant shrug.

'And a good cause and kind people,' I add, feeling slightly defensive on behalf of my Facebook 'friends' who are, in the main, good humans. I'm sure my real friends will be interested too, my slight subterfuge notwithstanding.

'Yes. That too,' agrees Viraj quickly.

'We better work out exactly what we have left then,' I say. 'We don't want to sell what we haven't got.'

I count the pairs. We have nineteen ready to go.

'Okay,' I say. 'We can take nine more orders . . .'

'Eight,' says Viraj as his phone buzzes again.

I can't stop grinning. This is such a high. I wonder if this is what it feels like to run a start-up!

'Seven,' says Ethel with an excited little squeak. 'You'd better start working on an out of stock post, Abbie.'

'We could just keep selling,' says Viraj. 'We can work to the orders.'

This makes me nervous.

'I'm not sure,' I say doubtfully. 'Let's see how much we sell this morning and then take stock. I don't want to put us under too much pressure. This is a sideline after all.'

'It'll be fine,' says Viraj. 'And if we start to sell too many to handle we can just put a hold on it.'

That doesn't sound too onerous.

We gather around Viraj's phone and watch as the sales keep clicking over.

'I can't believe it,' I say under my breath. 'Just look at that.'

When the sales match the amount of product we have to sell, I do an update post.

'Our AMAZING PJs have sold out in a matter of minutes. Don't miss out. PRE-ORDER YOURS NOW!'

I show the others.

'Smart,' says Ethel appreciatively. 'No need to tell them that we only had nineteen pairs in the first place.'

We all grin at each other, except Bob, who is staring blankly into the middle distance.

'Okay, Bob?' I ask.

He drags his focus back to us. 'Yeah. I was thinking. All that money. All those beds. It's bloody brilliant.'

'It's ace!' agrees Dawn.

Bob continues to shake his head, not quite able to take it in.

'Right,' I say. 'How shall we package them up? Recycled brown paper bags seems appropriate.'

And with that I start googling suppliers.

We don't make it into the café until the weekend and when we do Liz is quick to welcome us back.

'Where've you lot been?' she asks us. 'We thought you'd found somewhere better.'

'As if we'd abandon you, Liz,' says Bob, giving her a smile that positively twinkles.

It's the first time I've seen that part of him really shine through. There have been glimpses of it along the way, and the odd joke, but I wonder if he was like this before his life came apart at the seams.

'How's the fashion business?' Liz asks as she wipes down the table next to ours.

'Booming,' says Ethel at the same time as Dawn says, 'Brilliant! We sold nineteen pairs in, like, five minutes.'

Liz looks at me for confirmation of this rather unlikely statement and I nod.

'She's right. It was maybe closer to an hour but we did sell out pretty much straight away.'

Liz looks impressed. 'Is that it now then, my love? All done?'

'No! We're making more,' says Dawn. 'Loads more.'

'Good for you,' says Liz, and wanders back to the counter with her cloth and spray.

We settle at the table. I take a crafty look at the other patrons and wonder what they think about us, the group of misfits at the table for people with no friends. I bet they'd never guess that we are entrepreneurs!

'Have you mentioned to Bernie how well it's going?' I ask Bob.

He twists his mouth and shakes his head. 'Not yet.'

'How come? I thought you'd be dying to tell her how much we've made,' I say.

'I am,' replies Bob, 'but in my head, and you probably think this is stupid, I have a vision of me, Bob Hoskins, former client, presenting her with one of those giant cheques they give to lottery winners. And I want it to have a nice big number on it, with lots of zeros.'

'Nice!' Viraj nods.

We haven't talked about what success looks like to us. We didn't really look beyond selling the first five pairs.

'How many zeros?' I ask.

194

'Six!' replies Bob.

'No. Seriously?'

Bob looks up and narrows his eyes. 'Okay. Maybe not. But realistically,' he begins, 'given what we're selling and how we're making it . . .' He does the sums in his head. 'Maybe . . . ten grand?'

I blow my lips out. 'That's a lot of sewing.'

'Just shy of three hundred pairs, which doesn't include the cost of new fabric. It would be a commitment, that's for sure.'

Three hundred pairs of bottoms sewn by just five of us. That's only sixty pairs each. Put like that it doesn't feel quite so insurmountable.

'All right,' I say, casting my eyes around the table. 'If that's what we're aiming for then it's going to take a lot of work. And we're all busy people so I don't think anyone should feel obliged to help if they don't want to. We've done what we set out to do. We've made the money to provide some beds for the night. So, if anyone needs to drop out now then they can do, knowing that what we've already achieved is pretty special.' I pause and look round the group, trying to gauge the mood. 'But if you want to help carry on and help Bob reach his target then that would be amazing.'

I think about calling for a show of hands but there are so few of us and I don't want to put anyone on the spot. However, I'm struggling to think of an alternative way of getting the votes.

But I don't have to.

'I'm in,' says Viraj with barely a pause for thought about the commitment this will involve.

'I am also happy to continue,' says Ethel.

'And me,' says Dawn before taking a huge suck of her milkshake.

'And me too,' I confirm. 'That's a full house.'

We sit and grin at one another, excited about what's ahead of us. I look at Bob and his eyes are dewy. He makes no attempt to hide the tears as they start to trickle down his cheeks.

'You lot,' he says. 'You're the dog's—'

'Thank you, Robert,' cuts in Ethel. 'That's quite enough of that.'

'Right,' I say decisively. 'We're going to need some more fabric.'

43

I'm awoken on Sunday morning, as I am most days, by a hot scratchy tongue on my cheek and a slightly fishy aroma. I shove Elvis off me and lie on my back with my arms folded behind my head as I contemplate the slightly unusual place I find myself in. In the space of five weeks, I have gone from having my dream job with all the trappings that came with it to sewing pyjama bottoms in a borrowed studio with a bunch of new friends.

When you think of it like that, the whole thing is fairly surreal – but in a good way. I haven't been this happy in a long time and that has to say something. I do need to keep at least one eye on my actual life, though, so that it doesn't just wander off and get itself lost. I'm over a month into unemployment and by now I should probably be well along the path with interviews for something new but I haven't had one promising lead, or at least not for the kind of job I had before.

When I check my phone I have a message from Lucy.

Hi hun. Saw your post about this homeless stuff. New account at work? Nice new direction for the firm. Pro bono? Sal and me were saying that we've not touched base with you for a while. Let's fix that.

Mixed emotions. On the one hand, it's great to hear from Lucy, although the fact that she and Sal appear to have been talking about me behind my back makes me squirm a bit as I wonder how I came up in conversation. I bat that thought back down. These are my friends, after all. Why wouldn't they be talking about me and wondering?

I realise that as she didn't DM me on the post about the pyjamas she didn't get my round robin about the job situation so she, Sal and Meena still don't know. I have to tell them but the longer it goes on the harder it gets to do.

She says she wants to meet up, which is lovely, but she doesn't suggest a date. Does that mean it was just an empty promise, one of those things you say and might even mean but then never do anything about? Could I possibly be overthinking this?

There's also an email from a recruiter that I approached. When he'd asked which direction I was hoping to move in, I'd mentioned the charity sector, citing our pyjama project as evidence of my interest. His email tells me that he doesn't deal with charities and that perhaps on that basis we're not a great fit.

I go into a tailspin. I'd assumed widening my areas of interest would help me find a job, not hinder me. I tell myself that this is just one recruiter and I can apply for jobs without him. It's a scary moment though.

'Does it matter . . .' I ask Elvis, who is busy pouncing on my hand as I move it around under the duvet, 'that I have neither a job nor a plan?'

Elvis keeps pouncing so I stop whizzing my hand around like a demented mouse.

'Concentrate, Elvis. This is important.'

He paws at the duvet cover, trying to work out where his prey has gone, but offers no startling insights on my situation. He has many talents but conversation isn't one of them.

I will have to answer my own question and the answer is stark. Of course it matters. I must pay the mortgage, my utility bills, the council tax. The fact that I'm enjoying what I'm doing or that it's good to make a difference is neither here nor there. I have to get a job. And soon.

But I have made a commitment to the tablers. I have to sew sixty pairs of pyjama bottoms. I promised. So I need a job and to do that as well.

I decide to apply for anything that earns enough to pay my mortgage, but maybe not much more than that. It can't be the kind of all-consuming work that I was doing before. My priorities have changed.

There are also several voice messages from Mum. I knew this would happen as soon as the truth came out. I'm very tempted to just delete them but I don't. I dial into my voicemail and listen.

'Hi, Abigail. Your dad and I were just wondering about the job situation. It really is time you got something sorted out. We can't understand why it's taking so long. Is there an issue with your interview technique? I think you can get training for that. You should look into it. Anyway. I'll try again later.'

I hurl my phone down on to the duvet and Elvis jumps and then tries to pounce on it. Mothers can be so infuriating.

My phone buzzes again. If that's yet another message from her . . . I almost don't look but then I stretch for it and Elvis stretches for my moving arm. His claws are retracted, just about, but he catches my forearm with a rogue and extremely sharp pointy tip.

'Oww! No scratching!'

Elvis doesn't look even vaguely sorry.

It's a message from Spencer!

The dopamine hit is instant. I click, excited, in spite of myself, to know what he wants.

There's a video attached to the message, which I open. To start with all I see is grey. Then it comes into focus and I can tell that the grey at the top of the screen is the sky and the grey at the bottom is the sea. Judging by the shakiness of the footage, I imagine he's on a boat and not a very big one at that.

The camera pans around and I see the harbour with the coloured houses in the distance and then nothing but wide-open greyness in front of him. Something moves in the bottom of the screen. I peer at it. And then all becomes clear. It's a dolphin. It leaps out of the water right next to the boat, as if they're in a race.

It takes me by surprise and I gasp.

'Wow!' I say to Elvis. I know from previous experience that activity on a screen holds no interest for him so I don't bother to show him.

Then there's another one and then a third, all swimming along-side the little boat, leaping up and down in turn. It's amazing. The camera pans round and Spencer twists the phone so I see his face. My heart takes an inconvenient little leap at the sight of him. He raises his eyebrows in a 'well, would you look at that' kind of way. Then spray from a wave hits him square in the mouth and the video stops abruptly.

It's funny and it makes me laugh. I watch it again and then again. There is no message attached but I reply anyway with a little wide-eyed surprised emoji. I'm so tempted to add a kiss but I don't. I have to remember that he is my *ex*-boyfriend, sad though that is.

Scrolling up the thread, I realise that the last message I sent was when I (or at least Dawn) agreed to go and visit him. Since then, we've been so busy with the PJ orders that I've put the whole idea to the back of my mind. I watch the film again, pausing it when his face fills the screen. It would be nice to go and see the dolphins – there aren't many of those in Leeds. And it would also be nice to see Spencer. Lovely in fact.

But.

I'm about to type a message explaining that I haven't forgotten that I'm supposed to be going up there but life got a bit busy, but then I stop myself. He hasn't chased me. Perhaps this is one of those things that you promise you'll do but never quite get round to and everyone is okay with that. In which case I perhaps don't need to mention it.

So I don't. Do yourself a favour, Abbie. Move on. You have your new life to focus on. On that theme, I briefly consider the dating app that I downloaded and then deleted. Maybe going on a couple of dates might help me get over this inconvenient Spencer infatuation.

Instead, I go to the Time for Beds website. I can't see into the e-commerce part of the site so I have no way of knowing how many pre-orders are lurking there, but if yesterday's success is anything to go by then I imagine there will be a few. It's starting to look like this will be occupying all my spare time for a while. So with that and the renewed job-hunting campaign there wouldn't be space for a trip to the Outer Hebrides even if I was sure I wanted to go.

This is great, I realise, as I put my phone down and get out of bed. It means I can legitimately not think about Spencer.

And so I shan't.

44

We are so close to the end of our fabric stash that the impending supply issue needs to be addressed. I discuss this with Ethel over our morning drink in the café.

'What kind of things should I be looking for?' I ask her. 'When I go to the charity shop?'

Ethel tips her head to one side in her precise, bird-like way as she thinks.

'Cotton garments,' she says. 'It definitely needs to be cotton. Not too worn. We don't want any stains or thin patches.'

'They'll need to be fairly big to have enough fabric in them,' I muse. 'Unless we have more seams.'

'Indeed. It's hard to imagine that you'll find much that's suitable.'

Ethel's face contorts for a second, as if something that I can't see has just caused her some pain. She puts her hand to her chest.

'Are you okay?'

'I am,' she replies, the grimace gone. 'Old age is not for the faint-hearted, Abigail.'

'Do you mind me asking how old you are?' I chance, even though Mum once told me that a lady should never reveal her age.

Ethel pulls a face that suggests she agrees with Mum, but then she shrugs as if to say, 'what can it possibly matter now?' 'I'll be eighty-four tomorrow.'

My jaw drops. I knew she was old, but I would never have guessed she was as old as that.

'Wow! You look amazing!'

'Thank you,' she replies graciously. 'But since I turned eighty, life hasn't been quite as plain sailing as it used to be. We're only given three score years and ten, you know. I'm on borrowed time.'

She raises a finely plucked eyebrow and her lips turn up in a faint arc that I'm coming to recognise as her smile. It reminds me of the *Mona Lisa*. There, and yet at the same time, not quite there.

'What are you going to do to celebrate your birthday?' I ask without really thinking it through. What can she do? I suspect she has no friends left, no relations even. All she has is us.

She waves my question away with an irritated flick of her wrist. 'I have no need of celebration. It's just another day like any other.'

I let it go but make a mental note to pick up a card and the wherewithal to make a cake as I leave the supermarket.

Dawn is a ball of energy when she arrives and starts asking questions before she's reached us, calling them out across the café as she makes her way to our table.

'Did we sell out? Are they all gone? Should we go and get sewing *right now*?' She emphasises the last two words by raising her voice still further.

Other morning coffee drinkers turn their heads to see who's doing all the shouting and then, when they see how eccentrically she's dressed (this morning in a spring-green smock with a huge and very cheerful daisy print on it that I suspect was once a tablecloth), quickly return their attention to their cups.

'Morning, Dawn,' I say. 'Love your dress. Is that one of yours?'

'Yes,' she replies, nodding enthusiastically. 'Although I got a bit stuck on the armholes.'

She lifts an arm so that Ethel can inspect her handiwork. She has clearly struggled to make a seam on the curve and what's there is puckered and barely catches the raw edge. Ethel shakes her head and tuts. 'It's all in the cutting out. I'll show you when we're next in the studio.'

'I love it, though,' I say.

A woman of about my age is making her way with her tray across the café to a spare table. She stops near us and speaks to Dawn.

'I hope you don't mind me asking, but can you tell me where you got that dress? It's gorgeous.'

Dawn beams at her. 'I made it,' she replies proudly.

The woman's face falls a bit, like she's disappointed that she can't rush out and buy one for herself.

'Well, it's lovely,' she says. 'Sorry to interrupt.' And then she heads off to her table.

Dawn's lightbulb smile lasts for ages.

'I don't know about the sales,' I say, replying to her question. 'We need Viraj.'

But Viraj doesn't come. I don't think much of it because we are all free agents and aren't committed to turn up at ten every day, but when Bob arrives it's the first thing he asks.

'No Viraj today?'

'No,' replies Dawn indignantly. 'And he's the only one who can look at how many we've sold.'

'He's probably got something on at work,' Bob replies, and Dawn screws her nose up which I'm coming to recognise is her irritated face.

'We need to get to the studio and start making the pre-orders,' I say. There's a funny little twist in my stomach as I wonder just how many pre-orders there might be waiting for us. 'Ethel and I were just talking about fabric supplies. I'll go to the homeless charity shop today and talk to whoever is in charge, see if we can't cut some kind of deal.'

'Need any help?' asks Bob, but I shake my head. I think it will be easier if I don't turn up mob-handed.

'No, I'll be fine.'

Ethel has finished her mint tea and gets slowly to her feet, using the table to push herself up.

'I shall see you all tomorrow,' she says.

'Would you like me to pick you up?' The café is walking distance from her flat when you don't have bolts of fabric to transport, but I'm worried that she's struggling just at the moment.

My offer is met with one of her most withering looks. 'I'm perfectly capable of walking, Abigail,' she says, her tone crisp. 'I shall see you all in the morning.'

And with that she leaves us, her back characteristically straight and her head held high, even though her progress is a little slower than usual.

'She's one proud lady,' says Bob when she's out of earshot.

'You can say that again,' I reply. 'And it's her birthday tomorrow. She's going to be eighty-four! Eighty-four!! Can you believe that?'

Bob shakes his head in disbelief. 'I hope I'm as fit as she is when I get to that age.'

'Is that in, like, five years?' asks Dawn, and I can't tell if she's joking.

Luckily Bob seems to assume that she is. 'Cheeky!' he says.

'I thought I'd get her a card for us all to sign and maybe make a cake. You don't think she'll mind, do you?'

Bob gives me that twinkly smile that we're seeing more often. 'I reckon she'd be delighted.'

45

I decide on a lemon and elderflower cake for Ethel's birthday. Something about the delicate balance of flavours makes it seem appropriate for the former ballet dancer. I pick up the ingredients and set to at home and soon I have a pretty passable-looking cake. I decorate the top with some edible flowers that I think will probably blow Dawn's mind and put it in the fridge ready for the next day. Then I lick all the bowls clean, ignoring the judgey looks that I get from Elvis.

Next on my list for today is the charity shop. The one where Dawn and I went is as good as any, so I run through what I want to say as I walk. It's a fairly odd request after all, especially as we're hoping they will consider donating the garments for free.

When I arrive, the shop is busy. There seem to be two people working. The woman in charge of the till is short with a helmet of grey hair and a scowl. She is also busy with a long queue. I don't fancy my chances with her so I aim for the second woman. She is altogether gentler-looking. I guess she's retired too but her hair is a honey blonde and cut into a flattering long bob and she's wearing clothes that she probably bought this year rather than last century.

She is putting a huge pile on to hangers and I do a quick scan to see if anything might be suitable for my quest. Nothing doing.

'Hi . . .' I peer at her name badge. 'Angela. Do you mind if I ask you something?'

The woman smiles at me. 'Not at all. Although I've only just started working in the shop so I might not know the answer.' She speaks with a distinct Australian twang.

'You're not from round here,' I say without thinking and then immediately worry it's too personal a comment, but she doesn't seem to mind.

'I am actually,' she says. 'I've lived here since I was eighteen but somehow I've never quite managed to lose the accent. Now, what can I do for you?'

So, I explain about Time for Beds and what we need. Angela looks thoughtful.

'We do get plenty of donations but we sell pretty much all of it ourselves. I don't know for sure, but I doubt we could donate anything. If you wanted the fabric, then I think you'd just have to buy the item like anyone else. And I'm not sure we ever get much in that would be big enough to make pyjama bottoms out of.'

I sigh. 'Yes. I thought that might be a problem. Never mind. Thanks anyway.'

I turn to walk away but she calls me back.

'I might be able to help though. A friend of a friend runs one of those remnants shops. They carry some of their stock for years. The up-to-date lines fly out but the older fabric is just sitting on shelves at the back of the warehouse getting dusty. You could make her an offer for anything you could use. She can only say no.'

She gives me the name of the remnant shop and I go there next.

By the end of the day I have the offer of ten more bolts of fabric at a pretty good price. I don't buy them there and then, though, because I need to speak to Viraj to see how many orders we have. It's frustrating that I can't get hold of him and I make a mental note to ask for his phone number.

46

But there's no sign of Viraj the next day either. I turn up at the café a few minutes early with a huge box containing Ethel's birthday cake and a bad feeling in the pit of my stomach. Could I really have been so naive? I've always prided myself on my ability to read people, but I've had so many expectations challenged over the last five weeks that I'm starting to doubt myself. Maybe I have misread Viraj. Perhaps he isn't who I think he is.

Because I'm purposefully early I tell myself that it's not surprising Viraj isn't there yet and push my worries out of my mind. Liz and Joel are both working so I put the cake down carefully on our table and go to speak to them.

'Morning. It's Ethel's birthday today,' I say cheerfully. 'She's eighty-four! Can you believe that?'

They both confirm that they can't and wonder how it can actually be true.

'I know it's not ideal,' I press on, 'given that this is a café, but I've made her a cake. Do you think you could look the other way while we eat it? Of course, we'll buy drinks like we usually do.'

I give them my best 'pleeease' smile and Liz says 'Of course, my love' at exactly the same moment that Joel says, 'I don't think so.'

Liz nudges him in the ribs and I'm about to point out how much good we're doing for his altruistic profile at head office when he caves.

'All right. But try and be subtle about it,' he says ungraciously.

'Can I borrow some plates, please?' I ask quickly, before he changes his mind. 'And something to cut the cake up with.'

I scamper back to the table with the plates and a particularly vicious-looking knife, collecting some forks and paper napkins on my way.

Bob has arrived by the time I get back to the table and has his nose in my cake box. 'Nice. Did you make that?'

'I did. There's a card somewhere.'

I dig it out of my bag and pass it over. Bob signs with a flourish. He has lovely handwriting. Another surprise, although really you'd think I'd have learned not to be so judgemental by now.

'Are those real flowers, on the top?' he asks. 'I saw some dandelions on the way. I could have picked a few if I'd known.'

This man makes me laugh. I roll my eyes at him.

Dawn arrives next and as I predicted she is very taken with the idea that there are flowers you can eat. She keeps taking the lid off the box and poking at the pretty little violas.

'Are you sure, Thingy? They look just like what my gran used to grow in her garden.'

'They're probably the same,' I tell her.

'And they won't kill you, or anything?' she asks me anxiously.

My mind flicks back to Precious and the feared murder-by-reheated-rice situation.

'No, don't worry. These are meant to be eaten.'

'What are?'

Ethel is standing right behind me. She's so tiny that she can just sneak up on you. I jump and then drop the lid on the box before she can see what's inside.

'Ethel! Happy birthday!' I bellow, the shock of her sudden appearance playing havoc with my volume control.

We've been so distracted by the flowers that I realise that I haven't got Dawn to sign the card. I try to signal this to Bob via a combination of head tilts and eye movements. He quickly works out what I'm trying to say and goes to slide the card out of my bag, but Dawn is on to him.

'You can't go in other people's bags, Bob. It's private and it looks like you're stealing stuff.'

Bob is whispering to her that he's not stealing but Dawn doesn't really do subtle and continues to challenge him.

'I think,' says Ethel, 'that Robert is attempting to alert you to something surreptitiously, Dawn. I imagine it's to do with my birthday but I may be wrong about that. I shall go and get my tea which should give him enough time to explain.'

She heads for Liz and Joel at the counter and I hear them wishing her happy returns of the day. Bob whips out the card and a pen and Dawn signs. She adds at least a dozen kisses under her name.

'Leave some space for Viraj,' I say, but actually he's going to miss his chance to sign unless he arrives in the next thirty seconds. Which he doesn't.

'No sign of him again today?' asks Bob unnecessarily.

He throws me a look that wobbles me all over again. I can tell what he's thinking because it's the same thought that has been prowling across my mind. Viraj is the only person with access to the back pages of our website. This means he has exclusive access to the money that we've taken so far which will be around six hundred pounds.

'I'm sure it's fine,' I say, addressing Bob's apparent concern without directly voicing the fear out loud.

Before Bob can reply, Dawn is on her feet and cheering Ethel back to the table.

211

'Happy birthday to you . . .' she starts to sing.

I look over to Joel who has both eyebrows raised. Clearly this doesn't fall within the parameters of what he constitutes to be discreet.

'Sorry,' I mouth, and his expression lightens a little before he just grins at me and rolls his eyes. What's not to love about a woman dressed in a bright pink netting tutu and purple Crocs singing 'Happy Birthday' with great gusto to an eighty-four-year-old former ballet dancer?

I take out the cake and push it and the hastily signed card towards Ethel's customary seat as I join in with the rendition of 'Happy Birthday'. The volume is greater than me, Dawn and Bob could realistically be making, and I realise that most of the café's other patrons are joining in too.

It's joyous and Ethel looks truly delighted as she makes her steady way back to the table carrying her mint tea. I wonder when anyone last made such a fuss of her. My heart fills and I can feel my throat thicken as my eyes glaze. I'm so blessed to have these people in my life.

'Where are the candles?' asks Dawn. 'Thingy, you forgot the candles!'

Damn. I'd meant to pick some up in the shop before I came to the café. But there's no need to worry. Liz is on it. She comes racing across with a packet of silver candles and a box of matches and starts placing the little silver holders in a neat pattern around the top of the cake. By the time Ethel is sitting down the cake is aglow with a warm yellow light.

'Make a wish!' shouts Dawn as she bounces on her tiptoes, as excited as if it were her own birthday.

Ethel closes her eyes, puckers her lips and blows at the flames which flicker and then go out. Everyone cheers and Ethel nods her head graciously. I can picture her on a stage somewhere accepting the audience's rapturous applause with great dignity.

When the noise has died down, she looks over to me. 'Thank you,' she says. 'That was most thoughtful of you, Abigail.'

'You're very welcome. Now. Would you like a slice of this cake to go with your tea? It's lemon and elderflower.'

Dawn pulls a face. 'That's disgusting,' she says. 'I like chocolate best.'

'Well, I think it sounds delicious,' says Ethel. 'And it's my birthday.'

Dawn is still making puking noises as I cut the cake into slices and distribute it around the table. There's always that anxious moment when you try a new recipe because the first opportunity you get to taste it is when everyone else does. I prepare myself for the cake to be vile, but it's as I hoped it would be – light and delicate, just like Ethel.

Sounds of approval circulate as everyone tucks in. Even Dawn admits that it's 'not too yucky'. High praise indeed.

I'm just scooping up the final crumbs when I hear a familiar voice behind me.

'Sorry I'm late. Have I missed something?'

I look up to see Viraj there and I've rarely been so pleased to see someone.

'It's Ethel's birthday,' I say with huge enthusiasm, mainly fuelled not by the news but by the fact that he hasn't stolen all our money. 'She's eighty-four.'

Ethel glares at me. 'There really is no need to tell all and sundry,' she says with a sniff, but I see the shadow of a smile on her lips, and I can tell that she's actually proud of her age – and so she should be.

'Where were you yesterday, Viraj?' asks Dawn. Her tone is accusatory but she's smiling. 'We want to know how many pairs we need to make.'

'Sorry about that,' says Viraj. 'There was a crisis at work. We all got called into the office. Sorted now though. Hang on.'

He gets his laptop out of his backpack, opens it up and navigates to the Time for Beds page.

'I was thinking,' he says as he's waiting for it to load. 'I should probably share the log-in details with you so that it's not just me that can get in. For security. It's not safe that I'm the only one with the passwords.'

Immediately I feel guilty that I ever doubted him. Bob and I exchange a shamefaced glance. He must be feeling the same.

'Good idea,' I say, without adding that I totally did think he'd done a runner with our six hundred quid.

'So, here we go,' he says. 'We've sold out of stock, but we knew that, right. And we have . . .'

He looks at the screen and we look at him. His eyes widen and he puffs out his cheeks.

'Seventy-nine pre-orders.'

Shit.

47

A stunned silence falls across the table. Even Dawn is quiet, which is rare.

'Seventy-nine?' repeats Bob. 'So that's fifteen pairs each, give or take. Bloody hell.'

'That's a lot of sewing,' says Viraj. He doesn't look overly enthusiastic about the idea.

'It's going to take, like, forever,' says Dawn. That's not strictly true but it does feel a bit like that.

'Well, if we knuckle down, I'm sure we can get them done,' I say with more positivity than I'm feeling. Even on our most productive days we haven't made more than seven pairs in one session. By that reckoning, it's about eleven days' work and that's assuming that we sew every day, which I don't think we can.

'But maybe we should turn off the pre-orders for now,' I add. 'Just while we catch up.'

The others are so stunned that no one even agrees with me. So I am forced to agree with myself.

'Yes. That's what we'll do. Can you do that now, Viraj?'

He nods, clicks a few things and the online store is placed on hold.

'I've got some good news!' I continue, my voice all high and sing-songy like a nursery school teacher's. 'I went to the charity shop about the fabric. They put me on to a place that sells remnants and they have some stuff we can use. We'll have to pay for it so it'll mean slightly less money for the shelter. But, actually, given how many pairs we have to make, it's probably a good job we're not trying to cut the pieces out of existing garments. This will be much faster.'

The rest of them nod but they still have that glazed look about them. Bob is the first to come round.

'Yeah, good job sorting that out, Abbie. And it feels like a bit of a hurdle, but, hey, this time a couple of weeks back none of us could even sew. I'm sure we can speed up a bit.'

'Precisely, we'll get them done in no time. And just think how much we'll be making for the shelter. That'll be . . .'

I make a stab at the maths but Bob beats me to it.

'Nearly three grand,' he supplies. 'Less whatever we have to pay for the fabric.'

'That's loads,' says Dawn. 'I've never had that much money in my whole life.'

She's right. It is loads and that's what we need to focus on – how much we'll be helping, not how hard it's going to be to achieve.

'What's your mobile number?' Viraj asks me, and when I tell him he pings the log-in details to me on WhatsApp. 'Anyone else want that?'

'No use to me,' says Bob. 'I'm crap with computers.'

'I don't want it,' says Dawn.

'You could send it to me, please,' says Ethel. 'Always good to spread the load.'

I'm not at all surprised that she can use a computer. She is a woman of many talents. But I wonder whether she shared our doubts about Viraj. I hope not, but I'm obviously not going to ask her.

'In other news,' says Bob, 'I've got a job.'

Dawn wrinkles her nose. 'We know that. At the shelter.'

'Yeah. Well, that job and now I've got another one.'

As he speaks, I'm still panicking about our seventy-nine pairs of pyjama bottoms but I still manage a pleased smile.

'That's fantastic. What is it?' I ask.

'Bernie's sister-in-law's friend needs a new cupboard building in their downstairs loo and Bernie suggested me.'

Bob looks as pleased about this as he did about how much we were going to raise for the shelter a few moments ago. Possibly even more pleased.

'It's only a small job. But it's a start.'

'It very much is, Robert,' says Ethel. 'And an excellent one at that.'

'I'm kind of limited as to what I can take on because of the lack of tools situation but if I work then I earn money and then I can buy more. It'll take me a while to be able to afford a van again but at this point I don't care.'

'Can we eat more of Ethel's cake?' asks Dawn. She says exactly what's on her mind, that one.

'You may,' replies Ethel. 'Please help yourself.'

'That's such great news, Bob,' I say as Dawn cuts herself an enormous slice. 'And like you say, it's a start. Acorns and oak trees and all that.'

I cringe internally, worried about how that might come across, but Bob is grinning so wildly that I know it's okay. He turns his attention to Dawn and her wedge.

'I thought you only ate chocolate cake,' he says, nudging her gently in the ribs.

Dawn has just thrust a fistful of cake into her mouth.

'And cakes what Thingy makes,' she says through the crumbs.

48

It takes us a week to catch up with the orders and we only do that because Dawn and Ethel sew like the clappers and make far more than their fair share. Finally, I have the last pair packed and posted and we are up to date. We meet back at the café for the first time since the new orders all came in, but instead of triumphant, the mood around the table is sombre. We're all thinking the same thing, I think, but no one wants to be the one to say it out loud.

Of course it's Ethel who confronts the elephant in the room.

'I'm thrilled with what we have achieved so far,' she begins. 'And delighted that we have raised so much money for Bob's shelter, but this is quite unsustainable. We are not a clothing factory and we cannot keep producing at this rate. Either we sell fewer pairs or we find another way to make money.' She takes a sip of her tea, eyeing us over the rim of her mug.

She's right, so I am the first to agree. 'What could we do instead?' I ask, in an attempt to focus the discussion on what might come in the future rather than what we can't do now.

Fundraising is notoriously difficult. Just ask any charity. And enduring some terrible physical challenge in return for sponsorship is no use as between us we just don't have enough people to ask. Viraj and I have already tapped up most of our contacts, and the others . . .

'We need to find a fundraiser where people pay to receive something,' I say. 'Rather than a sponsored event.'

'What's a sponsored event?' asks Dawn.

'It's where people give you money to do something that's hard, like a long walk, say,' explains Bob.

A brief discussion about what might constitute 'long' ensues, during which I rack my brain for ideas but still come up with nothing.

'It needs to be something that we can all achieve, but which isn't easy for us. And there has to be something in it for the people who give us money too.'

No one makes any suggestions. A couple of times one of us opens our mouth but then we talk ourselves out of whatever it was before the idea can take shape.

Bob, who has been stirring his tea for far longer than it will have taken the sugar to dissolve, finally blows out his lips. 'Look. Raising ten grand was just a figure I plucked out of the air. We've done dead well. I can't believe we can pay for all them beds with what we've already made. Bernie and everyone at the shelter will be chuffed to bits. We could just call it a day now.'

I'm reluctant to accept this but I think he's probably right. And we must have made about five thousand pounds all told. That's not to be sniffed at. I'm about to chirp up to agree with him when Viraj speaks.

'We can't give up. Just because nothing's springing to mind right now doesn't mean it won't. We just need a bit of time to come up with the killer idea.'

'Yeah, Bob,' agrees Dawn. Her tone is accusatory. 'Bev says if something's hard we can't just stop trying.'

Bob throws her a fond look. 'And Bev is dead right,' he says. 'But some stuff is just enough as it is.'

'Well, this isn't!' Dawn snaps back. 'You want ten thousand pounds on your big cheque and we don't have that much. It's not enough.'

Bob looks like he's going to have a go at clarifying what he means but then changes his mind. 'Okay. We won't give up. What do you think, Ethel?'

Ethel looks thoughtful. 'We seem to have been enjoying the sewing. And Dawn has her yellow dress and the other things she's created recently. Might we find something to do with fashion?'

It's an interesting idea but I can't think what we could do and I say so.

'Like, I make clothes and we sell them?' asks Dawn, her eyes shining.

'I'm not sure that's entirely practical,' replies Ethel, not unkindly. 'We've already proved that we can't keep up with demand.'

We all fall silent again.

'There might be something in that, though,' I say. 'I'm thinking about converting one garment into another.' Then I follow my train of thought through. 'But, as you say, it's very labour intensive. And all the pieces would be one-offs which would be a lot of work on the website. There'd have to be a new page created for each item.'

Viraj nods. Then he taps his finger against his lips, thinking. 'What if we put together a pop-up shop, a real one rather than a virtual one?'

I shake my head. 'Same issue. Not enough stock. And we'd probably end up spending more on renting the space than we make.'

'I know, I know!!' says Dawn, bouncing up and down in her seat. 'We could have a catwalk. Like the supermodels do.'

I want to explain to her that this would fall foul of all the same issues as a shop when my mind starts to run with the idea.

'What if,' I begin slowly, 'it wasn't all about clothes we've actually made, but rather how we style them?'

Four blank faces stare back at me. 'Well, Dawn and I each have a particular look, and Ethel knows about costumes from her dancing days, and you two . . .' I look at Bob in his parka and Viraj in his ubiquitous black hoody and trackies. Bob raises an eyebrow, daring me to comment. I chicken out. 'Anyway, what if we joined forces with the charity shop and put on a fashion show showcasing what can be done with the clothes that other people give away?'

Ethel is nodding. 'We could charge for entry and sell refreshments beforehand and afterwards.'

Dawn is nodding but then her face tightens. 'What about the clothes what I make?'

'Well . . .' I begin. 'We could have them in a grand finale, like fashion houses sometimes have the bridalwear at the end of their shows.'

'This is sounding like a bit of a plan,' says Bob. 'But the logistics . . . ?'

'You mean where would we do it?' I ask.

He nods as I sigh.

Then we have the idea simultaneously.

'Here!' we both say.

There's a pause while we all consider what we're proposing. Ethel is the one to break the silence. 'I do believe that you may have hit upon something there, Abigail.'

49

I make a list. I love a list but I haven't had cause to write one since the day I was sacked. It feels good to be back in the flow.

My list goes:

1. Venue.
2. Charity shop agreement.
3. Where/how to sell tickets.
4. Refreshments – bar?
5. Chairs, etc.
6. Publicity.

Then I stop. Each point needs its own sub-list and of course, this isn't just about me. These ought to be team decisions. But perhaps I could go and sound out the charity shop, see if they might be up for a bit of a joint venture. I don't want it to look to the others like I'm taking over, but it needs doing and I have the time.

I dress carefully, choosing one of my vintage frocks over a modern copy. I'm particularly fond of this one because it's covered with blousy roses in bright yellows and oranges, and it always cheers me up although I realise that I don't actually need cheering up. Life is fine right now. I am fine.

Then I head back to the charity shop. I'm hoping that it's not the helmet-haired woman on duty today and I'm in luck because, as well as the lovely lady with the Australian accent who gave me the tip-off about the remnant shop, there's a perfectly benign-looking woman at the till.

First I speak to the Australian woman – Angela, her badge reminds me.

'Thank you so much for that contact of yours,' I say, hoping she will remember me. 'We managed to get all the pyjama bottoms finished. We've made almost five thousand pounds for the shelter so far.'

'You're so welcome,' she replies warmly. 'And that's fabulous. Which shelter are you fundraising for?'

I tell her and then the other woman, who is called Sara according to her name badge, comes over to find out what's going on and so I tell her too.

'That's amazing,' she says with genuine enthusiasm. 'They do such great work up there. They need all the help they can get. All the charities working with the homeless do. It's always tough, but times are particularly hard at the moment.'

'Exactly,' I agree. 'My friend had his tools stolen from his van and that led to him finding himself on the streets. He's actually one of the people helping with the fundraising now. He wants to raise ten thousand pounds.'

'That's brilliant,' says Sara. 'I love it.'

'Actually, that's why I'm here.'

Sara's expression becomes slightly more wary but to give her her due, she keeps smiling.

'We want to hold a fashion show, showcasing outfits that we've styled using items from your shop. The aim is to show people how stylish charity shopping can be. And one of our number likes creating new pieces out of clothes she finds here, so those will make up the finale.'

Sara and Angela are still listening so I press on to my request.

'We were wondering if we could come here early on the day of the show, pick out various outfits which we then borrow for the catwalk. Then people would be able to buy them on the night and if they don't sell we'll just return them and put them back out in the shop. The clothes would only be gone for a day so it wouldn't impact on you too much.'

There's a silence as Sara thinks about what I've just said. It's a lot to take in. She chews her lip as she contemplates, and I start to wonder whether I've jumped the gun a bit by coming in on my own before discussing it with the others. I'm just starting to run through a list of other local charity shops in my head when Sara replies.

'Yes,' she says thoughtfully, and then more decisively, 'yes. I can't see any reason why that wouldn't work. There's no real down-side for us apart from potentially losing sales on the day you have the clothes, but hopefully we'll more than make up for that with people buying the whole outfits rather than just the individual pieces. When were you thinking?'

This is a very good question. I decide to be honest. 'I have no idea. You are the first person I've approached. We have a contact at the supermarket up the road and we're hoping he'll let us use the space there out of hours but we haven't mentioned it yet. But if I can go to him with you on board then that should make it easier to sell the idea.'

'Well, I need to make a call or two myself,' says Sara. 'But I can't see any reason why the powers that be won't say yes. How about we reconvene in a few days and see where we're at.'

'Perfect.' I beam at her. 'Thank you.'

I leave the shop and walk up to the café. Already my head is full of how we can advertise the event to get the crowds in and how much we should charge for a ticket. I'm thinking about the logistics of where the models will get changed, how we'll transport the clothes. My mind is buzzing and I love it. I'd forgotten just how much I relish the challenge of coordinating something big.

If you'd said to me six weeks ago that I'd have lost my dream job and yet still be happy, I'd have laughed at you. And yet here we are. If anything, I'm happier than I was before. Yes, there's the tiny issue of not actually earning anything, but what I'm doing with Time for Beds feels important in a way that selling chocolate truffles never did. I know it sounds corny, but making a difference to something that matters is just more fulfilling than selling things to people who don't know they want them.

Then I have another, less encouraging thought. This is week seven and I still haven't heard from anyone else from my old team. It might have been awkward for them to get in touch at the start but that difficulty must have passed by now. So, there are only two conclusions I can reach. Either they didn't like me very much in the first place or I have just slipped out of their consciousness. Out of sight and very much out of mind.

Neither of these explanations is particularly palatable. I tell myself that it must be the latter option because that's marginally easier to come to terms with, but it still doesn't feel great. The buzz I was feeling a few short moments ago evaporates and I crash headlong into an existential crisis as I contemplate the stark reality of my life.

I'm thirty-one, single, with no job and apparently no friends except a bunch of oddballs and misfits that I met at a table designed for sad or lonely people. It feels like I've fallen off the planet and am lying in the gutter watching it as it spins on.

This isn't how it was meant to be. In the plan I had for myself I was supposed to be busy scaling the career tree with an eligible man at my side, a man just waiting for the perfect moment to ask me to marry him at a ceremony packed with all our fabulous (and very good-looking) friends. I hadn't fixed a timescale for all this to happen but I'm sure it was meant to be around now. And yet look at me. No career. No man. No wedding in the diary. No glamorous network of friends.

This smashing of my dreams takes some getting used to.

I take a deep breath and give myself a pep talk. Did I not just say that I was having more fun with the pyjama business than I was before? The fact that my life no longer looks like I expected it to is neither here nor there. It's still my life and it could be an awful lot worse.

I turn my attention back to my list. This is something I can do. Abigail Finch can organise a mean fashion show, one that people will be talking about for years to come. And that'll show them all, I think petulantly.

It's only when I get back home that it occurs to me: the only person I need to prove something to here is me.

50

At the café I explain my plan to the others. Much of it has come to me since we last met and so it feels a little different to what we had been discussing, but they seem okay with all my suggestions.

'So we don't have to sew anything?' clarifies Viraj, the relief clearly written all over his face.

'Nope. I mean, you can make something for the finale,' I add, and he shakes his head so emphatically that I fear it might actually leave his shoulders.

'I can though,' says Dawn.

'Absolutely,' I say. 'We need you to make a couple of fabulous creations for the finale and then people can bid for them at the end of the show.'

'Let's hope they all come with their purses bulging,' says Bob.

'And wallets,' I add. 'Call me a cynic . . .'

'Cynic,' says Bob.

I roll my eyes at him. 'Call me a cynic, but I wonder whether the way the supermarket headquarters jumped on Joel's ideas might point at a wider audience for us.'

'I don't get it. What are you saying?'

I'm not quite sure what I am saying so I start to pick my way gingerly through my thought process.

'Well, I think we'd imagined that the show would be for the people who might want to buy the outfits, people who already shop in charity shops.'

The others nod at me.

'But what if we looked wider than that? What if we invited the top brass from the supermarket, from the local, more corporate businesses and asked them either for sponsorship for the event or to come along and bring their corporate credit cards. All publicity is good publicity and they'd be seen helping out a local and very worthy cause.'

Then I suddenly wonder . . . 'Is that really exploitative of me?'

Bob and Viraj ponder this for a moment. I'm not sure Dawn has quite caught my drift and Ethel is with me at once, nodding and shrugging as if this is obvious.

'It is quite exploitative,' agrees Bob. 'But all's fair in love and fundraising. If they want to polish their halos by hitching their horses to our wagon, then I'm not going to stop them. Cash is cash. I don't think it matters how we raise it.'

'And the supermarket already has its charity of the year so we're ticking that box. Not that it's a box-ticking exercise,' I add quickly. For something so simple, raising money for charity, it feels like a minefield to pick my way through.

Viraj also seems to agree. 'I can see why it feels a bit off,' he says. 'But that's their problem, not ours.'

'Could we ask your bosses as well then?' I ask.

'Don't see why not. What's the worst that can happen?'

'But what about our fashion show?' asks Dawn. 'Are we still doing it? We have to because I told Bev and Precious and the others.' Her eyes dart around the table.

'We are,' I say. 'We just need to get Joel to agree.'

'Instead of merely asking him,' says Ethel, 'why don't we show him?'

'How do you mean?' says Bob. 'By staging a mini show?'

'Precisely.' Ethel's eyes shine. 'We can collect a sample outfit from the shop, and then imagine a catwalk in here and Dawn can show him what we're talking about. And if we pick a busy time . . .'

'He won't be able to say no in front of all the customers without tarnishing his "I really care" image,' finishes Bob. 'Now who's being exploitative?'

Ethel's eyebrows dance and she smiles her enigmatic smile as if this is the most fun she's had in ages.

'Right then,' I say. 'Who has time to come to the shop to pick an outfit?'

Dawn and I go to the charity shop that afternoon. Bob has a shift, Viraj says it isn't really his bag and Ethel says that she's busy, but secretly I wonder whether two outings in one day might not be a little much for her, not that she'd ever admit it. She has been looking tired though, since we started with all the sewing. We accept her excuse without further examination.

Sara is on the tills when I enter the shop for the second time that day, but when she sees me she waves and beckons me over.

'I've spoken to my boss,' she says. 'She thinks it's a great idea and is happy to help as long as it doesn't actually cost the shop anything.'

I confirm that it won't and thank her. Then I explain that we're looking for an outfit to use to try and persuade the supermarket café manager to support us.

'But I'll buy it,' I add quickly when Sara's expression suggests that she sees mission creep already. I can't really spare the cash but this is important.

Dawn and I start to scour the rails, lifting items up and then either choosing or rejecting them. 'Nothing too outlandish,' I say to her. 'I know we like to dress to turn heads but this is Joel we're trying to persuade. He's a bit more conservative than us.'

It occurs to me that we will really need to know our market before we put the outfits together for the actual show, and I scribble a note on my phone about including an age-range question on the ticket page of the website.

After several false starts, Dawn picks out a pair of wide trousers in a soft khaki and from there we build an outfit using a white blouse, a stone-coloured jacket and even a hat which Sara takes from a polystyrene head on top of a bookshelf.

Dawn nips into the changing rooms and comes out a few minutes later. She looks great but her nose is curling.

'It's very brown,' she says in a tone that makes it clear this is a bad thing.

She's right. The outfit is classy in neutral and expensive-looking natural shades, but very safe.

'Hang on.' I go back to the rails of men's shirts and find a pink one with blue and white pinstripes. I hand it to Dawn. 'Try that instead.'

The white blouse is tossed out of the cubicle, and I dive to pick it up before Sara notices. Moments later Dawn re-emerges. She has arranged the shirt so that the tails and cuffs peek out of the jacket. The outfit is transformed. Angela and I clap our hands in delight.

'That's perfect!' I say.

Dawn beams at us, strutting up and down the shop.

'Have you got some trainers, Dawn?' I ask, hoping that the question doesn't offend. The Crocs don't really work.

Dawn nods.

'Then we're good to go!'

51

The following day is Saturday, when we don't usually meet. Also, I'm not sure whether Joel works today.

I lie in bed, Elvis purring quietly as I rub his ears. The weekend is stretching out interminably. When I was working, I looked forward to Saturday as much as the next woman. I usually had something arranged, not wanting to waste a second of the time I had to myself.

Since I stopped working, things seem to have reversed themselves. Now the weekend has to be endured, with me watching the clock until it's time to meet the others at the café on Monday.

I'm turning into a recluse! Much as I love spending my mornings with Dawn and the rest of them, I can't let my old life just evaporate. The time will come, I assume, when I need to step back into it and at this rate there won't be anything left.

I think I've been waiting for some outpouring of support from my friends, but then again, is that a reasonable expectation? I've hardly been forthcoming about my situation. I haven't even mentioned it to Xander and Felix, although I assume Mum will have by now.

So, it's not at all reasonable for me to take umbrage that no one has been in touch since Lucy messaged me. Relationships are a two-way street and I am just as guilty of not making an effort as they all are, due to my own shame or embarrassment or whatever it was. For all I know, instead of forgetting all about me, they might have been giving me space to get my head round my new situation. Actually, this is a bit of a stretch, if I'm honest, but we do need to build a bridge or two and I'm not too big to make the first move.

I retrieve my phone from the bedside table, open WhatsApp and begin to type a message into the girls' chat.

> *Hi all. Sorry for disappearing on you. Weird times here since I lost my job. Have been taking time for a reboot. Still no real future plan but am feeling better about everything. Anyone free for a drink and a catch-up tonight? x*

My finger hovers over the send button. What if no one replies? What if I really have burned my boats? But then, I figure, at least I'll know where I stand.

I hit send and then immediately get out of bed to have a shower so that I'm not just watching and waiting for my phone screen to light up.

When I get back to it, wrapped in a towel and my hair dripping down my back, I'm gratified to see that I have nine notifications with messages from Sal, Meena and Lucy, all expressing concern about the ongoing job situation, checking that I'm all right, and the makings of a plan for later that evening. I smile at the phone, grateful that I still appear to have a circle of friends who care enough to at least catch up with my gossip, if nothing else, and push the thought that most of them didn't bother to check up on me during my silent period out of my mind.

I spend the rest of the day job hunting in earnest. There really is nothing in marketing at the level I was at. I could pivot into social media but the only ones around are more junior.

Then my eye lands on something. The logo at the top of the page is two simple stick people holding hands. It manages to be folksy and poignant at the same time and its mid-century colour palette appeals to me. I read on.

We are looking for a miracle worker.

I frown. I've not had much to do with recruitment but I'm sure you can't say that in an advert. Curiosity piqued, I continue.

Are you positive, capable, cheerful, good in a crisis, creative, innovative, tolerant, patient, great at making something out of nothing and above all a team player?

Well, yes. I can be all those things. I feel a buzz of excitement as my eyes scan the advert trying to work out what the job actually is and for whom. Instead of being swathed in the usual corporate speak that I'm growing familiar with, the copy reads like someone was having a chat with a colleague about their best friend. It's intriguing.

I think the position might be an office manager, but I can't work out what kind of business it is, and like many job adverts on these sites, it doesn't actually name the employer so I can't google them. I look at the pay and it's less than I was getting but not catastrophically so.

What do I have to lose? I rattle off a bubbly cover letter, attach my CV and send it off.

The only other thing that looks appropriate to my skill set is a junior account exec's job at a rival firm to my old one. I apply for that too.

There! That's two possibilities. No need to fret.

I meet the girls in a bar in the centre of Leeds. Sal has booked us a table, which is good because the place is full of gangs of women who look as if they've been out for a lot longer than we have. Lucy and Meena are already at the table with an open bottle of something white in a cooler. They wave enthusiastically as I approach.

I make my way over, trying to ignore the attention that my style always elicits. Once people have had a drink, any inhibitions about staring at me fade away and there's always an element of nudging and whispering as I walk past, although I think it's usually admiring rather than anything else.

I used to love the attention. It was all part of who I thought I was. Look at me with my confidence and my quirky style. Wouldn't you like my life?

It doesn't feel like that any more. Rather than being someone who turns heads I'd rather just float underneath the radar. The only part of my old life that I have left now is how I dress. I still love my look but making this much effort every day when everyone else is wearing leggings is starting to feel like I'm trying too hard.

Still, I'm out now and I need to own my style, so I make sure my back is straight and my head is held high to walk through them all. As I do, I think of Dawn and her catwalk and my stomach clenches. I'm not sure I can draw that much attention without the armour of the life I had to protect me.

But that thought is for another day.

'Hello stranger!' says Lucy as I sit down. 'Wine?' She slops a generous measure into the glass before handing it to me.

'So sorry about your job,' says Meena. 'That sounds like a pile of crap.'

'Personality clash,' I say vaguely. 'But now I'm free to try something new so every cloud and all that.'

'Like what?' asks Lucy.

I shrug.

'Haven't the foggiest. But I'm starting to think I need a change, try something completely different.' As I say this, I realise that it's true. Maybe this is what's been getting in the way of really looking for work.

'Had many interviews?' asks Meena.

I shake my head. 'Nope. Not one.'

Meena's eyes open wide. 'In nearly two months?! Aren't you terrified? How are you going to get back to where you were?'

I get how she's thinking. It's exactly how I thought when I first lost my job, but I seem to be less anxious about it as time goes on, not more.

'No, I'm okay for now, and I'm trusting the universe to deliver.' I pull a face to show them that isn't my entire plan, but in truth, it's not far off. 'Actually, something came up today that looks interesting . . .'

But then Sal arrives in a flurry of apologies both for her tardiness and her recent lack of communication and the moment is lost. She's been mad-busy with work it seems, and while my being out of the loop has felt fairly major to me, she confesses she was so caught up in her own stuff that she barely noticed.

'Have you heard from the lovely Spencer?' she asks first, more interested in my erstwhile romance than how I've been filling my days since I last saw her. 'Where did he go? The Scilly Isles, was it?'

She really doesn't listen. 'The Outer Hebrides.'

'That's it. Off Scotland, right?'

'Did you really just ask that?' Lucy laughs.

'Geography. Never my thing,' replies Sal dismissively. 'So, has he been in touch?'

'He has,' I say, hoping that the pink bloom to my cheeks isn't obvious in the bar's low lighting. 'He invited me to go up there. Not sure I want to.'

'Why not? He's cute.'

'Cute but ditched,' I reply.

'But he still asked you to visit?'

I nod and eyebrows are raised around the table.

There appears to be a consensus that this would be a good thing and I show them the pictures of the puffins which meet with general delight.

'You should definitely go,' says Meena. 'What else have you got to do?'

'Actually,' I begin. 'I've been pretty busy. You might have seen on my socials, I'm fundraising for a homeless shelter in Leeds. There's a team of us. We've been making pyjama bottoms to sell. And now we're going to have a fashion show to raise some more money, like a catwalk thing. You should all come!'

'Sounds great,' says Lucy. 'Who are you collabing with? Those boutiques in the Victoria Quarter? Or is there a fifties theme? I can see you doing something like that.'

All eyes are on me as they wait for me to fill them in on which high-end shops I've roped in to provide the clothes.

'It's not that kind of show,' I say, squirming in my seat as I anticipate their response. 'We're getting the clothes from a charity shop. We're going to style them.'

I scan their faces for a reaction. I think I see Meena wrinkle her nose, but Lucy and Sal look just as excited as they did when they thought I was working with flash designers.

'That sounds pretty cool,' says Sal. 'When is it? Can we come?'

'Of course you can. I don't know when yet but as soon as I do I'll be selling tickets. It would be great if you could tell people too. We want to make as much as we can.'

'Count me in,' says Sal. 'Now. Who's up for another bottle? And did you watch *Succession*? Can you believe Shiv?'

And just like that I am no longer the subject of conversation.

52

As soon as I arrive at the café on Monday, I'm scanning the place for signs of Joel. Liz is great but she can't give us the say-so for the show. We need the main man.

'Joel in today?' I ask her casually as I order my morning flat white.

There is a minuscule raise of an eyebrow before she answers.

'I have a business proposal for him,' I add quickly before her imagination runs off any further.

'Whatever you say, my love,' she says with a smirk. 'He's just in with the store manager. Should be back in ten minutes or so. Anything to eat?'

I resist the cakes and take my coffee over to the table. Dawn is next to arrive. She holds the bag for life containing her catwalk outfit over her head just in case I haven't noticed that she's brought it.

'I got some trainers instead of my Crocs like you said,' she says. 'White ones. They're Precious's. She said I could borrow them as long as I don't mess them up.'

'Joel's in a meeting,' I tell her. 'But Liz says he'll be here soon. Don't tell Liz what we're going to do,' I add as Dawn skips off in the direction of the counter. 'Remember, it's a surprise.'

Dawn puts a finger to her lips extravagantly.

Bob is next to arrive. 'Are we on for Operation Ambush Joel?' he asks.

'We are. Dawn just needs to get changed.'

'I can do that now,' says Dawn, putting her tray down on the table and starting to unbutton her shirt.

'Not here, love,' says Bob. 'Nip to the bogs and do it.'

Five minutes later she's back and looking fabulous.

'Nice threads,' says Bob.

'The trainers are Precious's, but we bought all the other things, didn't we, Thingy?'

'We did,' I confirm. 'And you look amazing.'

Viraj and Ethel arrive, agree that she really does look amazing and then we're all ready. Now we just have to wait for Joel to get back. We sit, staring at the entrance as if we're expecting royalty. Nobody speaks but there's a strange nervous tension in the air. We all want this to work out. There are other venues that we could approach, but something feels so right about here. In fact, I'd go as far as to say that it has to be here.

And then Joel arrives. Bob's hand shoots out to restrain Dawn who is up on her feet as soon as he appears.

'Hold your horses there, Dawn. Let Abbie speak to him first.'

I throw Bob a look that I hope says 'Why me?'

'Want Viraj to come with you?' he adds, neatly passing responsibility on to someone else.

Viraj looks horrified but before he can express exactly how much he doesn't want to speak to Joel, Ethel gets to her feet.

'I'll talk to him with you, Abigail,' she says. 'We'll show these cowardly men how to get things done.'

'Hang on. We need a signal for when Dawn should start.'

'I will raise my hand,' says Ethel. 'Like this.'

Her arm shoots up into what I vaguely remember as being fifth position from when I did ballet as a girl, a perfect balance of elegance and strength. Dawn nods and shuffles forward to the front of her chair, ready to leap up.

We make slow progress across the café, Ethel not being up for bursts of speed, but I doubt Joel has ever seen two women more determinedly on a mission. When we get close enough for him to see exactly how much business we mean, he even stops what he's doing and waits for us.

'Ladies,' he says, a slight question detectable in his tone. 'Can I do something for you?'

'It's more what we can do for you, young man,' replies Ethel. 'You are aware that we have been helping Robert to raise money for the homeless shelter where he works.'

'Indeed I am,' says Joel. 'Head office were very impressed with the photos of the pyjama bottoms.'

'We've sold over one hundred pairs of those,' I say proudly.

Joel's eyes widen as if he's finding this hard to credit but I don't rise to it.

'We are aiming to raise ten thousand pounds,' Ethel continues and Joel nods like he's impressed, which he jolly well should be. It's a lot of money. 'Our next venture will be a fashion show. People will buy tickets and will have the opportunity to buy the clothes if they so choose.'

'Sounds like an excellent concept,' says Joel. I can see his mind whirring as he tries to work out exactly where he fits in.

'We would like to hold it here,' I say, 'in the café. It seems appropriate as this is where we all met, and it's such a lovely space. And of course your charity of the year helps the homeless, so it really is just an extension of that.'

Joel's brow furrows. It's clear that he's not at all sure.

'You wouldn't have to do much,' Ethel continues, not giving him time to object. 'Abigail here is a marketing executive by profession so she can handle the finer detail. And I'm certain that your head office will be delighted to further support such an important and altruistic cause.'

Joel would make a terrible poker player. His every thought is written on his face and before he has time to express them verbally, Ethel's elegant arm shoots upwards and 'Think' by Aretha Franklin starts to pour forth from a portable speaker that has appeared by magic on the community table. Viraj grins and gives me a thumbs up sign.

And then Dawn makes her entrance. She must have moved to hide out of sight when we were talking to Joel, but now she struts into the café as if she owns the place. She sashays across the floor in time to the music. It's an excellent choice of song, just the right speed for her to strut with a sense of purpose, and with lyrics that hit home from the very first line. She swings her hips and juts her chin at a perfect angle. She is truly to the manner born.

Bob starts to cheer, and the other customers soon join in, looking at one another for clues as to what is going on but quickly becoming totally invested in the spectacle. It's impossible not to. Dawn's energy is infectious and it grows as more people begin to clap in time with the music. Joel doesn't quite know what to say, but he can't help but smile at her. The atmosphere is electric.

The song is coming to an end and Dawn heads back to the café entrance, timing her departure perfectly with the closing bars. Gradually the clapping subsides and people go back to their own conversations.

'So, can we count on your support?' asks Ethel, but really we've put him in a position where he can't possibly refuse us.

Joel knows that he's been backed into a corner. 'I'll speak to head office . . .' he tries.

Ethel throws him her hardest stare.

'But I'm sure it won't be a problem,' he adds quickly.

53

Dawn comes back into the café a few minutes later, dressed in her 'normal' clothes again. She's grinning from ear to ear.

'How was I?' she asks in her customary loud voice long before she's anywhere near us.

'You were very good, dear,' says an old lady at a nearby table.

Dawn performs a funny little curtsey and then comes over to us and drops back into her chair.

'I filmed the whole thing,' says Viraj and promptly shares it with me. 'Might be useful for publicity,' he says, and I nod.

'Well done, Dawn,' says Bob. 'That was amazing.'

'Thanks, Bob. I thought I was good. Everyone clapped me, didn't they?'

'That they did,' he says. Then he looks at us. 'So, did he agree?'

'I'm not sure he had much choice,' I say.

'Oh, he'll definitely agree,' adds Ethel knowingly.

'So, we probably need to start working out the details.' I think of my embryonic list. 'I'm happy to do that as I have the most time on my hands.'

'What details?' asks Dawn. 'We just need to know when it is so we can go and pick the outfits.'

'Well, we need to sell tickets too,' says Viraj kindly. 'That's how we'll make the money for Bob's shelter.'

'Oh, yeah,' says Dawn. 'But apart from that.'

We all nod, shabbily taking the path of least resistance rather than contradicting Dawn again, but I think the size of what we're taking on is starting to dawn on us.

Viraj looks up from behind his dark eyelashes. 'You know the show part?' he starts. 'Well, Dawn's doing that, right? We don't have to get dressed up and . . .' He mimics walking with his fingers across the table.

I haven't actually thought about who would do the modelling. I suppose I'd assumed we'd all take a turn but thinking about it now, I'm not sure there are enough of us, even with Viraj.

'Because I'm not really up for that,' Viraj continues. 'I'll do anything else but the modelling thing, that's not my scene.'

'And I'm not sure how quickly I can swap clothes,' chips in Ethel. 'When I was on stage, I was used to speedy changes but I'm not sure my limbs will cooperate these days.'

Naturally our eyes all turn to Bob, the only one yet to speak. It crosses my mind that it would be easier for everyone if someone suggested a shower to him before we start. But how would we do that without hurting his feelings? Maybe he won't be that keen on modelling either.

'I'm up for it!' he says with a huge smile. 'We're doing men's gear too, right?'

I hadn't thought about that either, but in light of our conversation about who we're intending to invite it makes sense.

'I think so,' I say, 'and it's great that you're keen, Bob, but I think we're going to have to recruit a few more models otherwise there'll be too big a gap between outfits.'

'I can do all the girls' ones,' suggests Dawn, but I can tell that she's already seeing the issues with this.

'Who can we get to help?' asks Ethel.

We all think. I have no one to ask. When I mentioned the show to Sal, Lucy and Meena, none of them offered to help.

'We could ask Liz and whichever Saturday person is currently employed here.'

'I can ask people from work too,' says Viraj with huge enthusiasm that I suspect is born from the fact that he might not have to model himself.

Ethel is looking thoughtful. 'Would it be fitting,' she begins, 'if some of Robert's friends from the shelter took part?'

I'm glad Ethel asked this. I think I might have chickened out. Bob stares up at the ceiling and runs his hands through his hair. 'I'm not sure,' he says. 'Homeless people aren't necessarily the most reliable. I'd hate it if they let us down.'

'Maybe not current clients of the shelter,' I suggest, 'but how about people like you. Former clients who now have their lives back on track?'

Bob shrugs but he still looks doubtful. 'I can put a notice up and see if anyone bites,' he says unconvincingly.

'What about your housemates, Dawn?' I ask her. 'Precious, is it? And Frankie.'

Dawn pulls that face I'm coming to know so well. 'Precious can't,' she says. 'I'm using her trainers.'

I could point out the obvious solution to that but I don't. Let Dawn have the moment to herself if that's what makes her happy.

This is getting complicated already. 'I'll give it some thought tonight, and then we can work out what we need to do.' No need to tell them that I've already started.

'You're telling me you haven't already done that?' says Bob.

Damn, he's good.

54

Joel says yes to the show – of course he does. We left him absolutely no choice. He comes over to the community table the next day to give me the details.

'Head office are happy to back your venture,' he says. Something about the way he delivers this news feels designed to make us think he's doing us a huge favour, but I don't care. A yes is a yes.

'It'll have to take place after the café closes but when the store is still open, so we don't have to pay for extra staff hours. You can have refreshments before and after and we're licensed so we can serve alcohol. We can talk through all the details. And I assume you're all over the publicity already.'

He looks at me expectantly and I realise that making sure the event is advertised everywhere will be part of how he's sold it to his head office. The supermarket being seen to be community-minded will be important to them. But to be fair, I can't knock that. Being community-minded is exactly what we should be shooting for, no matter how suspect the motive.

'I will be now I know we have the green light,' I say, my stomach lurching a little at just how much there will be to organise to make the show a success.

'The only thing is,' adds Joel, 'the café is due for a refurb, so you'll need to fit it in before then.'

'Okay. And when's that starting?'

'Two weeks today,' he says. At least he has the good grace to look shamefaced.

Two weeks.

TWO WEEKS!!

I have to tell my jaw to close as I stare at him in horror. How on earth can we squeeze everything that needs to be done into such a ludicrously short timescale?

'I realise it's a bit tight.'

A bit!

'But that's all I've got, I'm afraid.' He gives a little shrug. 'The shopfitters and decorators are all booked.'

'It's fine,' I gush brightly, hoping he won't hear the fear in my voice. 'We're just grateful that you can help.'

'You're welcome.' He pauses, lowers his gaze and then returns his focus to somewhere just over my left shoulder. 'Maybe we could go for a drink or something, to chat through the details?'

Is he asking me out on a date? I mean, he's a good-looking bloke and all that but any romantic interest I might have been harbouring evaporated when I found out how shallow he is. But I do need to keep him on side, so maybe I should go.

Flustered by the chatter going on in my head, I mutter something about that being a good idea and then Ethel arrives and rescues me.

'Joel was just telling us that we can have the fashion show here,' I say quickly. 'Isn't that great news?'

'Indeed.'

'It needs to be within two weeks today, though,' I add.

Ethel's expression says more than words could have done.

'I know it's not ideal, but that's the offer. Can we make it work, do you think?'

'Of course we can,' replies Ethel confidently. 'If anyone can work to a deadline then it's us.'

Joel hangs around for a moment, his eyes shifting from Ethel and then back to me and then finally he says, 'Great. Well, let me know if you need anything from me . . . and about that drink.'

'Will do!' I reply over-brightly.

Once he's gone I reach in my bag and pull out my new 'Fashion Show Plan' notebook which is a beautiful pale pink with a simple line drawing of a teacup printed across the front.

'Two weeks,' I say, shaking my head. 'It's really tight.'

'Let's work it through,' says Ethel calmly. 'See what needs to be done.'

'I started a list.' I open the notebook to show her but I haven't got further than my original six points. She looks at my meagre effort and then back at me.

'Let's each take a heading,' she suggests. 'I shall liaise with Joel about the requirements for here, chairs, fire exits, health and safety, that kind of thing . . .' She pauses and gives me a meaningful look. 'Unless you'd rather do that?' I swear she misses nothing.

'No, no,' I reply quickly. 'Happy for you to take that off my hands.'

'Very good,' Ethel continues. 'You can lead on publicity. Viraj can take on ticket sales and the website and Bob can be in charge of refreshments. Dawn is going to have enough to do sewing her outfits.'

This seems like a sensible division of labour. 'I can lend Dawn my sewing machine,' I say, thinking aloud. 'Save her having to go to the studio all the time. And I need to firm up the dates with Sara at the charity shop but that shouldn't be a problem.'

Ethel nods thoughtfully and my stomach flips as the enormity of what lies ahead settles on me.

'We're really doing this, aren't we?'

'Yes,' she replies. 'We really are.'

55

We go into overdrive, each of us working on our own parts of the show and then coming together every morning to share our progress and talk through any unforeseen issues which, thankfully, aren't too numerous.

Once we've agreed the ticket price, Viraj builds a new section of the Time for Beds website devoted to the show and I start to create a social media campaign. It's not easy without much in the way of imagery, so we opt for strong colours and text to make our message eye-catching, and I'm pretty pleased with the results, given the limitations.

I begin to share what we have across the various platforms, running a giveaway for a pair of free tickets for the show, and gradually interest begins to build. I mean, we're not talking hundreds of sales but realistically we can only sell as many tickets as Ethel can get hold of chairs!

Then I secure us a slot on BBC Radio Leeds by calling in a favour.

'Who wants to do the interview?' I ask at our next planning gathering.

Viraj looks at his feet. Dawn isn't there to volunteer. She's sewing madly I imagine, and Ethel shakes her head decisively.

'I think it should be you and Robert,' she says. She doesn't have to explain her thinking. Despite my reluctance, I know it makes sense for us to do it.

And so I have an appointment in my diary. Something I actually have to do. It's been so long that I can't quite remember how it feels to have a commitment.

And then all of a sudden I have two.

I'm making my lunch when an email pings in. It's from the application I made to the rival firm and they want to see me for an interview. Well, this is good. It's been a bit of a slow start but now we're under steam. I look at the job description they've attached. It is exactly what I was doing at McDougal & Wright but the pay is lower so they must have a less experienced person in mind for the position. I google the firm and peruse their client list. It's good. They have some big names on their books.

My spine tingles. This is more like it, what I need, what my life has been missing. You've got this, I tell myself. The job has your name all over it. Yes, it's a little bit of a step down but once I'm in the role I'm sure it won't take me long to get promoted. I'll be back on track. Abigail Finch will be in the building once more.

I toy briefly with the idea that I haven't actually got the job yet, but of course I will. No other candidates will have my experience. They might even have already decided that it's mine, the interview just a formality. They might even have been watching me and biding their time until I become available.

By the time I've eaten my sandwich the job is as good as mine. I email them back asking when they want to see me.

The email comes back by return and is, of course, at exactly when I'm supposed to be at the BBC with Bob. Shit.

Why is this my life? I have had literally weeks of empty days with nothing to do and now I get an interview at the same time as I'm supposed to be doing the only other thing in the diary.

The solution is simple. Bob will just have to go on his own. He's more than capable. And Ethel could go with him if he wants. There's nothing that says it has to be me.

But I *want* it to be me. I want to go and tell the world about this brilliant event for this amazing cause so we can get Bob to his ten grand.

But I also need a job and this one ticks the boxes. Shit.

I go backwards and forwards with the decision. Then I have an idea. I'll talk to the ad agency in terms they understand.

I email them back and tell them that I would love to come for interview but I have a prearranged appointment for an advertising campaign that I'm involved in at the time they've suggested. And then, because I'm super-proud of what we're doing and so they can see that I haven't just been sitting around waiting for a job to come to me, I tell them all about the pyjamas and the shelter. I end with a request for an alternative date. Simple.

I'm sure it will be fine. Interview dates get changed all the time and employers have to be flexible if they want to recruit the best people, but it would have been a whole lot easier if it hadn't fallen on exactly the same day as the radio interview.

I don't have to wait long for a reply. When the email arrives, I click into it expecting to see a new date for the interview, but the message doesn't say that at all. They tell me, in what can only be described as a supercilious tone, that news of my 'pyjama campaign' has caused them to reconsider my application. There is a concern, apparently, that my involvement with publicity of this type may have an adverse impact on their brand and those of their clients and that they are sorry but they are withdrawing the offer of an interview.

I have to read the email three times because it doesn't make any sense to me to start with, but once the whys and wherefores have settled, I realise there's nothing I can do to fix it. Their mind is made up and the only shot I've had at a decent job has gone up in smoke.

56

I meet Bob outside the BBC building just before we're due inside. I'm putting the shock of losing the interview behind me. I might have been resentful that my commitment to Bob and his cause has cost me a real job, but I don't think I am. What we have going on is more important. But the idea that I've blown the only chance of a job I've had so far does make me feel queasy.

I refocus on what we're here to do and find that I'm relatively relaxed about that. I've done radio interviews in the past and our message is simple with nothing in it to trip us up. It'll be fine.

Bob, however, is ghostly pale.

'Is everything okay? You look a bit on the pasty side. Honestly, there's nothing to be nervous about. He'll just ask us a couple of questions and we can bang on about pyjamas and the show and the shelter. It'll be child's play.'

Bob nods and tries a smile but it's a long way off the huge grin I've come to expect from him.

'Come on,' I say gently, putting my arm round his shoulder. 'What's up?'

'Do you think many people will hear it?' he asks in a quiet voice.

'Well, that's the idea,' I say with a little laugh. 'Not much point doing it if they don't. First-night nerves?'

'No, it's not that.' He swallows and blows out a long breath. 'It's hard, telling everyone about . . . all this. Even though most of them will be strangers, I'm still admitting to what a monumental screw-up I've made of my life, how I ended up on the streets . . .'

'Through no fault of your own,' I chip in. 'And then how you picked yourself up and started again. How many people can say that?'

Bob hangs his head. 'Not really something I'm that proud of,' he says. 'What if there are people I used to know listening?'

'Then they'll be astounded by how far you've come. And humbled by how hard you are working to put something back into the system that helped you get back on your feet.'

Bob still doesn't look convinced.

'You should be truly proud of yourself,' I say, but Bob shakes his head.

'Then how come I feel so crap?'

I give his shoulder another squeeze. 'Would you like me to do the interview on my own?'

Bob's face tells me that he would like this more than anything in the whole world, but his mouth says, 'No. I said I'd do it so I will.'

And then he straightens up, lets out a huge up-and-at-'em breath, and we push through the revolving door and into the lobby beyond.

Inside, the atmosphere is busy with lots of people coming and going, talking on phones and generally looking like they have people to see and places to be. Bob eyes the revolving door as if to go back outside would be deeply tempting.

'Come on.' I slot my arm through his parka-clad one and steer him towards the reception.

'We're here for an interview with Charlie Smart,' I say, trying to look as if I do this kind of stuff all the time. Charlie Smart's show is the breakfast slot and it's a big deal locally.

'I'll just tell him you're here,' replies the girl in a strong Leeds accent. 'What name is it?'

'Abbie Finch and Bob Hoskins,' I say, trying hard not to stumble over Bob's famous moniker but the reception girl doesn't bat an eyelid. She's probably too young to get the reference.

'Take a seat and someone will be here in a moment,' she says, and they are. The runner is younger still, so young in fact that I'm sure she should be at school. She swipes us through the door and leads us up to Charlie's studio. We can see him through the glass partition, his feet up on the desk in front of him, chatting away into his microphone. He sees us, gives us a wave and holds up a finger indicating one minute. Shortly after that he's standing at our sides.

'Hi,' he drawls. His voice is slow and languid. 'I'm Charlie. Great to meet you both. You're on after the news so we'll just get you set up with headphones. You can sit quiet until I've played a record and then we'll be off. I've read your stuff . . .' He wafts a sheet of paper that I assume is the press release I drafted. 'Amazing thing you're doing. Really cool. Right. I'd better get back in there. See you in a mo.'

And then he ducks back inside his studio, leaving us to get mic'd up. I see the man who is sorting our headphones wince slightly when his nose picks up Bob's scent and I come over all defensive. Yes, he might whiff a bit but you'd have to go a long way to find a nicer, more genuine bloke.

Instinctively I throw Bob a supportive 'you've got this' kind of face. He manages something in return but I'm really not sure I could call it a smile.

57

'And that was "As It Was" by the inimitable Harry Styles,' says Charlie in that upbeat voice that DJs must learn at DJ school. 'We all love Harry. If you're listening out there, Mr S, please feel free to pop in for a chat. Any time.'

My heart starts to beat a little harder in my chest. Charlie looks at us and I know we're on next.

'But for today, two people who have popped in to see me are Abbie Finch and Bob Hoskins. No, not the famous one, but someone who is doing fantastic things for the city of Leeds. Welcome, Abbie and Bob.'

We both say hi back in chorus and I immediately spot a potential issue with doing a two-handed interview – speaking over each other.

'So, you are involved in something a bit out of the ordinary. Want to tell us about it?'

Instinctively I take the lead. I smile before I speak, hoping it will show in my voice.

'Yes. We are raising money for a homeless hostel in Leeds. We started by making pyjama bottoms. We didn't know how to sew so we all had to learn. That was hilarious.' I roll my eyes and then remember that no one can see me. I rush on, hoping I'm not blushing too obviously. 'And now we're holding a fashion show with clothes sourced from the Help the Homeless charity shop. The idea is to show how stylishly you can dress without spending a fortune. It's all about recycling what's already in the world and saving money at the same time—'

'You're a bit of a style icon yourself, Abbie,' interrupts Charlie. 'For all our listeners, Abbie looks like she just stepped out of an Audrey Hepburn movie.' This irritates rather than flatters me. We're not here to talk about how I dress. This is about the fashion show.

'Well, I don't know about that,' I say, trying to bring him back on track by batting away the compliment, 'but we're hoping that people will come along on the night to support us. It'll be a fun evening with lots going on. One of our team is an incredibly creative seamstress, and she's making some one-off pieces for the grand finale. They'll be for sale on the night too.'

'That all sounds fabulous,' says Charlie. 'And I understand this is more of a personal story for you, Bob.'

I feel Bob tense up. Don't lose it now, I think.

There is a pause that stretches for slightly too long. Charlie raises an eyebrow at me, checking to see whether Bob needs rescuing, but then Bob speaks.

'That's right, Charlie. I was homeless for a bit me sen. I had a bit of bad luck and . . .'

No. I'm not going to let him make himself sound feckless or irresponsible when he was actually the victim of a crime.

I reach under the desk and squeeze Bob's arm. 'It wasn't bad luck, Bob,' I say to him and then continue to Charlie. 'Someone stole all his tools out of his van. And that led to him not getting work and then not earning anything and ultimately to him losing his home. All because somebody thought they could make a quick buck by taking things that didn't belong to them.'

'That's terrible,' agrees Charlie.

'So I ended up with nowhere to sleep,' says Bob. 'It was horrible on the streets. Cold, obviously, and dead scary when you don't know what to do next or where to turn for help. The hostel was there for me. They picked me up out of the gutter, gave me somewhere to stay and then helped me rebuild my pride. If it wasn't for the hostel . . .' His voice cracks and he shudders. There's a pause while he composes himself and I bite my lip. 'So now,' he continues, 'I'm trying to help them do the same for others.'

He sits up a little taller in the seat and looks Charlie right in the eye.

'It's dead important, the work they do,' he says, his voice stronger now. 'So, Abbie and me and three others, we're trying to raise ten grand for the shelter so they can help other people right when they need it.'

Charlie opens his mouth to speak but Bob doesn't let him.

'The homeless crisis isn't going away any time soon. It's getting worse year on year as more and more people can't make ends meet. And I get that it's confronting, seeing people in sleeping bags on the streets. Folk don't know what to do or say, so they do nowt. But this is something you *can* do to help. Buy a ticket for the show. Tell your mates. Make a donation. Every penny of what we raise is going direct to the hostel. And the bit that you give could make the difference between someone having a bed for the night or just giving up on their life.'

He speaks with such passion that it brings tears to my eyes. Even Charlie looks a bit overcome and has to pull himself round.

'So, where can people get tickets?'

'Our website is Time for Beds dot com. All the details are on there. And as Bob says, whatever little you can give will make a huge difference to the people that need it.'

'Well, we at the breakfast show wish you all the luck in the world,' says Charlie. 'Thank you so much for coming in and telling us all about it. Tickets for the fashion show are at Time for Beds dot com. Support them if you can. And next up it's "I'll Never Let Go" by Snow Patrol.'

Clearly someone has thought about today's playlist. Charlie mouths a thank you and gives us a thumbs up sign and then starts to cue up his next record.

We are ushered back out of the studio. My adrenaline levels start to return to normal leaving me feeling a bit shaky and emotional.

'I think that went okay,' I say to Bob when we're safe to talk. He nods. He looks a bit shell-shocked too, but the main thing is that we've done what we came here to do. The world now knows about the show and how to get tickets for it, or at least Leeds does, and that's much the same thing.

We're just heading out of the studio when Charlie's producer taps me on the shoulder.

'That was great,' she says. 'It makes you think, doesn't it?' and I know exactly what she means.

She fishes in her jeans pocket and then thrusts a twenty-pound note at me. 'Here,' she says. 'Add this to the pot.'

And then she disappears back into the studio before we have time to thank her.

Bob and I stare at the cash.

'Well done, Bob. You were brilliant.'

Bob shrugs. 'Well, let's hope it does the trick, eh,' he says.

58

It's family Sunday lunch time again. I toy with the idea of making an excuse. Mum is bound to ask lots of questions about how many jobs I've applied for and if I've had many interviews. She won't understand when I say I turned the only one I've had down so that I could go on the radio with Bob instead.

Felix and Xander will no doubt have questions too, although I imagine they will be far less searching than Mum's. Felix might even have a little dig – how the mighty have fallen, that kind of thing. Not showing up for Sunday lunch is starting to look quite appealing.

But if I don't go the questioning will probably be worse, and, anyway, I want to tell them about being on the radio and all the work we're doing for the fashion show.

I'm barely through the door before Mum starts at me.

'Have you got a job yet? You really mustn't leave it too late, Abigail. It's amazing how quickly these things can spiral out of control and I'm afraid your father and I don't have any cash spare.'

'Hi, Mum,' I say. 'Lovely to see you too.'

I'm tempted to tell her that I have everything under control, although that isn't strictly true. I do know there's no spare cash though. I'm pretty sure they spent most of what they had digging Felix out of his various holes.

I find Dad in the lounge watching the Grand Prix. I plant a kiss on his bald spot, and he greets me warmly but without taking his eyes off the screen. Xander and Lou and then Felix and a girl called Charice arrive not long after me and soon we're sitting round the table with me and Mum serving roast beef and all the trimmings to everyone.

'I have news,' I say when everyone has their food.

'I thought you said you hadn't got a job,' says Mum.

'No. It's not that.'

'You're not pregnant?!'

Honestly! I roll my eyes. 'No. I'm not.'

'Need a man for that, Abs,' smirks Xander, not unkindly.

I ignore him.

'I suppose it's a bit like a job,' I clarify, 'except I'm not being paid for it.'

'Sounds crap,' says Felix, grinning at Charice, who is hanging on his every word – she must be new and hasn't yet worked out what a gigantic pain in the arse my brother can be. 'Work for no pay. What's the point of that?'

I really can't be bothered explaining that concept to him.

'I'm working on a fundraising campaign for a shelter for home-less people in Leeds.'

Felix rolls his eyes but Lou nods encouragingly. I press on. 'We're selling tickets for a fashion show. It's next weekend at that supermarket near me. You're all very welcome to come – if you buy a ticket of course.'

Charice's ears prick up. 'Which brands are you working with?' she asks.

'Actually, we're going to style clothes that we'll find in a charity shop on the day.'

To give her her due, Charice does an excellent job of not react-ing, although I'm sure the idea won't have appealed to her going by the way she's dressed.

'My friend Bob and I were on the Radio Leeds breakfast show to publicise it.'

'*Breakfast with Charlie?*' asks Mum. 'Ooh, I like him. And you were on his show? On the radio? Well, why didn't you say? I'd have got everyone we know to listen.'

That's precisely why I didn't say, I think. But actually, with the radio show under my belt, I'm no longer nervous about what people might think. I'm really proud of what Bob and I did.

'It all happened quite quickly so there wasn't time to tell anyone.' I hope I'm not blushing too badly. 'But I think you can probably still hear it on catch-up.'

'Well, we'll do that, won't we?' says Mum with a nod to my dad. 'Wait 'til I tell people that my daughter's been on *Breakfast with Charlie.*'

Felix smirks and I'm tempted to kick him under the table as if we were kids again. I mutter something about it being nothing really and then move back to the main point.

'We want to sell out so it would be great if you could tell everyone you know, get them to come along.'

'Are you modelling?' asks Lou in her quiet voice.

I pull a face and nod reluctantly. 'We're looking for models actually. Anyone fancy it?'

Lou looks like she's trying to melt herself into the table top but Charice nudges Felix in his ribs.

'We could do that, babe,' she says. 'It might be a laugh.'

'Wearing skanky second-hand clothes,' replies Felix, nose curling in disgust. 'No chance.'

'Don't be ridiculous,' I say. 'They'll be clean.'

Much as my baby brother can be an idiot, he is tall and reasonably good-looking and we are short of male volunteers. I decide to play to his ego.

'And you definitely should, Fe. I've always said you could be a model.' In fact, I've never said this but Felix will believe it.

'You too, Charice,' I add. 'The better the models the more chance we have of selling the clothes. And there are some exclusive pieces in the finale. I'm sure there'll be a wedding dress too.'

I signal at her with my eyes and she in turn casts a quick glance at my brother. The poor girl. If she thinks Felix will propose she has another think coming, but all's fair in love and fundraising.

'I think we should do it, babe.'

'We can come to support, can't we, Xan?' says Lou. 'Put us down for a couple of tickets, please, Abbie.'

'Will do. Mum? Dad?'

'Will Charlie from the radio be there?' Mum asks deferentially as if the local radio DJ is royalty.

'Well,' I say doubtfully. 'I'm not sure. But I'll put you down for some tickets anyway, shall I? And maybe you could ask your friends?'

Mum nods happily, and I'm relieved that I seem to have done something right, even if it isn't getting a new job.

Charice looks delighted at the prospect. 'Well, how cool is this?' she says, looking round at us all in turn. 'Modelling. I'd love to do that, wouldn't we, babe?'

I notice the mixed pronouns and suppress a smirk. It looks as if I might just have made her month but Felix looks altogether less convinced, so in case Charice's enthusiasm isn't enough to win him round I drop another little ego boost to smooth the way.

'You two will be the stars of the show, I'm sure.'

Felix preens. He really can't help himself, and I chortle to myself at his predictability. For all his faults, I do love my baby brother.

After that, the conversation slides away to some new Roman event that has started up near Chester that Mum and Dad are keen to attend and a coach trip to Pompeii, which sounds like hell to me but about which they are very enthused. We get through the rest of the afternoon without Mum mentioning either jobs and the lack thereof or biological clocks. I'm barely out of the door before Mum is on the phone to one of her friends and I overhear her telling them that me and Charlie Smart are bosom buddies. As I cringe I suppose that all publicity is good publicity!

59

What happens next catches me totally off guard. After lunch at Mum and Dad's, I head home to work on the campaign for the show. So far, I've posted on Facebook and Instagram, but I wonder whether I'm missing a trick not having anything on TikTok, so I create one using the footage of Dawn doing her stuff in the café when we were trying to convince Joel about the show. She looks fantastic and I put captions over the top.

At the end, the video pans round to us all sitting at the table. You can see Bob grinning and clapping. Me and Ethel are there too.

My personal instincts want to cut the clip before it gets to me, but I decide against it. Bob's enthusiastic clapping means that it finishes on exactly the right tone, and it will be a bit abrupt if I just cut it without letting the pan complete, so I leave it as it is. The only person not visible is Viraj because he was doing the filming.

When it's finished, I post it, tagging Charlie Smart and thanking him for having us on his show. It's a little bit cheeky but he did seem genuinely interested in what we're doing so I hope he won't mind. He can always untag himself if he thinks it's a step too far.

It takes about twenty minutes before my phone starts to buzz. I ignore the first couple of notifications but then the buzzes are coming so thick and fast that I pick my phone up to investigate.

It's the TikTok. Charlie Smart has reposted it to his thousands of followers and they are all commenting. I start to read. Almost exclusively the comments are in favour of what we're doing. Local people like that we're raising funds for a Leeds shelter and everyone loves that we're going with charity shop finds instead of new clothes.

I sit agog and watch the numbers go up and up. I've had campaigns go viral before, of course, but when it's for work it doesn't have quite the same impact as it does when it's something personal. And they are our perfect market, local to Leeds, and exactly the people who might buy a ticket and come along or at least make a donation. I start to wonder whether we'll have enough chairs.

I'm so absorbed by watching this excitement unfold that I almost miss what else is going on. In and among all the TikTok notifications there's a message from Spencer. I've been dithering about the whole Spencer situation. Since receiving his invitation to visit (which Dawn replied to on my behalf) I haven't actually done anything about it. Instead I've pushed the possibility of heading up to Scotland out of my head while it's been filled with other things so that I don't have to make a decision about the best thing to do.

Now it appears that Spencer has tired of waiting.

Hi, Abbie, begins the message. *Wasn't sure you were ever going to sort your trip out, so I've done it for you. Attached is the booking with all the details on. You won't need your passport but you will need ID to get on the plane. And bring plenty of warm clothes. It can be perishing up here* 😆🥶.

I read the message again. Is he really saying that he's booked me a flight to go up there? My heart is soaring. This might be the most romantic thing anyone has ever done for me. It's so cute, even if we have split up.

But will I go? I give this question less than two seconds' consideration. Of course I'll go. The reason I've been so indecisive, I think now, is because I wasn't sure he really meant his invitation, and because I couldn't see his face when he issued it I had no way of judging how genuine it was. And then, on top of that, Dawn had replied for me with a one-word answer. Because my reply had been so casual I thought the invitation was too.

Maybe I've also been holding myself back because I thought I needed to get my old life on track before I tackled this, but now I'm wondering whether I actually want my old life back at all. Against the odds and despite still having no job, my new life seems to be shaping up quite nicely.

And now, Spencer has taken the initiative himself. This has to be proof that he really had meant his invitation. He's booked me a flight and I don't even have to arrange any time off work to go because I don't have a job. How perfect is that?

Immediately I'm excited, my head full of how it will be, what I should pack, what his new friends will be like, whether he has a spare room because we aren't a couple and he might have sent this invitation to me as a friend only. As I contemplate this, I realise how much I hope he hasn't. After all, we only split up because he was leaving. There's a good chance that whatever spark we found when we both lived in Leeds is still there. I cast that pretty woman from the photo out of my mind. He surely hasn't gone to all this effort just so he can introduce me to his new girlfriend.

And then I click on the attachment. It's not just a flight. There's a train ticket from Leeds to Edinburgh too. He's thought the whole thing through, bless him. I must offer to reimburse him, I think, as I look at the date to see when our grand reunion is going to take place.

No.

I peer at the numbers again, in case I've got it wrong. But obviously I haven't. The tickets are for Saturday, which is, of course, the day of the fashion show.

I've barely had an opportunity to get excited when I'm having to tamp down my disappointment. Of all the chances . . . But then of course it would be the one day this year when I can't possibly go because that is just the way the world works. It's the clashing interviews all over again but this time I am genuinely upset. I really want to go.

Tears start to prick in the corners of my eyes and my mouth pulls down ready to cry. It makes me feel like a little girl but I can't help it. My imagination immediately starts to torture me with images of Spencer and me dressed in thick sweaters with big scarves and those woolly hats that look so cute on models, running across white sands hand in hand, laughing. Then making hot chocolate in some gorgeous little cottage with an open fire. And then . . .

I stop myself. Spencer and I are not together. He issued his invitation because we're friends and he's probably even more lonely up there than I have been down here. Anything else I project on to it is just a result of my overactive imagination.

But I'm so, so disappointed. I stare at the tickets as if I can change what they say by the power of my mind alone but they stay resolutely for Saturday. Then irritation starts to build. What kind of an idiot goes to all this effort and expense without checking that the dates work? I don't really mean this, of course. I'm delighted that the tickets have arrived out of the blue. It's just . . .

I ignore all the TikTok notifications and begin to type a WhatsApp message to Spencer.

> *Hi. Thank you so much!! This is such a lovely thing and I'd love to come. But I've got something on next weekend that I can't change.*

I pause. Does this sound dismissive? The fashion show is a massive deal and I can't possibly not be there but will he think I'm just looking for an excuse not to go? Of course, Spencer doesn't know that because I've been treating him as if we've split up and so haven't bombarded him with the minutiae of my life. In fact, we *have* split up, so that really isn't a fault on my part. Spencer is to blame for not checking.

But it still feels rubbish.

I carry on.

> *I've organised a fashion show to raise money for a shelter for the homeless in Leeds and it's on Saturday night. Can the tickets be changed? I can literally do any other weekend. x*

I dither over the kiss. Too much? Not enough? God, I feel like a teenager, not a capable woman in her thirties. In the end, I leave the message as it is and send it. And then I watch the screen for a reply as the TikTok notifications continue to land.

60

I don't have to wait long for a reply and when it comes, instead of being shirty or annoyed, Spencer is contrite.

God. Sorry, Abbie. I'm an idiot. I should have checked. I just got carried away. There's a little festival thing happening on the island next weekend and I thought you'd like it. But don't worry. I'll just cancel the tickets.

That's it.

I watch the screen for an indication that he's still typing and that a second this-is-what-we'll-do-instead message is about to land. But there's no typing and then he's no longer online, leaving me wondering what he's feeling. Is he as disappointed as I am? Was this a romantic gesture or simply something born out of friendship? And how will I ever ask that question?!

I don't want him to cancel the tickets. I want to change them. The festival does sound fun, but surely we can have fun without it too.

But what do I do? If I message back and ask him to rebook the tickets, does that look a bit too keen? What if I offer to pay for the new tickets myself? Would that help or be an insult? He might have changed his mind already, be thinking that he should just cut his losses and run. God, what a mess.

I've never been lacking in confidence until recently. I was so sure of myself and my place in the world. I don't think I'd realised just how much of that came from what I was signalling about myself through what I did, rather than who I am. But now I worry that just me on my own isn't enough. I know that Spencer was never interested in my job and the trappings it brought, but we hadn't got far enough into our relationship for him to see how much I relied on it for my identity, and how unsure I am without it.

All this dithering is hopeless. I could just ring him and tell him that I want to go but not this weekend, but we haven't actually spoken since he left, and would this be the moment to do that anyway, when I have just spurned his kind offer? After driving myself mad with the possibilities for over an hour, I decide that I should at least wait until the morning. I get ready for bed, keeping one eye on the phone, but my screen just keeps lighting up with notifications from the reposted TikTok. There's nothing more from Spencer.

There are no messages when I wake up either, but I don't have bandwidth for these are-we-aren't-we plans. I need to be entirely focused on the show and not drop a ball. Spencer was lovely, I tell myself, but he's gone now and my life has moved on too. I am a strong independent woman and in control of my own destiny. This will become my mantra, I decide, and I tell Elvis just so that everyone is clear.

The TikTok has had almost a million views overnight. Dawn is a TikTok sensation. Everyone loves her and the comments are almost exclusively positive although there are so many that I don't have time to read them all.

I click over to the Time for Beds website to look at ticket sales. The total is very healthy. We must be pretty close to capacity now.

It feels both great and at the same time terrifying that we won't be strutting our stuff in an empty café.

My thumb, with a mind of its own, scrolls back to Spencer's message. So much for my new mantra! There's still no reply. I have to stop doing that. I can't make him respond simply by the sheer force of my longing!

Also, I don't have time to think about him. I need to crack on. Time is ticking down to the show and there is still so much to be done but instead of feeling daunted by it all, I'm buzzing. I've missed this, I realise. The pressure of a deadline, that raw nagging feeling deep in your gut, and you're a little bit scared that you can't quite deliver. This is what I used to get from my job. I thought I could only get that buzz from my work but it seems I was wrong.

But there's no time to ruminate too deeply on this today. I have a different kind of job to do. Looking at my list over breakfast, with Elvis wrapping himself around my legs, the main one is sourcing the clothes and creating the looks. I've been thinking about themes, and I reach for my iPad and open up Pinterest where I've been saving ideas.

In theory it looks fabulous but it rests or falls on what is available in the charity shop on Saturday and this is something I have no control over. My chest tightens as I ponder what we'll do if we get there on the morning to discover they've had a bumper week and there's only the thinnest of thin pickings left.

I snap myself out of it. There is absolutely no point in worrying about things that haven't yet happened.

My phone buzzes and I dive on it, hoping that it's Spencer with a new plan, but it's just another TikTok notification. If it doesn't calm down soon, I'll have to turn them off or I'll be a nervous wreck by the end of the day.

Maybe I should just message him back and nudge him into rearranging the dates. My finger hovers over the screen as, yet again, I dither about how I should phrase what I want to say. But realistically it's only been a few hours and we've been asleep for most of them. I just need to be patient and see how it pans out.

'Not known for my patience, am I, Elvis?' I say, rubbing at the space between his pointy little ears. He cocks his head towards me and our eyes meet.

I think he agrees.

61

'We've sold out!!'

Dawn is shouting at me before I've even had a chance to walk from the entrance of the café to our table. As soon as she spots me she's on her feet and waving as if she hasn't seen me for a month. As ever, people turn and stare and then smile at the slightly eccentrically dressed woman who is so excited about something that she cannot wait the ten seconds that it will take her friend to cross the space so that she can pass on her news without shouting it. A proud glow radiates through me.

'Thingy!!' she hollers again in case I didn't hear her the first time. 'There are no tickets left. Viraj says they're all gone. All of them.'

She's grinning from ear to ear and I can't help but grin back. I look at Viraj for confirmation and he nods.

'She's right. There was a massive run on them last night. Not sure what happened but something worked like magic.'

'I know exactly what happened,' I say, pulling my phone out and navigating to the TikTok. 'Look!'

They dip their heads around my phone and watch.

'That's me!' says Dawn, looking up at me, eyes shining.

She goes back to watching, her delight growing. When it gets to the end she claps her hands.

'Again! Again!'

I run the clip again and Dawn wants to see it for a third time. I oblige but don't watch it again.

'Have you seen the number of views?' Viraj asks me, his tone incredulous.

'I have indeed.'

'How many people have watched me?' asks Dawn, not taking her eyes from the little version of herself in my phone.

I peer at the bottom of the screen for the up-to-date figure. 'Currently . . . about 1.4 million.'

The number still takes me back a bit, but Dawn looks totally floored by it. Her jaw drops and her eyes stretch as wide as the plates we have our cakes on.

'1.4 million,' she repeats. 'That's, like, more than all the people in this whole supermarket.'

'It is,' I agree. 'And a lot more besides. You're a TikTok sensation, Dawn.'

'Hence the spike,' says Viraj, rubbing at his stubbly chin. 'Pretty cool.'

That tiny acknowledgement is all it takes to make me feel like a million dollars, and I soak up the warm feeling that comes with it like a sponge.

'I've got us a couple more models too,' I add. 'My brother and his girlfriend say they'll come and help.'

'Nice,' replies Viraj.

'How are your outfits coming along?' I ask Dawn. 'Nearly finished?'

Dawn taps her nose. 'You'll have to wait and see,' she says, which doesn't really answer my question.

'But they'll be ready?' I ask, unable to stop myself.

'Yeah,' is all the response I get and it will have to do to calm my inner control freak.

I fish my notebook out of my bag and turn to the master list, running my finger down it as I mentally check items off. It does seem like we're pretty much ready for Saturday. The lack of available time to get everything lined up, which had felt like a problem at the start, has turned out to be an advantage. Everyone has been forced to focus rather than letting matters drift.

Bob appears just as I'm putting my notebook back in my bag.

'Morning all,' he says.

'I've gone viral!' Dawn tells him gleefully.

Bob's eyes slide over to me and Viraj to fill in the gaps, but Dawn has got this.

'Thingy made a TikTok of me and she posted it and now millions of people have seen it,' she announces breathily.

Bob's brow creases and he looks to me. 'Millions?'

'Well, 1.4 million actually,' I clarify. 'But it's pretty much the same thing.'

I grin as Bob absorbs this.

'TikTok is that video app, right?' he asks.

I nod.

'I don't use it. Don't know anything about it.'

I explain about tagging Charlie Smart and how he reposted it.

'Bloody hell,' Bob says. 'Let's see then.'

I cue the TikTok up again and pass him my phone. He watches it through, his smile steadily growing. Then he reaches the end and sees himself applauding Dawn. For a few seconds his whole face fills the screen.

'Hey! Look at that! It's me!'

'It's mainly me, though,' says Dawn, sounding slightly put out.

Bob agrees quickly. 'Spot on, Dawn, love, and you look as pretty as a picture.' He hands the phone back to me. 'So what about ticket sales?'

'They're all gone,' I reply, and he nods approvingly.

'Good effort, Abbie. Well done!' He looks around the café. 'No Ethel this morning?'

I shake my head. 'Maybe she had something else on,' I say, although these days no one misses a morning gathering. Meeting up at the community table has become an integral part of our day, and particularly now when the show is so close.

'Maybe,' Bob agrees. 'Anyway, my ducks are behaving.'

I'm confused and my face must tell him so.

'They're all in a row,' he explains. 'I spoke to Joel. He's going to serve drinks and some canapés and he's agreed to let us have them at cost so any markup we make can go straight into the fund.'

'Nice negotiating,' I say, genuinely impressed.

'What can I say? If you've got it, you've got it.' He flicks some invisible dust from his shoulders.

There seems to be a bit of a kerfuffle going on in the supermarket itself. Lots of busyness and some shouting.

'She's over here,' someone says, and then I hear, 'Excuse me. Can you let us through, please?'

'What's going on out there?' I ask.

Dawn is up immediately, unable to resist the drama.

'I'll go and see,' she says like this is a major public service she's providing.

But she comes back a couple of minutes later, her face tense. 'There's an ambulance. They're putting someone on to a stretcher. I think it's Ethel.'

62

Leaving our drinks unfinished, we race out of the café to see what's going on. Dawn is right. There's an ambulance parked right outside the main door, its blue lights flashing and lighting up the whole of the entrance foyer. We're just in time to see the paramedics wheeling a stretcher with a very small-looking Ethel strapped on it. She has an oxygen mask over her face and doesn't appear to be conscious.

'What's the matter with her?' Dawn asks me as if I must know everything.

'I'm not sure,' I reply, but you have to worry when someone as old as Ethel is taken ill.

I rush to the paramedics. A quick glance at their patient confirms our fears.

'This is our friend Ethel. What's happened?'

'She collapsed and she's unconscious. We don't know why as yet. We'll do more tests in the ambulance. Do you know her full name?'

My mind goes blank and I wonder if I've ever known Ethel's surname.

'It's Ethel Hunter,' says Bob. 'She's just turned eighty-four. She lives alone. No known medical conditions other than the kind that come with old age.'

He's so calm and gives over the information like he's done it a hundred times before.

When he sees me looking at him curiously, he just shrugs. I suppose he's had experience of dealing with ambulances in recent times.

'Thanks, mate,' says the paramedic. 'We're taking her to St James's if you want to follow on.'

'Can I go with her?' asks Bob. 'So she's not on her own.'

The paramedic readily agrees.

'We'll see you there,' I say as the ambulance doors close.

'I don't know which bus it is,' says Dawn urgently. 'I don't know where to go.' She has gone very pale and her voice is full of panic. 'Where do we go, Thingy? We have to get to Ethel but I don't know which bus.'

I stroke her arm, trying to calm her down. 'It's okay, Dawn. I have a car. I can drive us there. We just need to go to my place to get it.'

'I came in my car,' says Viraj, and he grimaces at the confession. 'I know. Not very green but walking's not my thing. I'm parked over there.'

He leads us to a sporty little Audi in the most surprising shade of cherry red. I definitely didn't have Viraj down as a red car kind of guy.

'Nice wheels,' I say admiringly, momentarily forgetting why we need them.

Viraj shrugs and tries to suppress a proud smile.

'Your car looks very fast,' says Dawn. 'That's good. Ethel needs us to get there quick.'

There isn't really a back seat but I'm smaller than Dawn so Viraj tips the driver's seat and I fold myself into the tiny space behind.

'Seat belts,' says Dawn officiously.

We do as we're told and then Viraj is pulling out of the car park and into the stream of traffic.

'Is Ethel going to die?' asks Dawn as we crawl along.

I have no idea what to tell her. 'I hope not, Dawn,' I say vaguely. 'I'm sure everything will be okay.'

Of course, I'm not sure. How can I be? But I really, really want it to be and for now that will have to be enough.

It takes what feels like an age to get to St James's but it's probably not more than fifteen minutes. Viraj parks the car and then we race across the car park in search of information. I assume that the ambulance will have taken her to A&E to be triaged so that's where we start.

As ever, it's busy. Is there ever a time when it's not? Bob is already there, sitting and waiting among the walking wounded.

'What's the news?' I ask him.

'She's with the doctors now,' he says. 'They're trying to establish what made her collapse.'

'Did she come round in the ambulance?' I ask but Bob shakes his head tightly.

My stomach gripes. I've only known Ethel for a couple of months, and she is hard to get close to, but she's such a vital part of our team and I really, desperately, want her to be all right with all my heart.

'Is she going to die, Bob?' asks Dawn.

Immediately, I feel like an outsider. Bob, Dawn and Ethel were friends before Viraj and I came on the scene, so it makes sense that Dawn will look to Bob for information and support, but it leaves me feeling excluded. For God's sake, Abbie, I think. This is not about you.

'I don't know, Dawn, love,' he says. 'We just have to hope for the best and prepare for the worst.'

I have to admire his honesty. There's no sugar-coating.

Dawn nods and then sits quietly and waits. I have never seen her so still.

Time crawls by at a glacial pace. As we wait, I run through every worst-case scenario I can think of, trying to dismiss each one. Surely she will be fine. Ethel is fit and healthy, as far as we know, but what do any of us really know about what is going on inside our own bodies, let alone anyone else's?

After we've been waiting for what feels like an age, Bob slaps his hands on his thighs decisively and goes to speak to the man on the desk. The receptionist checks something on his screen and they discuss it for a moment. Then Bob comes back to us. I try to read his expression as he makes his way over but he's giving nothing away. I bite my lip and prepare for the worst.

'Well?' says Dawn. 'Is Ethel alive?'

Bob seems anxious still but is clearly relieved. 'Yes. She's still alive. And she's come round too. They're running tests. They're going to keep her in overnight for observation.'

'Can we see her?' asks Dawn, getting to her feet.

'Hold your horses,' says Bob. 'She's very tired. She needs rest. The bloke said we can ring tomorrow to see if she's up to visitors. I told him we'll collect her when she's well enough to go home but obviously I don't have my van any more so . . .'

'No worries,' Viraj says.

'Ethel will like his car,' says Dawn, less panic in her voice now that the danger appears to have passed. 'It's dead low down to the ground and everyone stares at you when you drive past.'

I hadn't noticed the car drawing attention, but then I had other things on my mind and was folded in half in the back.

'There's always my car too,' I add. 'Not as impressive as Viraj's but it does go.'

'That's great,' says Bob. 'So, I've got to work this afternoon so I'd better head back. Why don't you come with me, Dawn? Your place is on the same bus route.'

Dawn agrees meekly. 'I didn't know which bus it was, Bob,' she says. 'I didn't know where to go.'

Bob's tone is soothing. 'It's okay. I've got it. See you two as usual tomorrow?' he adds, looking at me.

'Yep,' I say. 'I'll ring here beforehand so we know what's what.'

We head out of A&E, a little band of four instead of five.

It feels all kinds of wrong.

63

Viraj and I go back to his car and I climb into the passenger seat. He and I probably have the most in common of all of us. We're a similar age, have the same kind of corporate jobs (if you ignore the fact that I don't currently have a job, of course) and I think we were drawn to the community table by a similar need.

Or at least that's my best guess. Viraj doesn't give much away but I think he must be lonely.

And so am I.

There are so many people just like us, I think, people with no partner or a family of their own. People who live alone, earn decent money but work long hours so it's not always easy to find the time to have fun. People whose friends are starting to pair off and make new families while they are being left behind. It's strange because people like us probably don't look lonely from the outside, and yet there we all are. There seems to be a hole in our lives, a space that I always expected would be easily filled but which seems to be empty. I've found everything I've ever dreamed of and yet something is still missing.

All this is far too much to actually discuss with Viraj, however, and definitely not in broad daylight and sober. And, while we do have the most in common of the tablers, he is also the one I feel I know the least well.

I wonder if he would say the same about me. Do I come across as guarded too? Maybe a lifetime of sharing everything online has had an impact on us millennials, made us retreat into ourselves somehow. We curate this life for ourselves on social media but then are wary of sharing what's really going on in case it doesn't match up.

Maybe I'm just massively overthinking the whole thing!

'This is a great car,' I say instead of anything that might tiptoe over the line into personal.

He turns to grin at me. 'A present to myself when I moved north,' he says. 'I decided that if I was going to be buzzing up and down the M1 all the time I wanted to do it in style.'

'Do you go back to London often?'

He rolls his eyes. 'Haven't been once.'

'Ah. It's still a nice car.'

'Yeah.'

He looks across at me and catches his lower lip between his teeth. 'I don't suppose you fancy a little road trip? I never seem to get round to going exploring on my own.'

'Why not?' I say without thought. 'I'm hardly rushed off my feet.'

A wide smile blossoms across his face. 'Great. Right. You're the local. Where shall we go?'

I think for a moment. 'How about Wetherby? Have you been there? It's straight down the A58 from here.'

'Never been,' he says, and types the name into the car's navigation system.

We quickly make it out of Leeds and into open countryside. As we drive through Scarcroft and Bardsey, Viraj makes appreciative little noises at how pretty the villages are.

'Not that grim up north, is it?' he says as we pass a particularly lovely house with manicured lawns and electric gates.

'Best-kept secret. Known only to real northerners. Don't tell them down south.'

As we drive we catch up on the kind of basic details that you would usually know about your friends. We talk about his work (challenging but sometimes dull), where he lived in London (Kentish Town) and where his family live (Wood Green and Bangladesh). I tell him about my family and losing my job, and he laughs when I describe Mum and Dad's Roman adventures. I forget how peculiar they sound to an outsider.

'And how are you finding Leeds?'

There's a pause, like he's deciding what he wants to say, and I hope he isn't going to be rude about my home town.

'Honestly?' Another pause. 'I don't know. I barely see anything of it. I thought it would address the work/life balance thing, moving up here. But actually . . .'

'You're working more because you haven't got anything else to do?' I suggest.

'Precisely. I assumed I'd meet people, through work or whatever. Plus, I thought my mates would come north to visit.'

Immediately I think of Spencer's invitation, still unresolved due to Ethel being taken ill.

'And they haven't?'

Viraj shakes his head. 'They're busy. They don't make the time. And I can't keep asking. It looks so . . .'

'Desperate?'

He sighs. 'Yeah.'

'Is that why you let Dawn drag you to the table that day, in the café?'

He nods. 'Who knew I'd end up being friends with an ex-homeless guy, a woman who's as bonkers as a bag of frogs and an octogenarian.'

'And me! Or am I the bonkers one?'

283

He turns and grins at me before sliding his gaze back to the road ahead.

A few more fields roll by and I add, 'They're not a bad bunch, really.'

'They're great. They've really grown on me. They know what they're about too. Have you noticed that?'

'They make me feel very humble,' I say simply.

As we approach Collingham the traffic thickens and we end up sitting in a queue.

'Did something major happen here?' he asks.

'Not that I'm aware of. Why?'

'All the houses have those blue plaques. Like famous people lived in them.'

Then I remember that I once read something about it. 'I think it's a local history thing. The villagers researched who lived in the houses one hundred years ago. It was to do with marking the end of World War One.'

'That's cool,' he says.

As the car slows again we peer out at one of the plaques.

'George Wray. Born 1893. Brewery worker. Married with two children. Royal Field Artillery. Killed in action 1917. Grew up here with five siblings,' I read. 'Isn't it fascinating? Just a few facts and I can almost picture them.'

'All those stories,' says Viraj thoughtfully. 'I wonder what they will make of the way we live in a hundred years.'

'Well, we're not going to be here to see it,' I say with a wry laugh.

'No. That's true enough.'

We muse for a moment or two and then the traffic starts moving again and we carry on towards Wetherby.

'I hope Ethel is okay,' says Viraj.

'Me too.' I stare out of the windscreen at the road ahead. 'What do you think we should do if . . .' I don't dare vocalise what I'm thinking but there's no need.

'If she dies, you mean?'

I nod tightly, my eyes starting to glisten.

'We carry on,' says Viraj, his voice confident. 'That's what she'd want. I don't know much about Ethel but you don't get to be a ballerina by being a quitter.'

'True enough,' I say. 'But hopefully . . .'

'Yeah. Hopefully.'

64

I ring the hospital in the morning for an update.

'Are you family?' asks the nurse suspiciously.

'No. I'm not sure she has any family. I'm a friend. I came in with her yesterday,' I say, hoping that Ethel would agree with my credentials and consider me someone to whom information could be given.

There's a pause while the nurse seems to consider this. 'She had a comfortable night. We're still running tests to find out what caused her to collapse but she's awake.'

'Can we visit?'

'Yes. But you mustn't tire her. She's still quite weak.'

She gives me the visiting times and the ward number and I make a note so I can tell the others.

I check my phone for a new message from Spencer as I have done a hundred times since he said he'd cancel the trip he planned for me, but there's nothing. I wonder whether enough time has gone by to follow up with a question about rebooking but I worry that he'll have lost all the money he spent on the tickets and will be annoyed with me for making something other than a visit to him my number-one priority. And anyway, right now Ethel is more important.

At the café, I pass on the news and we decide to meet back in the supermarket car park later so that I can drive us over to the hospital. Lovely though Viraj's car is, we can't all get in it.

It's a motley crew that turns up at Ethel's ward later that day. Dawn is wearing her yellow satin dress in honour of Ethel and is carrying the remainder of a bag of grapes. She's picked at them on the way and now there are more unappealing sticky stems where grapes used to be than actual grapes.

I've also made an effort, choosing to wear the vintage skirt that Ethel once complimented me on. She probably won't notice but I'm wearing it just in case.

The hum coming off Bob is slightly more pungent than usual, which might be because we were all in such close proximity in my car. It feels rude to open the windows. I assume Bob doesn't know that he smells – if he did, he would surely do something about it – and so wouldn't have been offended, but Dawn might well have drawn attention to me letting fresh air in.

Surprisingly, Viraj has been the most thoughtful of us. He has bought a copy of *Vogue*, which I can imagine Ethel reads, and a puzzle book and pen. He's even bought some of those reading glasses you can get without a prescription as Ethel might need them and we can't get into her flat to collect anything for her.

'That's so kind,' I say when I see what he's brought.

He looks at his feet sheepishly. 'My gran is often in hospital,' he says by way of explanation.

We are buzzed into the ward and make our way to the nurses' station to ask where Ethel's bed is. It's an old people's ward and as we walk down the corridor I see many of them are in bed, eyes closed and gummy jaws drooping. There is something so intimate about seeing people at their most vulnerable and I look away quickly, feeling like I have no business looking.

Ethel is apparently in the room at the end of the corridor. We walk quietly and even Dawn drops her voice. But when we stand on the threshold, I think the nurse must have made a mistake. I can't see Ethel in any of the beds.

I'm just starting to turn round when one of the very old people speaks.

'Abigail. How kind of you to come. And the others too.'

I have to stare hard. The speaker is tiny, shrunken. With no make-up on and white wispy hair wild around her face, it's so hard to see the Ethel I know. Her eyes seem to have slipped deep into their hollows and her cheeks are sunken beneath her sharp cheekbones.

It is her. I can just about make that out but she looks about twenty years older than the last time I saw her.

I step towards her bed, smiling and hoping that my surprise at her appearance doesn't show on my face. 'Ethel. How are you? It's good to see you. You gave us all a bit of a shock.'

'I gave myself a shock,' she says. Her voice is still as clear and precise as it's always been. 'So undignified, collapsing in front of all those strangers.'

'I'm sure it went barely noticed.' I wink at her and she manages a weak smile back, although it lacks its usual sparkle. 'Have they told you what they think caused it?'

'Tests and more tests,' she says, 'but basically they haven't got a clue. It'll turn out to be one of those things that happens to old ladies. I merely fainted. That could have been caused by anything.'

I want to say that I hope it's nothing serious but that's too trite for Ethel, so I just nod instead.

'When will they let you out?' I ask.

'Yeah. Because it's the show on Saturday,' chips in Dawn, 'and we need you.'

I'm about to tell Dawn that Ethel doesn't need to worry about that now when Ethel replies, her tone, if not her volume, forceful.

'If I am still here by the weekend then they will be holding me against my will and I shall discharge myself.'

'That's the spirit,' says Bob cheerfully, although while I admire the sentiment, I'm not sure we should be encouraging her down this line.

Still, it's a long time until Saturday and lots might happen.

We pass an hour going through the details for the show, each of us ticking off our individual areas of responsibility. We are pretty much ready, which is a relief. Dawn borrows my phone and shows Ethel the viral TikTok, and then she parades it round the room to show the other ill old people, who seem, in the main, to be glad of the distraction. One of them takes a purse from her bag and thrusts a five-pound note into Dawn's hand.

'Here,' she says, closing her frail hand over Dawn's. 'There's not enough looking out for the have-nots in this world. The old and the poor, we all get left out with the rubbish. No one's interested in us.'

Actually, the fact that we are all here visiting Ethel goes against that but, judging by how few other visitors there are in the ward, we may well be the exception that proves the rule.

'Thanks,' says Dawn and then passes the note to me for safekeeping.

After an hour, Ethel's eyelids start to flutter and then close and so we tiptoe out.

'We'll be back tomorrow, Ethel,' I whisper to her as I leave, and her hand hovers above the blanket for a second in a tiny gesture of acknowledgement.

'Is she going to be okay?' asks Dawn as we troop back down the endless corridors to the car park.

'Yeah, I reckon so,' says Bob.

'Good,' she replies.

65

Ethel is released from hospital on Thursday and I pick her up and take her back to her apartment. She's physically frail, although she's never been what you might call robust, but mentally she's as sprightly and alert as ever.

'This is most kind of you, Abigail,' she says as we pull into the large car park in front of the mill conversion.

'No problem. I think I should come up with you, make sure you're settled. Would that be all right?'

Ethel nods tightly. She is usually entirely independent so I can see how difficult it is for her to rely on other people. But at least she is admitting that she needs a little help, for now at least. This is a good sign.

Her apartment is just as breathtakingly beautiful as I remember. Sunlight streams in through the tall windows and fills the space with a golden glow. There is a large vase of white lilies on the table which are just reaching their peak. The scent of the pollen sits heavily in the stale air.

'Shall I open a window?' I ask, looking around to see which would be easiest to reach.

Ethel lowers herself gracefully into a chair and points at a smaller window in the kitchen area.

'The key is in that dish on the windowsill,' she says. I would mention home security but we're three floors up so only Spider-Man could burgle the place through the windows. 'Shall I just make you a cup of peppermint tea and then leave you in peace?'

'Yes please to the tea,' she says. 'But would you stay for a moment or two, Abigail. There's something I'd like to discuss with you.'

This is unexpected but I'm delighted to say yes.

She goes to get changed and I make the tea. I find a surprisingly modern bone china cup and saucer comically decorated with a photo of a naked man and woman, which I hand to her on her return as if I serve tea in cups like this every day of the week. Then I settle on the chair opposite and wait.

She has put her hair back up into its elegant chignon and applied a lick of mascara and some blusher. She looks more like herself, although the slightly haunted look that she had in the hospital hasn't quite left her. Lifting the teacup to her lips with a tiny smirk at its design, she takes a sip and then replaces it on the table deliberately.

'Now,' she begins. 'There is nothing like a spell in hospital to make one examine one's mortality.'

I open my mouth to make reassurances about the long years still ahead of her, but she silences me with her palm.

'As you know, I have no family, or at least none that has bothered to keep in touch. My friends are dead – AIDS, cancer, old age. Something will get us all in the end. So I find myself in difficulties when it comes to my will. I have a will already, of course, but the events of the last couple of months, due in no small part to you, Abigail, have made me reconsider my wishes.'

She clears her throat as I wonder what on earth is coming next.

'I am not a rich woman,' she continues, 'but I do have some savings, and there is this place of course. I would like to change my will and would be grateful if you could help me, in confidence, of course.'

'Of course,' I say, wondering if she's basically asking for a lift to the solicitor's.

'I intend to leave a couple of small bequests to individuals, but I wish the bulk of my estate to go to whichever homeless charity in Leeds my executors believe is doing the best work when I die. It's hard to be specific when I don't know how much longer I shall live for.'

She pauses and so I wait and wonder.

'Could I ask you to be an executor, Abigail? I believe you would be the best person for the job.'

I'm overwhelmed by the request and my eyes flood with tears, both because she trusts me enough to ask, but also because the thought of Ethel dying is suddenly so very upsetting.

'Of course,' I splutter. 'It would be an honour.'

She takes another sip of her peppermint tea.

'You have become quite the addition to our little flock, Abigail,' she says after a moment or two of silence. 'We were close before, in our own way, but you have brought something quite unique with you. There's a new sense of purpose which we lacked before. I, for one, am very grateful. And I feel it from the others too. Dawn has her sewing now. With careful steering she could turn that into a career for herself and move away from the infernal cleaning.'

I hadn't thought about this, but it makes perfect sense. Dawn has a real talent. She has more to learn but she's quick to pick things up, and keen. I'm sure it won't take her long.

'And I see new hope in Robert too,' she continues. 'There is work to do there, but gradually he is regaining his self-confidence. He still needs to shower more frequently.'

This is the first time anyone has mentioned Bob's personal hygiene and I try not to let my surprise at her frankness show.

'And he needs to find a way to reconnect with his children, but the difference is that whereas before he saw it as a hopeless labour, now he can picture it happening. I can't overstate how important that is.'

She focuses all her attention on me, her pale grey eyes boring into mine so that I can't look away.

'And I believe you have done that, simply by being you.'

I press my lips together in a pointless attempt to control myself but the tears come anyway. It is the nicest thing that anyone has said to me in as long as I can remember.

'Thank you,' I mumble. 'That means such a lot. It's been hard, losing my job and not being quite sure of where I fit in the world. Meeting you all has made me rethink what is important to me. I don't know what I'd have done without . . .'

But I can't quite finish what I want to say because I'm sobbing, all the stress and fear and doubts of the last two months all finally being released.

Ethel stays where she is and lets me cry.

66

The day before the fashion show dawns and I wake up sick with nerves. Obviously I've known what is coming but somehow, with all the organisation and then the worry over Ethel, I have managed to push it to the back of my mind. But I can't any longer.

I am going to have to get up in front of a room full of people and perform. All eyes will be on me, and it doesn't matter how many times I tell myself that it's only a bit of fun and all in a great cause, I still feel like throwing up at the mere idea of it.

I try to give myself a talking-to. This makes no sense. I dress to be seen every day of my life so why should having people stare at me suddenly be such an issue?

It's the job thing again. I know it is. When I was an account exec, my confidence as high as the sky, what I wore was just an extension of how great I felt about myself. It was part of the quirky persona I had created and what I was known for.

It still is now. I think my fifties style is as much a part of me as my eye colour or my hair. But this modelling business – specifically setting out to make people look at me – that's a different thing altogether. I'm no longer hiding behind the shield of confidence that my job gave me and without it . . .

Perhaps I can wriggle out, I think, on the basis that there are enough other models, making me surplus to requirements, but we won't really know until tomorrow when we can see how many people have turned up, and that'll be too late.

In an attempt to distract myself from one horrible problem, I turn my attention to another. Spencer. The time has come, I decide, to accept that visiting him was a one-time-only offer and as I spurned it (and by implication him) I have lost the chance to go.

I could push him one more time but my dignity won't let me. I have to accept that I cocked that one up. I let Spencer slip through my fingers because I thought my life was strong enough to withstand his departure.

How different things look now. And isn't hindsight a smart-arse?

I take a deep breath and, with shaking fingers, delete Spencer's number from my phone and thus relegate him to my past. I have no idea what will be in my future but, for now at least, I'm not going to worry about that. I have far more immediate problems.

There's a new email from the company that withdrew my interview when they found out that I was working on the homeless shelter fundraising. I can't think what they might want. They made their position resoundingly clear. Curious but also bracing myself for yet another blow, I open it.

Dear Ms Finch,

We hope you are well.

We have seen the TikTok campaign for your pyjama project. It is an interesting piece of work and we would like to talk to you about it. Please attend an interview at . . .

I don't read the rest. There's no point. I won't be going. I don't need a job working for a company like that no matter how desperate things get. They had their chance. They blew it and I have more important things to do.

I delete the email and I can't tell you how good that feels.

When we get to the café, we don't even sit down. There isn't time. Joel appears with a list of one or two last-minute issues and we buzz around with him, working out where the catwalk will be and where the chairs will go. He suggests we section off an area in the kitchen to use as a changing room and has a first-aid screen, but it's pretty tight for all of us and I think we're going to have to abandon our modesty for the evening and just get on with it.

A couple of people from Viraj's office have offered to model and there will be Felix and Charice and the four of us. Ethel is still at home and while I hope she'll be well enough to come, I can't guarantee it, although of course she would take being in the spotlight in her stride. I can tell from Viraj's face that he's as nervous as I am, but Bob and Dawn strut up and down the improvised catwalk with no concerns at all.

By the time we leave at lunchtime we are as ready as we'll ever be, except for the actual clothes – no small part of the overall event.

As Dawn and I cross the car park my phone buzzes with a text. It's from Sara, the charity shop manager.

> *Been thinking. Why don't you come over after we close tonight? We can make a start.*

This is a great idea and will take the pressure off no end. Dawn says she'll swap her shift with Precious and I text back saying that we'll be there at five thirty.

When we arrive, Sara has cleared a hanging rail for us. It looks ominously empty and my stomach churns. Getting the clothes right is the most important part of the entire event and it's weighing heavily on my shoulders. Dawn, by contrast, is barely able to stop bouncing on her toes. I almost have to hold her back.

'I've been putting one or two things in the back,' Sara tells us conspiratorially. 'I know that's kind of cheating but we want to show off our stock at its best and there's no guarantee what we'll have in on any given day.'

When I see what she's saved I have to agree that it was a wise move and I'm incredibly grateful. The pieces are perfect and will form a great base to work from. Then we begin working our way through the rest of the shop.

'Is there a jacket that might go with this dress?' I ask, and Dawn homes in on a little cropped number which will highlight the dress's nipped-in waistline.

'Don't forget we've got male models too,' I say, when the rail is becoming increasingly full of outfits more suited to women.'

'I think my friend Jody is coming,' says Dawn. 'She likes both.'

'Perfect. But we need some things for the boys to model too.'

We work well as a team, with Dawn and I pulling together outfits we like and Sara adding the finishing touches because she knows her stock well and can often put her hands on the perfect accessory.

By around nine o'clock we have the makings of a show. I run a discerning eye over the outfits, now tightly bunched together on the hanging rail, and nod appraisingly. 'You know, that really isn't bad at all. I think we've done it!'

Dawn is still bouncing. Her energy knows no bounds.

'I agree,' says Sara. She lifts her chin proudly and smiles. 'People will struggle to believe it's all come from a charity shop. It'll be great publicity for us. And I gather you've made the pieces for the finale,' she adds, looking at Dawn.

'I have,' replies Dawn, her face suddenly serious. 'I've made two.'

'And they're top secret,' I add, hoping that I don't sound as anxious about this as I feel. Not having seen anything of what Dawn has done is a little bit risky as her creations will be the grand finale to the whole event. I just have to trust that she's moved beyond making clothes using staples and Sellotape.

'It's so exciting,' says Sara, opening her eyes wide. 'I can't wait to see them.'

'They're going to be ace,' says Dawn, but is then uncharacteristically tight-lipped. My stomach turns over again. Who knew this event would have so many moving parts?

I take a deep breath to steady myself. I never got nervous like this when I was working at McDougal & Wright. Then again, I don't remember anything I did there being as important to me as this show is, as these people are.

This really matters. I'm beaming from ear to ear. It really matters and I'm right at its heart, which feels truly amazing.

'Shall I take these clothes with me now? Save us disturbing you tomorrow.'

Sara agrees and I decide that it's just as easy to wheel the rack of outfits through the streets to my flat as it is to go and get the car and bundle them all into that. It's not so far, especially if Dawn can take one end.

We set off slowly, steering the rail along the pavement. One of the wheels has a mind of its own and keeps spinning off in random directions like a shopping trolley but we manage to keep it pretty much under control. We get a couple of odd looks from passers-by, but Dawn and I are well able to deal with odd looks.

'Can I go now?' asks Dawn as we get to the bottom of my road, as if I'm a schoolteacher or her boss.

'Of course. Thanks for your help. I'll see you tomorrow around five?'

Dawn nods and then she's gone, leaving me to woman-handle the unruly rail to my front door. I stop at my gate, fumbling in my bag for my keys.

'Abbie?' someone says and I look up, not sure who I'm expecting to see at this time of night.

It's a man in a fleece and a knitted Aran hat. He has a beard and a wind tan.

'Hello,' I say. 'Can I help you?'

And then I recognise him.

It's Spencer!

67

My heart has gone from a perfectly normal rhythm to something that must surely be off any scale in a split second.

'Spencer!' I squeak because I seem to have lost control of my vocal cords as well. 'What are you doing here?'

'I thought I'd surprise you?' he says, his voice going up at the end of the sentence as if he's not quite sure.

I don't know how to react. Every tiny part of me wants to throw my arms around his neck and hold on to him tight so he can't run away from me again. I want to shower him in kisses right here on my doorstep and have him kiss me back. I want the neighbours to peep round their curtains and think 'Get a room!' when they see us.

But I can't do any of that. I finished things between us. I don't get to play this scene as the epic homecoming. It would send out horrible mixed messages and it's the wrong thing to do. So I hold myself back.

'Mission accomplished,' I say instead. 'I am very surprised! And, actually, your timing is excellent. Can you help me with this lot?' I gesture at the unruly clothes rail.

'Did you rob a Marks & Spencer's?' he asks, looking dubiously at the mismatched selection of garments.

I laugh. 'No. It's for the fashion show I mentioned. It's tomorrow and . . .' Then I realise that we're still standing on the doorstep. 'Let's get inside. I can explain, and then you can.'

Spencer helps me lift the rail up the stairs and into the flat. The rail felt quite manageable in the larger spaces of the shop and the street, but in my little flat it seems to fill most of the available space, leaving Spencer and me trapped on either side of it. I push it to one side so that I can squeeze past and then usher him into the kitchen.

'I'm sorry,' he's saying. 'I suppose I shouldn't have landed on you with no warning. But I booked the flight and then I was coming anyway so I thought . . . Well . . .'

'What would you have done if I hadn't been in?' As I say this, I'm wondering where he thinks he's going to stay. Could he stay here?

I close the thought back down. Spencer and I are over. I ditched him. I need to remember that.

'I don't know,' he says. 'It was a terrible plan. I've got a hotel room, though,' he adds quickly. 'I wasn't . . .'

How is this so awkward? I'm embarrassed. He's embarrassed. Even Elvis looks a bit uncomfortable.

'Look, descending on you like this unannounced was a daft idea. I'll go to the hotel and then maybe we can meet up tomorrow . . .'

'Tomorrow is the fashion show,' I remind him. 'Which is why I couldn't come to you.'

I sound dismissive, even to me. I try to smile to show how pleased I am to see him but he's looking at his feet.

'Oh yes.' His shoulders slump and he looks so dejected that I just want to hug him to make him feel better.

'It's okay,' I say, more kindly. 'Why don't you stay for a cup of tea at least. You can tell me about your puffins.'

He looks at me gratefully and settles himself in one of the chairs at my kitchen table while I bustle about making tea.

'So, what's this show all about?' he asks, and yet again I find myself explaining about Time for Beds and the shelter and how much Bob wants to raise. The figure clearly surprises him but he doesn't question it. I don't mention the community table. It's not that I'm in any way ashamed of my connection with it, but I really don't want him to know how lonely I've been since he left.

We exhaust the subject of the show and then the obvious next one is his life in Scotland, but when a gap opens up in the conversation, he doesn't fill it as I might expect.

'And how are your family?' he asks, even though he's never met any of them.

I lift my mug and eye him over the rim. 'Why are you really here? What's going on?'

Spencer picks at an invisible mark on my table with his fingernail. I wait. Elvis rubs himself against my legs and I give his ears a gentle stroke.

'Not much to tell really,' he says eventually. 'The Outer Hebrides are beautiful. The people are lovely, really friendly. And puffins are super-cute.'

'Well, that all sounds great.'

The 'but' hanging in the air is so loud that it's virtually beating a drum. When it becomes apparent that he's not going to say it, I do.

'But . . . ?'

He won't meet my eye although I don't understand why. None of this is anything to do with me any more, no matter how much I wish that it were. Yet he has sought me out to talk to me about it. That has to mean something, doesn't it?

'But. I don't think I'm cut out for island life.'

I wait for him to elaborate.

'It's cold and dark and there's nothing to do. You can't nip out for a pint of milk or a drink.'

'They do have pubs on Lewis,' I say. I know this because when he first left I spent a fair bit of time on Google Maps exploring his environment and imagining how life might have been if I'd gone too.

'Yes. Lewis is great. But I wasn't on Lewis most of the time. I was on the nature reserve counting birds. I swear if I ever see another gannet, I'll lose my mind. And those Arctic terns! Vicious little buggers. You need a helmet or they'll turn your scalp into a sieve.'

He does an impression of a fast-diving bird with his hand and it makes me laugh.

'What were the other rangers like?' My mind automatically reaches for the image of the pretty woman in the photo.

'The other blokes?' he asks, and the image fades away. 'Happy to spend nights on end playing Uno and watching logs burn,' he says. 'Quite earnest.'

I picture a group of bearded men in thick fisherman's sweaters and try to slot Spencer in among them. It's not easy. And maybe that woman has been a red herring all along. I hope so.

'And I think they all came out of the womb with binoculars round their necks. There isn't anything they don't know about the wildlife and there isn't much I do know. They tried to teach me but, well, it turns out I'm just not that interested.'

'Oh dear. It really wasn't for you then?'

Spencer shakes his head. 'No. Pretty huge mistake.'

'Leaving your life here to go to Scotland?' I know I'm fishing but I can't help myself.

He nods. 'I don't think I've ever been so lonely in my life.'

Now I'm just confused.

'But I thought you were having the best time,' I say, thinking of the perky little messages he's sent me, the ones that made me feel even more wretched.

'I think I was trying to convince myself. I thought I'd get used to it.'

'But you didn't?'

He shakes his head sadly.

'So have you left?'

'Not quite. But I'm not sure I'll be going back for long.'

'And you invited me up because . . . ?' I'm not sure I want to hear the answer. Was I merely a distraction from the tedium or did he genuinely want to see me?

But I don't have the headspace for that conversation. I have a show to run. The team are counting on me and I absolutely can't let myself get distracted by my own personal nonsense.

'Actually,' I add. 'Don't answer that.'

I stand up, signalling an end to the conversation and surprising myself at the same time. It would be the easiest thing in the world to move on to the sofa, sit next to him, snuggle in. Isn't that what I've been longing for?

But not like this. Not now. My head is too full of everything else to deal with surprises and romantic interludes.

'Right,' I say. 'I've a big day tomorrow, so . . .'

'I'll go,' says Spencer, taking my hint at once and jumping to his feet so quickly that Elvis hisses and flies out from under the table. 'I'm sorry. I shouldn't have just turned up like this.'

He's right. He shouldn't. His unexpected arrival has completely ruined my equilibrium and I have enough to do trying to find space in my head as it is.

But I couldn't be more pleased that he did.

'It's fine. I'm just a bit . . .'

'Busy. Yes. I see that.'

At the front door we might have had one of those will-they-won't-they moments you see in films, but I stand far enough back that a kiss is not on the cards. To give him his due, he reads the room correctly and doesn't try, but he's still loitering on my step. There's obviously something else on his mind. I put my hand on the door and begin to inch it closed because I really don't think my self-restraint can handle much more pressure.

'Can I come?' he asks, the words coming out in a rush. 'To the show?'

I'm uncomfortable enough about the whole modelling business as it is. The last thing my confidence needs is Spencer in the audience. My lack of enthusiasm must be obvious, because he backs away.

'Sorry. I can see you don't want me around. Stupid. Well, I hope it goes really well for you. Goodbye, Abbie.'

And then he turns and lets himself out, leaving me wondering what just happened.

68

Because it's the night before the most important event in my diary for some time and I need to be at my sparkly best, I can't sleep. My head buzzes with Spencer and how unresolved that situation suddenly is. Why didn't I just tell him how I feel, that I wish I'd never finished things, that I've missed him every day?

But he didn't say any of that either. He's upset at making a mess of his life and he just wanted someone who knew about it to chat it through with. And him coming to see the show. That's probably just because he hasn't got anything else to do and he's curious. Again, not really anything to do with me.

Those thoughts segue neatly into my anxiety about the show and how wrong it all might go, and from there it is only a short hop to what am I doing with my life, how quickly the time is flying by and how will I pay my bills?

And the result of all this nocturnal analysis?

No sleep.

Instead I use the wee small hours to put name labels on all the clothes so we know who is supposed to be wearing what. I have to guess at some of the sizes but I manage to split the outfits fairly evenly between all the models.

It crosses my mind that I could just appoint myself dresser and not allocate myself any clothes at all. But I know I can't do that. This is a team event and we all have to join in.

It's not quite true that I don't get any sleep. When I've finished with the labels, I tumble back into bed and finally drift off around six thirty, a mere two hours before my alarm wakes me up again. When I look at myself in the bathroom mirror, I most definitely don't see a supermodel staring back at me.

Oh God. What was I thinking, volunteering to do this? The idea of walking up that catwalk is still making me feel sick. What if I fall over in front of all those people? 'Because you fall over in the street all the time, Abbie,' my rational head tells me. And it's right. There is no reason to suppose that I will fall or even trip or let my clothes drop down around my ankles or do any of the other stupid things that my imagination is convinced are going to happen. I am perfectly capable of putting one foot in front of the other without incident so I need to stop imagining disaster and just crack on.

I haul myself into the shower and try to run through my to-do list but my head keeps going back to Spencer and how forlorn he looked.

What does he want?

And more importantly, what do I want?

The day crawls by with me getting more and more nervous as the appointed hour approaches, but eventually the time arrives and I make my way to the café with the clothes. I had to dismantle the clothes rail to get it back out of the flat and ended up putting it and the clothes on the back seat of my car. I then rebuild it in the supermarket car park. As I roll the laden rail across the tarmac, people smile at me supportively. The posters for the show have been prominently displayed inside so I assume they know what I'm doing with a rail of clothes and it's not just because they think I've come unhinged.

The café has closed for the day and the current Saturday girl is sweeping up between the tables. Joel is then moving them to one side to make room for the catwalk and Liz is lining the chairs up along the edges in neat lines.

Bob sees me struggling with the rail and rushes over to help.

'This is it,' he says in a voice that seems over-bright. 'Our big moment.'

I grimace at him.

'Come on. It'll be fine. We're just walking around in some second-hand clothes. How hard can it be?'

And when he puts it like that I have to agree.

We wheel the clothes through to the makeshift dressing area, him peering at the labels as we go to try and work out what he will be wearing.

'Don't mess up the order,' I say sharply but with a smile. 'You'll see what I've picked for you soon enough.'

It's Bob's turn to pull a face. 'I hope you've been kind.'

'Of course. You'll look fabulous, darling!' I say in an affected tone. Bob gives a little shimmy of his shoulders, which makes me laugh.

When we get back out into the main café, we find Ethel directing a slightly chagrined-looking Joel on how to arrange the refreshments without any concessions made for the fact that this is what he does for a living.

'No,' she says as if she's talking to a small and particularly stupid boy, 'put the drinks at the far end of the line or no one will buy any food.'

Joel nods like this is a revelation.

'Ethel!' I say, delighted to see her. And then, 'Should you be doing this? Are you . . .'

I am going to say 'up to it' but one of her arched-eyebrow looks stops me mid-sentence and I do a quick U-turn. '. . . happy with everything?'

She gives a single nod to acknowledge how well I changed direction and continues.

'I am. I've checked final numbers with Viraj and we have the correct number of chairs with a couple spare in case, glasses, etc., for the attendees. Joel has done an excellent job with the refreshments and you have the clothes in hand, I see. This has the makings of quite an event.'

She winks at me and I see that her spirit is back.

'I hope you're right.'

She reaches out her tiny hand and rests it on my arm. 'It will be perfect, Abigail.'

Her eyes find mine and they say more to me than words ever could. A huge wave of gratitude for her friendship washes over me. I don't know what I've done to deserve these wonderful people in my life but I couldn't be more delighted.

Sal, Lucy and Meena arrive first, followed by two women from Viraj's office. They bring with them an air of bubbling excitement dusted over with a tiny pinch of nerves, which is demonstrated by them talking ten to the dozen and laughing over-loudly and often. Soon the little gang appears to be as thick as thieves.

I'm pleased to see Sal and the others and I really hope they like what I've been doing for the last two months. It's important that they are on board with this new version of me, and also, I realise, that they forgive me for the old one.

Felix and Charice are next to arrive, and are more or less on time, which must surely be Charice's doing as Felix is never punctual if he's under his own steam.

I smile a greeting. 'Hi, you two. Thanks for coming. We'll be starting to get ready in a few minutes if you can just wait over there with the others.'

'Has anyone seen Dawn or Viraj?' I ask the general throng. I have a phone number for Viraj but I've no way of getting in touch with Dawn. I'm just thinking that this was a pretty major oversight and am making emergency plans for the finale in the event that Dawn fails to show, when I hear Bob swear.

'What's up?' I ask, my already panicked state thrust on to an even higher alert.

Bob is staring at the entrance to the café. There's a pretty blonde woman standing there with two teenage children. She lifts a hand waist high and waves it uncertainly in our direction.

'It's Sonia,' Bob says, incredulity dripping from his words. 'And they're me kids – Chloe and Jake. What the hell are they doing here?'

He turns to face me, and his expression is pure terror. 'Do I look okay?'

'You look fantastic. Go and say hello.'

He stares at me and then over at his family, and then he drops his shoulders and gives himself a little shake. 'Right,' he says. Then he plasters a huge smile over his face and heads towards them.

69

I try to watch Bob with his family without making it obvious that I'm watching. His body language signals nervousness. His frame looks smaller than it usually does, his arms held tightly in against his body and his head bowed. He reminds me of a dog that is expecting to be beaten.

But a glance at his family suggests that this isn't what they have in mind. Sonia wears a tentative smile but his daughter seems thrilled to see him, waving enthusiastically as he approaches. I watch as Bob relaxes, looks surprised and then delighted. Then he starts to tell them something. He turns to point at me and I'm caught staring at them. Embarrassed, I quickly turn away, looking for something to do. I decide to go and invite the models to start getting into their first outfits.

'Thanks so much for coming,' I tell the collected bunch. 'We really couldn't do this without you. I've put the clothes out in the order that we'll walk and I've labelled everything. Do you want to come and see?'

They follow me, making jokes about what I might have chosen for them to wear as we go. I see that Bob is laughing now, his head thrown back. It's hard to drag my attention from him as we round the corner and go into the changing area.

'I've grouped the outfits into themes,' I say. 'Everyday, work-wear, "out out" and vintage. I wanted to do a whole seventies section but it's almost impossible to pick that stuff up in charity shops these days so that part is more retro-inspired than actual retro.'

I explain how they get one outfit in each theme to give them time to get changed between runs – not much time, it has to be said, but this was always going to be a bit pressured.

Charice finds her outfits and is surprisingly appreciative. I like her more and more. Felix takes more convincing, but Charice is all over it, cajoling him into cooperation in a way I've rarely seen anyone manage. Everyone else is happy just to do as they're told.

'What've you got for me?' asks Viraj, who has appeared from nowhere and is peering at the rail anxiously.

'Nothing awful, I promise, but my brother and Bob are here. They can take your outfits and you can bow out gracefully if you want.'

It has to be said that he looks tempted, but then he shakes his head with as strong a display of mind over matter as I've seen.

'All for one and one for all,' he says, and he actually looks like he might believe it.

'That's the spirit.'

And then Bob appears at my shoulder with a smile so broad it makes the rest of his face crinkle up so much that I can barely see his features.

'Chloe saw the TikTok.' His eyes are glistening. 'She said she was proud of me. Sonia said so too. She said, and I quote, "I knew the real Bob Hoskins was still in there somewhere." Those were her exact words. They've got tickets for the show. They want to see me strut me stuff.' His head does a little dance on his shoulders. He's clearly delighted.

I'm delighted too, and I throw nasal caution to the wind and hurl my arms around his shoulders.

'Oh, Bob. I'm so pleased. That's fabulous.'

I see that his cheeks are wet and I wonder whether I should give him some space to compose himself, but either he's not aware or, more likely, he just doesn't care.

'They're proud of me,' he says again quietly, as if he's reassuring himself rather than telling me. 'Proud.'

I'm tempted to say that they jolly well should be, but that's not my place, so instead I murmur again about how wonderful it is. Then he puts a hand on my arm and steers me gently to the back of the space where we can talk without being overheard.

'Listen, Abbie,' he says without meeting my eye. 'If I ask you something, will you be honest with me?'

'Of course,' I say, hoping that I can deliver.

'It's a bit . . .' He screws up his face, clearly embarrassed about what's coming next. 'Jake just said that I smell a bit. Of BO. I don't know if he's just saying that because he expects me to smell or because it's actually true. The thing is, no one's ever said that to me before. And they would surely have done if it was right, wouldn't they? So I don't know what to make of it.'

I feel like a total heel. But what can I say? I am that person who called myself his friend but never mentioned that he has a body odour issue. I swallow and nod.

'You do smell a bit,' I say. 'Just sometimes.'

My chest tightens as I wait to see how he's going to react. Have I just single-handedly blown our friendship apart?

There's a beat whilst he takes in what I've said. 'Okay. Wish I'd known that sooner but thanks for being honest,' he says.

I could shoot myself on the spot, but there's nothing dark in his tone. It seems to be a genuine thank you.

'Do you reckon they have a staff shower here?' he asks.

'I've no idea but I can ask Liz. Would you like me to? Discreetly.'

Bob nods. 'If my lot are proud of me again, I don't want to do anything to mess it up.' He's grinning again and then he adds, 'I can't believe they saw that TikTok.'

'Almost two million people saw that TikTok,' I say. 'It's not that surprising that your family were among them.'

'When you put it like that . . . Chloe said she showed everyone at school. Told them all it was her dad. Can you believe that? After all those months of them not wanting anything to do with me. Suddenly I'm TikTok famous and not embarrassing. You couldn't make it up.' He chortles to himself. His laughter is infectious, setting me off too, although mine is touched with an element of hysteria too. 'Do you know what,' he adds. 'I'll ask Liz about the shower me sen.'

And then he virtually skips away to find her.

70

And then Dawn arrives, dressed in her usual array of colours. She glides down the newly created café catwalk as if she'd been born on a red carpet, flicking her head left and right, greeting her crowds, although we haven't opened the space up to the audience yet so there's no one to see her except us. She's got a couple of suit carriers slung over her shoulder, which I assume contain the outfits for the finale.

'Bev lent me these special bag things,' she shouts to me as she approaches. 'They're like they use at real fashion shows. Look!'

'They're great. Shall we hang your outfits up so they don't get creased?'

Even as I say this, I'm wondering what the carriers are going to contain and whether creasing will actually be an issue. The clothes might be made out of scrunched-up newspaper for all I know. But Dawn nods like this might be a good idea and takes the garments out of the carriers and hangs them up. They look promising. Very promising indeed.

After that it's all a bit of a blur. Joel starts to let the guests into the café and the background noise increases as they buy glasses of fizz and eat the dinky little canapés. Backstage we get ourselves organised with everyone putting on their opening outfits – the first theme is daywear, and we have some great pieces, styled in a slightly quirky manner by Dawn and me.

Liz pops over to wish us luck.

'Well, look at you lot,' she says, shaking her head in disbelief. 'Who'd have thought it, eh? I'm dead proud of you all, I really am. Break a leg!'

There are five minutes to go until the show is due to begin. I peep out from behind the canvas screen and beckon Joel over.

'Can you get them to take their places so we can start?' I ask him.

'Will do,' he says with a little salute. I think he's quite enjoying himself. 'Is someone going to say a few words before we kick off?'

Shit! I hadn't thought of that but of course we should.

'Hang on!' I gather the other four together. 'Someone needs to say a few words, to introduce the show and what we're trying to do. Any volunteers?'

Viraj instantly loses two inches in height.

'It should be Robert,' says Ethel in her crisp voice. 'He's the obvious choice.'

Bob appears to have found a shower because his hair is still slightly damp and he smells of mint and eucalyptus. Dressed in his first outfit instead of his customary navy-blue parka he looks like a new man. He rubs his chin thoughtfully and then he nods.

'Okay,' he says as if he's convincing himself. 'I can do that.'

Then he makes a move towards the audience who are settling themselves into their seats.

'Hang on!' I say in an urgent stage whisper. 'You can't go out like that. You'll spoil the reveal.' I look around for something for him to wear over the top of his outfit but there's nothing to hand, and I don't want him to put that infernal anorak back on.

316

'I know!' Dawn pulls open cupboards until she finds what she's looking for – a huge roll of black bin bags. Then she pulls a hole in the top of one and passes it back to Bob.

'A bin bag for the homeless rubbish,' he says, nodding his head slowly. 'Very appropriate, Dawn.'

Dawn's brow furrows at this. 'You're not really rubbish though, Bob,' she says just to be sure.

'No, Dawn,' he replies with a gentle smile. 'I'm not.'

Moments later we hear Joel welcoming people to the evening and then he introduces Bob, and Bob, bin bag over his head so that it shrouds the top half of his outfit, goes out.

The clapping dies down and Bob begins to speak. We huddle together out of sight and listen.

'A while back, some little bastards, excuse me language, nicked me tools out of the back of me van. They didn't care. They just wanted some quick cash to score. But that one thing was the start of me whole life falling to bits. I lost me business. I lost me house. I lost me wife and kids.' He turns to one side and I assume he's looking at Sonia. 'And caught up with all of that, I also lost me dignity.'

The hush is so complete that I hardly dare breathe for fear of spoiling it.

'No one wants to be on the streets without a pot to piss in. But sometimes that's where life takes you. They talk about a downwards spiral and that's just what it felt like. One minute I was a respected member of society. The next I was lower than a stray dog.

'And that's where the hostel came in. They gave me a bed and some food. They gave me somewhere I could spend time without worrying about getting me head kicked in or someone peeing on me when I was asleep.'

He pauses to let the reality of his words sink in. He's good at this, I realise. He has a natural command of the room. Then his body language changes. We can't see his face but I know he's smiling.

317

'Fast forward a bit and I had a few coins in me pocket and somewhere to stay and I saw a notice in here.'

He looks around the café and then walks towards the huge plate-glass window. Our sign is leaning there and he plucks it up and starts reading.

'Community table. A place to sit and make new friends. Joel over there, he started a scheme where customers could put a price of a cup of coffee on the tab too.'

Joel acknowledges the praise and tries, not that successfully, to look modest.

'So I came. And I sat. And then I met some of the best friends I've ever had.'

A lump comes to my throat and I feel tears pricking my eyes. Ethel reaches for my hand and squeezes it gently.

'We're a proper mixed bunch and you'd never have put us together. But together we are. The community tablers. Stupid name, I know, but that's us. The mismatched, the lonely, the ones who at that particular moment didn't quite fit in, didn't know which way to turn.'

My chest tightens as he describes me like that, knowing that my friends and family are listening. But he's right. Difficult though it might be to hear, he's hit the nail on the head.

'And now you're all here too,' he continues, 'to help us make ten grand for the shelter so that average people, just like me, can get themselves back on their feet when their life turns to shit. So let's have a great night. Open your hearts – and your wallets – and we'll get this show on the road.'

The applause is deafening, and then Bob, in his black bin bag, reappears, his cheeks flushed but his smile wide.

'Was I okay?' he asks.

'You were brilliant,' I say, hugging him as hard as I can.

71

Joel starts the music and 'I Gotta Feeling' starts booming out over the sound system. According to my list, Viraj and I are the first out. I did that on purpose so we didn't have too long to feel nervous. I'm entirely terrified but I take his hand and pull him out on to the catwalk.

Bob has rigged up some spotlights, which is great because it means we can't really see the audience. It's too bright to see further than the end of the catwalk.

'We've got this,' I whisper to Viraj, although given the volume of the Black Eyed Peas it's unlikely he's heard me.

At the start of the catwalk, I feel him falter. I could just keep hold of his hand and drag him with me but I don't. Instead, I take a deep breath, pull my shoulders back and raise my chin as if I'm walking through a crowded restaurant in my most beautiful vintage dress. And then I set off, matching my steps to the beat of the music. The audience claps. Bob's speech has hit its target and they are totally with me.

I'm wearing a plissé skirt in lavender with an oversized chunky-knit sweater in neon yellow. The colour combination is striking and I love the feel of the skirt as it swishes around my legs when I move.

I've only gone a few steps when I see Viraj out of the corner of my eye. He looks great, his long, lean shape totally rocking a classic roll-neck and chinos combination. He has that rabbit in the headlights look though, and I wink at him as the applause sounds around us. Then he too seems to find his confidence and he even manages a little twirl.

By the time we get back to the changing area where Sal and Meena are waiting to take our places, I'm as high as a kite.

'Okay?' I mouth at Viraj over the noise.

He turns the corners of his mouth, raises his eyebrows and nods like he can't quite believe that he survived.

But there's no time to congratulate ourselves – we need to get changed into our next outfit. We throw ourselves into the chaos of the changing room and virtually tear the clothes off before struggling into the next set.

Everything runs remarkably smoothly. We have a sticky moment when a zip on a pair of polyester trousers eats itself and won't move up or down. Viraj's colleague, who is in the trousers at the time, remains calm, however, and Ethel manages to ease it back into action. The audience continues to clap with as much enthusiasm as we had at the start and the atmosphere crackles.

And then all too quickly we are down to the last two outfits, the ones that Dawn has created.

Ethel is to go out first. Her outfit is an elegant evening dress. The bodice is a pale pink silky fabric and Dawn has sewn in tulle sleeves so that Ethel's arms are visible but covered. It then drops down to a skirt also made of tulle, this time in pale grey, that cascades like a waterfall to Ethel's ankles. It could be a costume for a ballet but it still looks like a dress.

There's barely time to appreciate it, however, before Ethel slips beyond the fabric screen and out into the lights. The clapping increases considerably as she appears. I assume it's something to do with both her age and the fact that people know Dawn made this one, but then Bob says, 'My God. Look at her go!' and we all rush over to the screen and peer out.

Ethel is making her way down the catwalk in the beautiful pink and grey gown en pointe. She raises her willowy arms above her head and courus her way to the end, taking tiny little steps on the tips of her toes like a real ballerina – which, of course, she is.

'Did you know she could still do that?' I ask Dawn.

Dawn looks totally unfazed. 'Yeah,' she says, like seeing an eighty-four-year-old woman walking on the tips of her toes is an everyday occurrence. I love Dawn.

Dawn is ready in her outfit too. She has taken the brief of it being a wedding dress but missed the part about it being white. She's used scraps of fabric in all the brightest jewel colours she could find and sewn them all together to make a rainbow of a gown. There is even a rainbow train that drags on the floor behind her.

The audience are applauding wildly and we all push the screen aside now so we can watch her do her thing.

Dawn laps up the attention, strutting and twirling so that it takes her at least three times as long to get to the end of the catwalk as it took everyone else. It doesn't matter though. The audience loves her. They clap and whoop so loud that Justin Timberlake's 'Can't Stop the Feeling!' is almost drowned out.

Finally, she gets back to our end of the catwalk and then beckons for us to join her. The other models go first and then the four of us follow, each dressed in a pair of our by now surely world-famous pyjama bottoms and a white T-shirt. I feel like I'm flying. This is the best moment of my life so far!

Gradually the clapping dies down and Joel takes the microphone once again.

'Well, what a show!' he says. 'When they first asked me if we could host this here I knew that we were on to a winner. As you know, our café has always tried to show support for those that need it. Our community table and the coffee-for-a-stranger scheme have been so successful that the business wants to roll them out to other cafés across the chain. And now this! Thank you all for coming and showing so much support for our supermodels.'

He turns and claps in our direction, encouraging the audience to do the same. We beam and swell with pride, nudging each other in embarrassed disbelief.

'As you know,' Joel continues, 'everything you've seen tonight is for sale, and we have card readers available for those of you who just wish to donate to the fund. Please be generous.'

Bob sneaks up behind him and grabs the microphone. 'Don't forget,' he says, his tone suddenly serious, his smile gone. 'We are all just a few short steps from calamity.'

72

Sara and her team from the charity shop leap into action to help with the sales and within twenty minutes almost everything we showcased has been sold. I spot Sal and Meena with bulging bags and it makes me smile. I catch Sal's eye and mouth 'thanks' at her across people's heads. 'Well done you,' she mouths back.

We also get several offers for Dawn's dresses. I had intended to auction them off but in all the excitement of this week I forgot to set it up. Dawn, however, is all over it. She finds out who is wanting to buy and then shouts from one customer to the other.

'Oi! You who wants Ethel's dress . . .'

The woman, herself quite elegant and understated and definitely not used to being shouted at, is startled but points to her chest questioningly.

'Yeah. You. This one wants to buy it for one hundred and fifty pounds. But you want it. So what will you pay?'

The woman looks very taken aback but then throws herself into the spirit. 'Er, two hundred,' she calls back.

Dawn looks at her other potential purchaser. 'Well?'

'Two hundred and twenty-five?' she says obligingly.

Dawn nods. 'Did you hear that,' she bellows across the café.

The elegant woman nods, raises her chin and shouts, 'Three hundred, but that's my final offer.'

The first bidder, looking relieved that this is at an end, bows out graciously and the winner looks delighted with her success, before realising that everyone is watching, at which point she blushes furiously.

'Can we have a photo?' asks the reporter from the *Evening Post*, there to cover the event and appearing like magic at the woman's elbow. 'Of you and your dress.'

'It's not hers yet,' says Dawn as she presses through the crowds with the card reader.

The transaction is completed and the woman is swept away by the reporter.

'Happy?' I say to Bob.

'Yep,' he replies, shaking his head from side to side. 'We did all this,' he adds. 'Wait until I tell Bernie.'

'Do you reckon we have enough for your giant cheque? Ten grand. It's a lot of money.'

'The cheque doesn't really matter,' he says. 'It was just a little dream of mine.'

'I hear that little dreams are all the rage,' I reply and he gives me another hug.

Then Chloe, his daughter, is at his side. 'You were ace, Dad, I filmed it all. It's on my story.'

Bob scoops her into his arms and hugs her. 'Thanks, Princess,' he says, his eyes shining.

Next to appear are Xander and Lou, both grinning. Lou raises a bag that I assume contains something she's bought.

'That was fantastic, sis,' says Xander, kissing me on both cheeks just as Mum and Dad appear.

'That was super, love,' says Dad with a broad smile.

'Aw, thanks, Dad. Bit different from my usual kind of gig.'

I bite my lip while I wait for his reaction.

Dad gives me one of the winks that he used to give me when I learned to ride my bike or fly a kite on my own.

'Yes,' he says. 'I think you might have finally found where you fit.'

I bristle, not sure how to take this or what he's really saying. But the look on his face is so genuine that I realise it's not a criticism. And he's right. I do fit in here. I relax and grin back at him. 'I think you're right,' I say.

The moment is interrupted by Mum. 'That was super. Wait until I tell everyone that my daughter has given up her marketing job to be a catwalk model.'

I don't correct her, ridiculous as it is. Let her have her moment.

'Thanks for coming,' I say instead and then Felix and Charice appear too. 'Thanks so much for your help, you two.'

'It was a right laugh,' says Felix. 'I reckon there might be something in this modelling lark. I'm going to contact some agencies, see if I can't pick up a bit of work.'

Charice, standing just out of his line of sight, bites her lips together to suppress a giggle. I like her more and more.

And then I spot Spencer. I had no idea that he was coming, and I'm very glad I didn't know he was out there when I was on the catwalk, but now my heart is in my throat at the sight of him standing there looking all awkward and handsome. I've missed him so much.

He's loitering, clearly not sure whether he should come across or not, so I wave him over and then move in his direction, leaving my family to listen to Felix planning his new career. We meet in the middle.

'You were great,' he says when we're close enough to hear one another.

'Thanks. It was fun. In the end.'

We stand, self-consciously staring at one another until a switch in my head flicks over and I pull him in to me and squeeze him tightly.

'I've missed you,' he breathes into my hair.

'Oh, me too. So much. It was such a horrible mistake, letting you go. I didn't realise at the time and I've tried so hard to move on. But I've done a really bad job of it.'

I squeeze a little harder.

'Can we go back to where we were?' he asks. 'Before I went to Scotland?'

And I'm just about to answer when I hear Dawn's shrill voice.

'Is this Spencer? We saw your puffin pictures. You shouldn't have left, though. You made Thingy dead sad.'

God bless Dawn!

'Spencer, meet Dawn,' I say without turning round. 'And I wasn't that sad.'

'You didn't cry much but you were sad. I could tell.'

Note to self. Never, ever underestimate people. 'I was a bit sad,' I admit.

Spencer touches my cheek with the back of his hand. It's rougher than it was before he left, weather worn from all that puffin spotting.

'Me too,' he says.

I savour this moment to the extent that I can with Dawn looking on and the café in chaos around me. Then I pull myself back into practical mode.

'We're going to clear up here and then we're all going for a drink to celebrate. Please come with us.'

'I'd love to,' he says. 'Can I help with anything?'

We get stuck into the clearing up and by ten o'clock it's all over. The floors are swept and mopped, the rails packed away and the tables and chairs put back where they belong.

Viraj plucks the community table sign from where Bob put it down.

'Do we still need this?' he asks. 'I think we can sit where we like now.'

He's right. We're no longer a disparate group of the lost and lonely. Now we're the tightest bunch of mates you could ever wish for.

'It's not just for us though,' says Dawn. 'What about all the other lonely people?'

Viraj replaces the sign carefully.

Dawn is, as ever, right.

73

It's Monday morning. The spring sunshine blasts through my kitchen window and Elvis almost trips me up as I make my way to the kettle.

All is right in the world.

'Tea?' I shout through to Spencer.

'Please,' he says, 'but then I need to go and catch my train.'

He's heading back to Scotland to resign and collect his stuff, but then he'll be back. Neither of us has a job and he has nowhere to live, but right now none of that feels even vaguely troubling.

'Do you mind if I don't come with you?' I say as I fill the kettle and flick it on. 'I need to be at the café at ten.'

'No worries. You have some serious celebrating to do. Any idea how much you've made?'

I shake my head and I realise that I'm nervous about this. I know it was always an arbitrary figure plucked from the air, but I really want Bob to have made his ten thousand pounds for the shelter.

We sit at the table and drink our tea. Elvis paces between us and then goes and rubs himself against Spencer's leg. That cat has great taste.

An email pings in on my phone and I open it.

Dear Abbie,

*You sound like exactly the kind of miracle worker
we have in mind. Fancy coming in for a chat?*

Best wishes,

Ali Dale

Miracle Worker in Chief

'Anything interesting?' asks Spencer as he crunches his toast.
'Yes. I think it might be,' I reply.

When I get to the café Bob and Ethel are already sitting at the
table. Not the community table but another one with a view over
the car park. I get a flat white and a celebratory piece of rocky road
and join them.

'Well, this feels all kinds of weird,' I say, tipping my head
towards our erstwhile home.

'Indeed,' agrees Ethel. 'But we need to vacate the space to allow
others to discover it. I assume Joel will reinstate the table after
they've done the refurbishment.'

'I reckon he will,' replies Bob, and we all signal our agreement.
How could he not now?

And then something else occurs to me.

'Ethel,' I say, shaking my head at her. 'I can't believe you did
your catwalk en pointe!'

Ethel had disappeared quickly after the show, no doubt
exhausted by her efforts on the back of her stay in hospital, and so
we hadn't had the chance to talk to her about it.

'I'll admit it's not as easy as it once was,' she says. 'But I try.'

'You were ace,' says Bob. 'Bloody incredible, in fact.'

Ethel wafts the compliment away with an elegant wave of her dancer's hand, but there's that tiny *Mona Lisa* smile at her lips.

'Do we know how much we made yet?' I ask, but Bob shakes his head.

'Waiting for Viraj,' he says.

Dawn arrives next.

'Can we do another fashion show next week?' she asks before she's even sat down.

Laughter ensues.

When Viraj arrives he has his backpack with him. He sits down and slips his laptop out. We all wait with bated breath as he opens it up and navigates to a page.

'And the grand total is . . .' he says, turning the laptop round so we can all see the screen.

We peer at the rows of numbers, trying to work out what we're looking at.

Bob gets there first. 'Not . . . ?' He looks up at Viraj. 'Not that . . .'

Viraj nods.

'Bloody hell,' says Bob, leaning back in his chair and puffing out his cheeks.

'How much? How much?' squeals Dawn.

'Ten thousand, three hundred and forty-six pounds and eighteen pence,' says Viraj.

Dawn looks from one to the other of us. 'So, is that the same as ten grand then?' she checks.

'It is,' says Bob. 'And a bit extra for good measure.'

Dawn leaps to her feet and proceeds to do a little happy dance in the middle of the café. I don't bat an eyelid.

Liz looks over from her station at the counter. 'Good news, love?'

'We've made ten grand for Bob's shelter,' says Dawn in a voice loud enough that the entire café can hear.

'Well done,' comes a voice from a neighbouring table.

'Yes, very well done indeed,' comes another.

A little shimmer of pride runs from my head all the way down to the tips of my toes.

We get the giant cheque made up and Bob tells Bernie that he'd like to see her. I ring the nice reporter from the *Evening Post* too. Then we all go and watch as Bob, in his new clothes with his hair clean, hands the cheque over to Bernie.

I swear there isn't a dry eye in the house.

'This is just wonderful, Bob,' says Bernie gratefully in her lovely Irish brogue. 'When you said you wanted to raise some cash, I had no idea you were talking on this scale.'

'Couldn't have done it on me own,' he says. 'It was a team effort.'

'That's some team you've got there,' she says.

And I couldn't have put it better myself.

ACKNOWLEDGEMENTS

Thank you for reading my book. I really hope you enjoyed it. The idea for the story came to me when I saw a sign for a community table outside the café at my local supermarket. I have since wondered whether I dreamed it because when I went back to investigate more fully the sign had gone.

However, the idea stayed with me and gradually grew into the story. I was interested to explore modern loneliness. We all live such busy lives with so much happening online, and sometimes it can be difficult to make the time for old-fashioned human contact. One day you might look round and realise that you haven't actually seen your friends for weeks. It's easily done.

As you'll know, it takes more than just me to write a book. Thank you so much to all the team at Amazon Publishing. They really know publishing and are a joy to work with. Special mentions go to my editors Victoria Oundjian, Victoria Pepe and Sophie Wilson, who put up with my panics beautifully and steered me through to calmer waters.

Thanks also to my wonderful family. They are my biggest supporters and are always there in the background cheering me on.

And finally, thank you to you for taking the time to read the book. None of this works without you, and I am more grateful than I could ever express.

As you may know, I also write as Imogen Clark and you can find out all about me and my books at https://imogenclark.com/. Please follow me on Amazon as both Izzy Bromley and Imogen Clark and then you'll be the first to hear any news. Finally, if you enjoyed the book please consider leaving a rating or review to help other readers to find it too.

THE COACH TRIP

Looking for more from Izzy Bromley? Turn the page for an extract from *The Coach Trip*.

1

I'm SO sorry

'Mel, what can I say? I'm SO sorry.'

I press my hands together in a prayer of sorts as I try to get across to my best friend just how very, very sorry I am.

Mel stands, arms folded and her head tipped to one side, and stares at me. In the twenty-odd years that we've been friends and over the very, very many cock-ups I've made in that time, I've rarely seen her look as cross as this. Even her hair looks cross.

'You had one thing to do, Emma,' she says. 'One thing!'

I wish our grotty carpet would split and swallow me up so that I wouldn't have to look at her any more. It's not so much her anger. I know that'll pass. Mel's temper is like a firework – all bangs and sparks and then lost to the night sky as quickly as it arrived. But it's the disappointment that lies beneath that's harder to deal with. I've let her down.

Again.

I hang my head.

'If I could turn back time . . .' I try, which sounds pathetic even to me.

Mel is having none of it.

'And it's not only me that you wrecked things for. There's poor Jonathan too. All that effort he made. Ruined.'

This isn't entirely true. I didn't ruin the entire evening. And actually, I bet this was the most interesting thing to happen to Mel's new boyfriend in years. But of course, this isn't the moment to point that out.

'Well, at least you managed to salvage the end of the night,' I say, and then, when I see Mel's raised eyebrows, instantly wish that I hadn't. I shake my head and look down at the swirls on the carpet again. 'I know, I know,' I say. 'That's not the point.'

'What I don't get,' continues Mel, 'is how you could have forgotten. It's not like we didn't talk about Valentine's night. We've talked about virtually nothing else for days.'

This isn't strictly accurate either. Mel talked about Valentine's for days. I, having no one in my life to surprise me with a huge romantic gesture, just listened to her endless speculations about what Jonathan might have planned.

She's right, though. I'm not sure how I could have forgotten. He'd sneakily passed me the card, all cloak and dagger, with instructions to hand it to Mel before she left for work on Valentine's Day.

And somehow the blessed thing slipped my mind.

How was I supposed to know that it contained all the instructions for the romantic night that he'd arranged? He should have mentioned that it was more than just your common-or-garden card when he gave it to me and then I might have taken more notice.

But no.

There is no excuse.

Whichever way you cut it, I am a rubbish friend.

'I don't know what to say,' I try again. 'I really am sorry. But I'll make it up to you. I promise.'

This is a rash statement as I doubt there is anything I can do to fix her ruined night. It was a once-in-a-lifetime experience, the kind of story you'd be telling your grandchildren decades later, and I'd blown it for her.

'I keep picturing Jonathan waiting on that train platform,' Mel says, her eyes straying to the stained ceiling as she imagines the scene. 'He must have thought I'd stood him up. And he had that massive bunch of red roses. It was all so romantic.' And then she tightens her lips into a thin line. 'Or it would have been. If you'd just given me the card.'

Suddenly, and I'm really not proud of this, I want to laugh. The desire to giggle is almost overwhelming, even though giggling now would be about the most inappropriate thing I could do. This is the time to be contrite, remorseful, repentant. I need Mel to understand that even though I am a crap friend and I let her down more often than Northern Rail, I am very, very sorry.

But my mouth doesn't seem to understand the importance of this moment and my lips start to twitch. I bite them together, but I fear it's too late. The giggle is building from my stomach. I can feel it making its bubbling way up my spine.

I tense my shoulders to try and stop it escaping, but it's a determined little blighter and before I can say 'sackcloth and ashes' it's out of my mouth. A full-blown guffaw made all the worse by my trying to contain it.

Mel looks at me as if I've just produced a steak at a vegan barbecue. Her jaw drops and she begins to shake her head slowly in disbelief.

'God, I'm sorry,' I say, trying to stifle my laughter with a futile hand. 'But it is kind of funny.'

'What is? You single-handedly wrecking my extraordinarily romantic Valentine's night out? Oh yes, Emma,' she says coldly. 'It's absolutely hilarious. Pardon me while I pee my pants.'

'But Jonathan standing there at the station waiting for you,' I splutter, 'with all those roses and the table booked and everything, and you waiting here for him to turn up, getting crosser and crosser. You've got to see the funny side.'

And then Mel's mouth creases a little at the edges. It's not much, but it's enough, and I know that it's going to be all right. She rolls her eyes and lets out a sigh.

'I suppose it is a bit funny,' she concedes. 'If you ignore the fact that you wilfully forgot . . .'

'It wasn't wilful,' I interrupt. 'A genuine accident.'

She looks at me down her nose like our headmistress used to do.

'. . . that you wilfully forgot to give me a Valentine's card that my boyfriend had entrusted to you. And on Valentine's Day, which should have been a pretty big memory jogger.'

'But you did get to the club,' I say. 'After he texted to find out where you were. I mean, I know you missed the candlelit dinner, but the evening wasn't a complete disaster.'

Mel holds up a warning finger.

'Don't push it, Em,' she says, and I know that if I'm not entirely forgiven already, it won't be far away.

'Listen,' I say. 'What if I pay for you and Jonathan to go for a romantic dinner somewhere to make up for it?'

As I say this, I'm thinking of my meagre bank balance and the overdraft that I absolutely promised myself I wouldn't dip into again this month. But needs must.

Mel considers my offer and nods slowly, as if it's a good start. My mind is running into overdrive now as I scrabble for other ways to make it up to her, because I really am sorry, and I can't bear the idea that I might have wobbled our friendship. Mel has a lot to put up with, living with me and my chaos. I want her to know that I really appreciate her.

'And how about we go away for a girly weekend?' I add. 'Just the two of us.'

Mel is smiling at me now in the way you might smile at a puppy that's just walked dirty paw prints all over a clean floor but is just so cute that you can't get annoyed.

Encouraged, I press on.

'How about the weekend of your birthday?' I suggest, ignoring the fact that she'll probably want to spend her birthday with boring Jonathan. 'We could go to Edinburgh. We've always wanted to go there together. What do you say? Shall we do it? I can find us a nice Airbnb.'

It's on the tip of my tongue to offer to pay for that too, but luckily I manage to restrain myself. I haven't been that bad a friend.

I can tell from her face that she's considering saying no because I'm not quite forgiven. But then she can't resist, and she grins.

'Okay,' she says. 'You're on. Let's do it! But if you let me down like that one more time, Emma Lewis, then I swear we are over. *Finito.*'

I nod vigorously. Mel's birthday is a few weeks away. Plenty of time to clear my diary and get something booked in Edinburgh. It'll be fabulous, just like the weekends we used to go on before grown-up life started to get in the way. I can feel excitement fizzing in my stomach already. This is the perfect way to make it up to Mel and show her how much she means to me.

And I'll make sure that everything runs like clockwork.

ABOUT THE AUTHOR

Photo © 2022 Carolyn Mendelsohn

Izzy Bromley is a storyteller. She is never happier than when she is creating characters and dumping them in hot water to see what happens next. When she leaves her keyboard, she loves the cinema and learning to do new things. She lives in Yorkshire with her family.

You can learn more about Izzy at her website izzybromley.com and follow her on Facebook and Instagram as izzybromleyauthor.

Izzy Bromley has also sold over a million books writing as Imogen Clark.

Follow the Author on Amazon

If you enjoyed this book, follow Izzy Bromley on Amazon to be notified when the author releases a new book!
To do this, please follow these instructions:

Desktop:

1) Search for the author's name on Amazon or in the Amazon App.
2) Click on the author's name to arrive on their Amazon page.
3) Click the 'Follow' button.

Mobile and Tablet:

1) Search for the author's name on Amazon or in the Amazon App.
2) Click on one of the author's books.
3) Click on the author's name to arrive on their Amazon page.
4) Click the 'Follow' button.

Kindle eReader and Kindle App:

If you enjoyed this book on a Kindle eReader or in the Kindle App, you will find the author 'Follow' button after the last page.